英语国家101位诗人
101首爱情短诗及其汉译并注

解　红　王永胜◎译著

安徽师范大学出版社
ANHUI NORMAL UNIVERSITY PRESS
·芜湖·

责任编辑:汪碧颖
责任校对:辛新新
装帧设计:丁奕奕
责任印制:桑国磊

图书在版编目(CIP)数据

英语国家101位诗人101首爱情短诗及其汉译并注 / 解红, 王永胜译著 . —芜湖 : 安徽师范大学出版社,2020.5(2020.11重印)

ISBN 978-7-5676-4234-8

Ⅰ.①英… Ⅱ.①解… ②王… Ⅲ.①英语诗歌 – 诗集 – 世界②英语诗歌 – 诗歌研究 Ⅳ.①I12②I106.2

中国版本图书馆CIP数据核字(2019)第142878号

英语国家101位诗人101首爱情短诗及其汉译并注

YINGYU GUOJIA 101 WEI SHIREN 101 SHOU AIQING DUANSHI JI QI HANYI BING ZHU

解 红 王永胜◎译著

出版发行:安徽师范大学出版社
芜湖市九华南路189号安徽师范大学花津校区
网 址:http://www.ahnupress.com/
发 行 部:0553-3883578 5910327 5910310(传真)
印 刷:苏州市古得堡数码印刷有限公司
版 次:2020年5月第1版
印 次:2020年11月第2次印刷
规 格:700 mm × 1000 mm 1/16
印 张:21.75
字 数:356千字
书 号:ISBN 978-7-5676-4234-8
定 价:68.00元

Preface
前　言

在群星璀璨、光芒四射的英语诗歌天空中，有一类篇幅短小的诗歌，它们有一个共同的主题——爱情。这类诗歌，有些出自名家之手，如威廉·莎士比亚、珀西·比希·雪莱、托马斯·哈代等；有些出自非知名诗人之手，如查尔斯·汉森·汤等。但是，这些诗歌都歌颂了爱情的美好。

本书精选的爱情诗歌，大部分为格律诗，少部分为自由体诗，都具有短小精悍的特点，本书将这些诗界定为短诗①。这些诗歌或直接抒发爱情，或借助某些意象间接歌颂爱情，让人读后回味无穷。在这个“快餐文化”盛行的时代，选择这样的短诗加以翻译，无疑会适合人们的“胃口”，节省他们宝贵的时间和精力。

本书从各类英文媒体中精选出101位英语国家诗人所作的101首爱情短诗（一人一首）②，并根据诗人和诗歌的特点，分为“英国诗人的韵体爱情短诗”“美国诗人的韵体爱情短诗”“其他英语国家诗人的韵体爱情短诗”和“英语国家诗人的自由体爱情短诗”四大篇章。每首诗由诗人小档案、英文诗、原诗注释、简明导读及汉语译诗组成。

对这些诗歌的翻译所形成的汉语译文，简称“译诗”。由我们翻译、加

---

① 收录的个别诗歌篇幅稍长，但相比于长篇诗歌，仍属短篇诗歌范畴。

② 本书的英语诗歌来源广泛，我们对所选英语诗歌的“诗题”和“诗体”，从多个媒体中加以比对、甄别，最后选入。因有些诗歌在不同媒体会略有差异，本书根据需要对诗歌的大小写、标点及个别用词等略作处理。“诗人小档案”部分根据需要稍加调整和处理。

工、处理过的译诗“可口”与否，恐怕是“众口难调”之事了。

这样说，不是在推脱诗歌译著者的责任，实则因为诗歌翻译乃难中之难的事情。这里所说的“英诗汉译”不仅涉及英诗的“内容”翻译，而且涉及英诗的“形式——格律”翻译。虽然英诗格律具有多样性以及英汉语言具有差异性，但英诗汉译领域仍然出现了“百花齐放、百家争鸣”的现象。译者各有方法：民族化译法、移植译法、格律化译法等。译诗形式也有很多样：有的译成汉语的格律诗形式，有的译成汉语的自由体无韵诗形式，有的译成汉语的散文体形式，有的译成汉语的韵体诗形式，等等。

英诗汉译是以原诗为基础的，所以要在观照英诗形式即格律的基础上，忠实英诗内容，此乃英诗汉译的根本。因为，形式是为内容服务的，无论形式多么完美，内容不符，甚至背离了原诗，也就失去了英诗汉译的意义，翻译的目的也就无从谈起。由于英汉语言本身具有较大的差异性，英诗汉译过程中力求对原诗内容的“信”，以及译诗内容的“达”，而在形式上则有所“归化”。除一些格律较为特殊的英诗外，本书大多数英诗在汉译时采用了“节奏弹跳式自由体韵诗（Free Verse with Sprung Rhythm）”的形式，也就是说，译诗形式并不严格紧扣汉语古体诗或近体诗的格律形式，但基本保留其押韵形式，即偶数行押韵，首行可押也可不押，并尽可能做到平声入韵，有时也押仄声韵，采取平仄通押的押韵方式，以求最大限度做到对原诗内容的“忠实”。这里的“节奏弹跳式”借用的是英国诗人杰拉尔德·曼利·霍普金斯提出的“Sprung Rhythm”（“弹跳韵式”或“弹跳节奏”），算是“洋为中用”了。

> Prior to Hopkins, most Middle English and Modern English poetry was based on a rhythmic structure inherited from the Norman side of English literary heritage. This structure is based on repeating groups of two or three syllables, with the stressed syllable falling in the same place on each repetition. Hopkins called this structure “running rhythm”, and though he wrote some of his early verse in running rhythm, he became fascinated with the older rhythmic structure of the Anglo-Saxon tradition, of which Beowulf

is the most famous example. Hopkins called his own rhythmic structure "sprung rhythm". Sprung rhythm is structured around feet with a variable number of syllables, generally between one and four syllables per foot, with the stress always falling on the first syllable in a foot. It is similar to the "rolling stresses" of Robinson Jeffers, another poet who rejected conventional metre. Hopkins saw sprung rhythm as a way to escape the constraints of running rhythm, which he said inevitably pushed poetry written in it to become "same and tame." In this way, Hopkins can be seen as anticipating much of free verse.

在霍普金斯之前，多数中世纪英语诗歌及现代英语诗歌所基于的韵式结构，是从英国文学遗产中诺曼人一方继承下来的。这种韵式结构的基础是重复的群组，每个群组由两至三个音节构成，而且重音落在每一次重复中同样的位置上。霍普金斯称其为"奔跑韵式"（或"奔跑节奏"）。尽管霍普金斯早期的一些诗运用奔跑韵式写成，但他却对更为古老的"盎格鲁-撒克逊"传统的韵式结构着迷，古英语史诗《贝奥武甫》就是最为有名的一个例子。霍普金斯称自己的这种韵式结构为"弹跳韵式"（或"弹跳节奏"）。弹跳韵式围绕音步展开，每个音步的音节数量不固定，但每个音步一般由一至四个音节组成，且重音总是落在每个音步的第一个音节上。这种结构类似于鲁滨孙·杰弗斯创造的"滚动重音"。杰弗斯是另一位厌弃传统格律的诗人。霍普金斯将弹跳韵式视作挣脱奔跑韵式限制的一种方式。他认为，奔跑韵式势必将以此韵式写成的诗推向"同模和驯服"。这样看来，就可以说，霍普金斯预先写出了大量的自由体韵诗。

就译诗而言，若以汉语停顿的次数即所谓的"顿数"来代替英诗音步，则每一顿数的汉字数量是不固定的（这一点与汉语近体诗中严格的格律要求有所不同）。这样做的目的，就是最大限度地忠实于原诗的内容、意义和意象。

不同的译者对英诗原文内容思考的角度不同，因此在英诗的理解上不能公式化或程式化，所谓“诗无达诂”也。关于这一点，从美国现代派诗人比利·柯林斯为他的学生所写的一首现代诗《诗歌入门》（*Introduction to Poetry*）中可见一斑，算是理解诗歌内容“以诗论诗”的典范。

I ask them to take a poem
and hold it up to the light
like a color slide

or press an ear against its hive.

I say drop a mouse into a poem
and watch him probe his way out,

or walk inside the poem's room
and feel the walls for a light switch.

I want them to waterski
across the surface of a poem
waving at the author's name on the shore.

But all they want to do
is tie the poem to a chair with rope
and torture a confession out of it.

They begin beating it with a hose
to find out what it really means.

我要求学生拿出一首诗，
对着光线举起来，
就像举起一张透明的彩色幻灯片；

或者将一只耳朵贴近诗的蜂房。

我说的是，把一只老鼠扔进诗中，
看老鼠如何找到出口；

或者在诗的房间里走动，
摸索四周的墙壁，找到灯的开关。

我想要学生
在诗的表面滑水，
同时向岸边的诗作者招手。

可是，学生想做的
却是用绳子把诗绑到椅子上，
严刑拷打，逼其招供。

他们开始用软管带抽打，
要查出它到底有什么意义。

本书在尽最大可能观照原诗的意义和意象的基础上，对英诗进行汉译探索。

本书遵循以下翻译原则：

1.人名、地名的翻译主要依据《世界人名翻译大辞典》（中国对外翻译出公司2007年修订版）、《世界地名翻译大辞典》（中国对外翻译出公司2008年第1版），个别人名、地名的翻译兼顾了流行的译法。

2.译诗在忠于英诗原文的基础上尽量杜绝“翻译腔”，以保持汉语语言的纯洁性和规范性。

3.译诗多采用“归化”的翻译方法，即充分观照汉诗的押韵特点，以求最大限度地适合汉语读者的阅读习惯。

需要说明的是，为了那些“查找式”阅读者的需要，有些注释的条目反复出现，而未给出“交叉引用条目（Cross Reference）”，从而免除读者来回“参见”之苦。

匆忙且蹒跚的步履有时会迈出“不和谐”的步伐，在对这101位诗人所作的101首爱情短诗的翻译过程中，不当之处在所难免，还望读者不吝赐教。

解　红　王永胜

2020年初春

Contents
目　录

Chapter 01

Short Love Verse by Poets from the United Kingdom of Great Britain and Northern Ireland

第一章

英国诗人的韵体爱情短诗

001 William Shakespeare
威廉·莎士比亚

◆ *The Poet's Profile* （诗人小档案）

威廉·莎士比亚（1564—1616）：英国戏剧家和诗人。莎士比亚的戏剧多以无韵诗的形式写成，包括喜剧、悲剧、历史剧、希腊和罗马剧，还包括他戏剧生涯的收官之作——悲喜剧。莎士比亚写了150多首商籁体诗歌，多于1609年出版。此外，莎士比亚还写过一些叙事诗。

◆ *Shall I Compare Thee to a Summer's Day?* （*Sonnet 18*）

Shall I compare thee to a summer's day?
Thou art more lovely and more temperate.
Rough winds do shake the darling buds of May,
And summer's lease hath all too short a date.
Sometime too hot the eye of heaven shines,
And often is his gold complexion dimmed;
And every fair from fair sometime declines,
By chance, or nature's changing course, untrimmed;
But thy eternal summer shall not fade,
Nor lose possession of that fair thou ow'st,
Nor shall death brag thou wand'rest in his shade,
When in eternal lines to Time thou grow'st.
So long as men can breathe, or eyes can see,
So long lives this, and this gives life to thee.

◆ Annotations （原诗注释）

1. thee: *pron.* [second person singular] archaic or dialect form of you, as the singular object of a verb or preposition （古英语“thou”的宾格，同“you”）你；汝

2. thou art = you are

3. thou: *pron.* [second person singular] archaic or dialect form of you, as the singular subject of a verb （古旧用法或方言用法）（作动词的单数主语）你（同“you”）

4. art: *v.* archaic or dialect second person singular present of be （古旧用法及诗歌中用法）“be”的第二人称、单数、现在时形式

5. hath = has

6. complexion: *n.* the natural colour, texture, and appearance of a person's skin, especially of the face 天然肤色（尤指面色）（e.g. an attractive girl with a pale complexion肤色苍白的漂亮女孩）

7. ow'st = ownest = owns

8. wand'rest = wanderest = wanders

9. grow'st = growest = grows

◆ A Lead-in Note （简明导读）

此诗为商籁体诗，即十四行诗，为典型的英国式十四行诗。因莎士比亚的运用，将商籁体诗推向了顶峰，所以也称“莎式十四行诗”。诗体采用三节四行诗和最后一节双行对句体的形式，韵式固定为“ABAB，CDCD，EFEF，GG”的形式。但译诗基本上遵从中国传统的古体诗押韵方式，即偶数行押韵，但首行未入韵。这算是译诗押韵的“归化”处理策略，避免了复制原诗押韵方式可能带来的“水土不服”问题。同时，为使汉译诗具有良好的节奏感，译诗字数控制在十三个汉字之内。

此诗是莎翁商籁体诗中最著名的一首。此诗中，爱情得以升华，成为永恒的主题。若将“你”比作夏日里的一天，则局限性太大，因夏日转瞬即

逝，且炎热无比，令人烦躁。“有时候太过火辣的是老天的眼，而老天的金容则经常昏暗不清。”意思是说，太阳有时候太炎热，还经常被乌云遮盖。

◆ 我可否将你比作夏日里的一天？（商籁体第18首）

我可否将你比作夏日里的一天？
你可是更加美好，更加温和。
烈风定将五月迷人的蓓蕾摇颤，
而夏日的时光瞬间飞逝而过。
有时候太过火辣的是老天的眼，
而老天的金容则经常昏暗不清。
美人再美再多终有衰退那一天：
衰退于不测或者自然的进程。
而你的夏日不会衰退，直至永远。
你的美流芳百世，就连死神
也不应吹嘘，说你漫步于其边缘。
因永恒的诗中，你得以永存。
若人以呼吸为生，或者以眼观看，
若此诗长存，你此生则得以续延。

002 Percy Bysshe Shelley 珀西·比希·雪莱

◆ *The Poet's Profile* （诗人小档案）

珀西·比希·雪莱（1792—1822）：英国诗人。雪莱是英国浪漫主义文学的领军人物，政治观点激进。他的代表作有政治诗歌《麦布女王》，诗剧《解放了的普罗米修斯》，论文《诗辩》，以及悼念济慈的挽诗《阿东尼斯》。

◆ *On a Faded Violet*

The odour from the flower is gone
Which like thy kisses breathed on me;
The colour from the flower is flown
Which glowed of thee, and only thee!

A shrivelled, lifeless, vacant form,
It lies on my abandoned breast;
And mocks the heart, which yet is warm,
With cold and silent rest.

I weep—my tears revive it not;
I sigh—it breathes no more on me;
Its mute and uncomplaining lot
Is such as mine should be.

◆ *Annotations* （原诗注释）

1. violet: *n.* a herbaceous plant of temperate regions, typically having purple, blue, or white five-petalled flowers, one petal of which forms a landing pad for pollinating insect s 堇菜；紫罗兰

2. thy: *adj.* （also "thine" before a vowel） archaic or dialect form of your （元音前亦作"thine"）（古旧用法或方言用法）你（您）的（同"your"）

3. thee: *pron.* [second person singular] archaic or dialect form of you, as the singular object of a verb or preposition （古英语"thou"的宾格，同"you"）你；汝

4. shrivel *v.* wrinkle and contract or cause to wrinkle and contract, especially due to loss of moisture （尤指由于失去水分而）（使）枯萎；（使）收缩

5. revive: *v.* restore to life or consciousness 使复活；使苏醒 （e.g. Both men collapsed, but were revived. 两人都倒下了，但又都被抢救过来。）

6. lot: *n.* a person's luck or condition in life, especially as determined by fate or destiny 命运（e.g. schemes to improve the lot of the disadvantaged 改善弱势人群的命运的方案）

◆ *A Lead-in Note* （简明导读）

此诗基调低沉，令人感到压抑甚至是沮丧。人生、命运、死亡、悲痛等元素充斥全诗，直至诗的结尾也不见希望的火花。凋萎的紫罗兰代表一个人的离去，或许是亲人，或许是朋友，但更大可能是诗人深爱的一名女子。死而无法复生，面对死亡，诗人无能为力。于是，"我哭泣，眼泪无法令它复苏；我叹息，它的气息不再将我弥漫"。

◆ 凋萎的紫罗兰

紫罗兰花的气息已经消散，
如同你的吻，曾经在我身上弥漫；
紫罗兰花的色彩已经消失，
那色彩曾经只闪耀出你的容颜。

紫罗兰躺在我空荡的胸膛，
没有生机，干枯而黯淡，
却在寒冷而寂静的长眠中
嘲笑我那颗心——心仍温暖。

我哭泣，眼泪无法令它复苏；
我叹息，它的气息不再将我弥漫。
它那无言无怨的宿命，
映照了我自己命运的短暂。

003 William Strode
威廉·斯特罗德

◆ *The Poet's Profile* （诗人小档案）

威廉·斯特罗德（约1602—1645）：英国诗人、神学博士和牛津大学校方发言人。斯特罗德很小的时候就表现出勤奋好学的天性，先后被送到威斯敏斯特学校及牛津大学基督教会学院学习。在牛津大学学习期间，斯特罗德的诗歌天赋开始崭露头角。1629年，他被推选为校方发言人。如果没有伯特伦·多贝尔先生这位伯乐将斯特罗德的诗歌重新挖掘的话，他在诗歌领域就默默无闻了。1907年，多贝尔先生将斯特罗德的诗歌编辑出版，书名为《威廉·斯特罗德诗歌作品选》。作为诗人，斯特罗德在抒情诗和挽诗方面出类拔萃。

◆ *Kisses*

My love and I for kisses play'd,
Shee would keepe stake, I was content,
But when I wonne shee would be paid;
This made mee aske her what she meant.
Pray, since I see （quoth shee） your wrangling vayne,
Take your owne kisses, give me myne againe.

◆ *Annotations* （原诗注释）

1. play'd = played

play: *v.* bet or gamble at or on 打赌；赌博 （e.g. He didn't gamble or play the ponies. 他没有赌博也没有赌马。）

2. shee = she

3. keepe = keep

4. stake: *n.* （usu. as "stakes"） a sum of money or something else of value gambled on the outcome of a risky game or venture 赌本；赌注 （e.g. playing dice for high stakes 掷骰子赌大钱）

5. wonne = won

6. mee = me

7. aske = ask

8. pray: *adv.* （formal or archaic） used as a preface to polite requests or instructions（正式用法或古旧用法）请；务请 （e.g. Pray continue. 务请继续下去。）

9. quoth = quotes

10. wrangling: *n.* an angry, noisy argument or dispute 愤怒地争论；大声地辩解

11. vayne = vain

vain: *adj.* having or showing an excessively high opinion of one's appearance, abilities, or worth 自负的；自视过高的（e.g. Their flattery made him vain. 他们的吹捧使他自命不凡。）

12. owne = own

13. myne = mine

14. againe = again

◆ *A Lead-in Note* （简明导读）

诗人以诙谐幽默的笔触写出了爱情中一个具体的场景。爱情中没有谁对谁错，甚至可以说女子总是"对"的，男子若一本正经地跟女子讲道理，那他就输定了，或者说他根本不懂爱的"真谛"。以吻作赌金，"可我赢了，她却将赌金兑了现"，与其理论一番肯定无果。最终，女子说："请把你的吻拿走，再把我的——物归原主。"蛮横、淘气的样子令人忍俊不禁。

◆ 吻

吻作赌金，我跟我爱人开赌；
她持续下注，我心满意足。
可我赢了，她却将赌金兑了现；
我问她用意何在，我很糊涂。
好吧，我明白（她说）你气愤力争，自命不凡，
请把你的吻拿走，再把我的——物归原主。

004 Edward FitzGerald 爱德华·菲茨杰拉德

◆ *The Poet's Profile* （诗人小档案）

爱德华·菲茨杰拉德（1809—1883）：英国学者、作家及诗人。菲茨杰拉德是第一个英译欧玛尔·海亚姆的《鲁拜集》的诗人，这是他最为知名的英文译作。在所有最不引人注目的作家当中，菲茨杰拉德却凭借着自身非凡的个性，逐渐对英国文学产生了影响。

◆ *The Three Arrows*

(*Porcia's Song*)
Of all the shafts to Cupid's bow,
The first is tipp'd with fire;
All bare their bosoms to the blow
And call the wound Desire.

Love's second is a poison'd dart,
And Jealousy is named:
Which carries poison to the heart
Desire had first inflamed.

The last of Cupid's arrows all
With heavy lead is set:
That vainly weeping lovers call
Repentance, or Regret.

◆ *Annotations* （原诗注释）

1. shaft: *n.* an arrow or spear 箭；矛

2. Cupid: *n.* （Roman Mythology） the god of love. He is represented as a naked winged boy with a bow and arrows, with which he wounds his victims. Greek equivalent Eros. （罗马神话）丘比特；爱神（他是长有双翅的裸体男孩，在寻找到目标后就搭弓射箭，相当于希腊神话中的爱神"Eros"。）

3. bow: *n.* a weapon for shooting arrows, typically made of a curved piece of wood joined at both ends by a taut string 弓（一种武器）

4. tipp'd = tipped

tip: *v.* attach to or cover the end or extremity of 附在……的顶端；覆盖在……的顶端

5. bare: *v.* uncover （a part of the body or other thing） and expose it to view 使（部分身体等）裸露 （e.g. He bared his chest to show his scar. 他露出胸膛展示伤疤。）

6. bosom: *n.* the chest of a human （人体的）胸部

7. poison'd = poisoned

8. dart: *n.* a small pointed missile that can be thrown or fired 镖

9. jealousy: *n.* the state or feeling of being jealous 妒忌；妒羡；嫉妒

10. inflame: *v.* （poetic/literary） light up with or as if with flames （诗/文用法）点燃（e.g. The torches inflame the night to the eastward. 火炬点燃了东方的夜晚。）

11. set: *v.* mount （a precious stone） in something 镶嵌（宝石）

12. vainly: *adv.* to no avail; to no effect 徒劳地；无益地

13. repentance: *n.* remorse or contrition for past conduct or sin 悔悟；悔改；后悔；忏悔 （e.g. Considering the signs he showed of genuine repentance, we shall deal leniently with him. 鉴于他有真诚悔改的表现，我们将对他宽大处理。）

◆ *A Lead-in Note* （简明导读）

此诗取材于古希腊罗马神话中的爱神丘比特——长有双翅的裸体小男孩。他寻找到目标就搭弓射箭。射中谁，谁就会受其箭“伤”，而“伤情”则视其箭的性质而定。此诗中，丘比特的三支箭可分别命名为“欲望”“嫉妒”和“后悔”或“痛悔”，每一支箭都颇具威力。

◆ 爱神丘比特的三支箭

(写给波尔恰的歌)
丘比特的弓，搭箭数量无穷，
可第一支，箭头火焰红彤彤。
男男女女赤裸胸膛被箭射，
伤口以欲望来命名。

第二支，名字叫作嫉妒，
毒药涂抹在其尖端。
它带着毒一路奔向心脏，
那里已被欲望点燃。

爱神的最后一支箭，
有沉重的铅镶嵌。
哭泣的情侣称之为后悔
或痛悔，但为时已晚。

005 Christina Georgina Rossetti
克里斯蒂娜·乔治娜·罗塞蒂

◆ *The Poet's Profile* （诗人小档案）

克里斯蒂娜·乔治娜·罗塞蒂（1830—1894）：英国女诗人。罗塞蒂写下诸多宗教诗、情诗、浪漫诗和儿童诗。她的代表作品是《〈妖怪集市〉及其他诗》。罗塞蒂是丹蒂·加布里埃尔·罗塞蒂的妹妹。

◆ *Remember*

Remember me when I am gone away,
Gone far away into the silent land;
When you can no more hold me by the hand,
Nor I half turn to go yet turning stay.
Remember me when no more day by day
You tell me of our future that you plann'd:
Only remember me; you understand
It will be late to counsel then or pray.

Yet if you should forget me for a while
And afterwards remember, do not grieve:
For if the darkness and corruption leave
A vestige of the thoughts that once I had,
Better by far you should forget and smile
Than that you should remember and be sad.

◆ *Annotations* （原诗注释）

1. plann'd = planned

2. corruption: *n.* （archaic） decay; putrefaction （古旧用法）腐坏；腐烂（e.g. The potato turned black and rotten with corruption. 土豆变黑腐烂了。）

3. vestige: *n.* a trace of something that is disappearing or no longer exists 残余；痕迹 （e.g. the last vestiges of colonialism 殖民主义的残余）

◆ *A Lead-in Note* （简明导读）

此诗笔调苍凉，情感细腻，既表达了诗人对美好爱情的向往，又表达了诗人因受病疼折磨而对爱情产生的顾虑。其实，此诗为意大利式十四行体诗（Italian Sonnet），由于意大利诗人彼特拉克的推广而得以流行，因此又称“彼特拉克体十四行诗”（Petrarchan sonnet），共分两部分：第一部分为八行诗节（Octave），韵式固定为“ABBA，ABBA”；第二部分为六行诗节（Sestet），韵式不固定。对于克里斯蒂娜的这首诗而言，韵式为“CDD，ECE”。这与本书第001首的英国式十四行诗有所不同。此诗中，诗人在“记住”（Remember）和“忘记”（Forget）之间似乎出现了矛盾（Contradictions）。那么，这到底是怎样的一段爱情？是刻骨铭心，还是去留无意？

◆ 记 住

记住我，在我离开之际：
远远离开，进入静谧之地。
那时，你将无法握着我的手，
我也无法回头，但欲离又止。
记住我，在你规划好我们的未来
却又不能日复一日将之谈起之际。
只需记住我，因你理解：

那时，忠告或祈祷为时晚矣。

然而，要是你忘记我一小会儿，
随后又将我记起，也不要悲戚：
无论多黑暗，多腐烂，都会遗留
一丝我曾经拥有的思想痕迹。
至此，最好遗忘且微笑，
而不要悲伤并记起。

006 George Gordon Byron
乔治·戈登·拜伦

◆ *The Poet's Profile* （诗人小档案）

乔治·戈登·拜伦（1788—1824）：英国诗人。拜伦的诗对浪漫主义文学，尤其对欧洲大陆的浪漫主义文学，有着极大的影响。他参加了希腊独立战争，但还没投入激烈的战斗就死于疟疾。拜伦的代表作品有《恰尔德·哈罗尔德游记》和《唐璜》等。

◆ *When We Two Parted*

When we two parted
In silence and tears,
Half broken-hearted
To sever for years,
Pale grew thy cheek and cold,
Colder thy kiss;
Truly that hour foretold
Sorrow to this.

The dew of the morning
Sunk chill on my brow—
It felt like the warning
Of what I feel now.
Thy vows are all broken,
And light is thy fame:

I hear thy name spoken,
And share in its shame.

They name thee before me,
A knell to mine ear;
A shudder comes o'er me—
Why wert thou so dear?
They know not I knew thee,
Who knew thee too well:
Long, long shall I rue thee,
Too deeply to tell.

In secret we met—
In silence I grieve,
That thy heart could forget,
Thy spirit deceive.
If I should meet thee
After long years,
How should I greet thee?
With silence and tears.

◆ *Annotations* （原诗注释）

1. sever: *v.* divide by cutting or slicing, especially suddenly and forcibly （尤指突然或用力）切断；切割（e.g. The head was severed from the body. 头从身体上被砍下。）

2. thy: *adj.* （also "thine" before a vowel） archaic or dialect form of your（元音前亦作"thine"）（古旧用法或方言用法）你（您）的（同"your"）

3. foretell: *v.* predict （the future or a future event） 预言；预示（未来之事）

4. brow: *n.* a person's forehead 额头；脑门子 （e.g. He wiped his brow. 他擦

了擦前脑门。）

5. thee: *pron.* [second person singular] archaic or dialect form of you, as the singular object of a verb or preposition （古英语“thou”的宾格，同“you”）你；汝

6. knell: *n.* （figurative） used with reference to an announcement, event, or sound that is regarded as a solemn warning of the end of something （比喻用法）丧钟；警钟 （e.g. The decision will probably toll the knell for the facility. 该决议可能会为这项服务敲响丧钟。）

7. o'er = over

8. wert = were

9. thou: *pron.* [second person singular] archaic or dialect form of you, as the singular subject of a verb （古旧用法或方言用法）（作动词的单数主语）你（同“you”）

10. rue: *v.* bitterly regret （something one has done or allowed to happen） and wish it undone 对……感到懊悔；对……感到后悔；对……感到悔恨（e.g. She might live to rue this impetuous decision. 她可能会对一时冲动做出的这个决定后悔一辈子。）

◆ *A Lead-in Note* （简明导读）

诗人拜伦的这首诗应该是写给他曾经爱过的一位异性的，也许拜伦曾经刻骨铭心地爱过她。据考证，拜伦写此诗的灵感来自曾经有段时间他对弗朗西丝·韦德伯恩·韦伯斯特女士的爱恋。但是，她后来却与威灵顿公爵有染而成为人们说长道短的对象。对此，深爱着她的拜伦也颇感不齿：“你的名字有人当面提起，如警钟敲响耳畔。”但拜伦对她依然留恋：“若是你我再见时，会是经年后的某段时光。我该如何向你致意？默默无言泪成行。”当然，此诗后来就具有了普遍意义，成为一首悲伤情诗。

◆ 你我分离时

你我分离之际，
默默无言泪成行。
心碎两半儿，
不知要碎碎多少时光。
苍白寒凉的，是你的面颊儿，
你的热吻则更加寒凉。
那一刻真实无比，
预示了此生的悲伤。

那天早晨的露滴，
冷冷落到我的眉头——
摸起来就像某种预示，
预示着如今的感受。
你的誓言破碎难觅，
你的声名已落俗陋：
你的名字有人提到时，
我感到的只是愧羞。

你的名字有人当面提起，
如警钟敲响耳畔。
一阵惊栗传遍身体——
曾经为何那么把你迷恋？
人们不知你我以前相识：
相识到亲密，相识到无间。
我的懊悔如今无休止，
懊悔多深已难辨。

你我曾经约会，很隐秘——
如今，独我暗地悲伤：
伤感你的心竟忘记，
伤感你的情已成霜。
若是你我再见时，
会是经年后的某段时光。
我该如何向你致意？
默默无言泪成行。

007 Edmund Spenser 埃德蒙·斯宾塞

◆ *The Poet's Profile* （诗人小档案）

埃德蒙·斯宾塞（1552—1599）：英国诗人。斯宾塞被公认为现代英文韵诗发端期技艺超群的诗人之一，被称为“诗人中的诗人”。斯宾塞最知名的作品当属长篇寓言式浪漫体史诗《仙后》。《仙后》颂扬伊丽莎白女王一世，采用的是“斯宾塞式诗节”（每节九行，前八行用五音步抑扬格，最后一行用六音步抑扬格，韵式为“ABABBCBCC”）。此外，斯宾塞还写了一部商籁体组诗《小爱神》，其中包括“商籁体第75首”。对于商籁体组诗，斯宾塞做了两件相当温馨又颇具创意的事情：其一，他创造了一种商籁体诗歌的变体形式，就是现在所称的“斯宾塞式商籁体”（包括三个四行体诗节和一个双行体诗节，每行皆为五音步抑扬格，且每节的最后一行与下一节的第一行关联，韵式为“ABAB BCBC CDCD EE”）。其二，斯宾塞改变传统商籁体诗凄美的爱情主题为完美的爱情主题。如《小爱神》讲述的是他成功追求到妻子伊丽莎白·博伊尔以及与她婚姻美满的故事。

◆ *One Day I Wrote Her Name upon the Strand* （*Sonnet 75*）

One day I wrote her name upon the strand,
But came the waves and washed it away;
Again I wrote it with a second hand,
But came the tide, and made my pains his prey.

“Vain man,” said she, “that dost in vain assay,

A mortal thing so to immortalize;
For I myself shall like to this decay,
And eke my name be wiped out likewise."

"Not so," quoth I, "let baser things devise
To die in dust, but you shall live by fame:
My verse your virtues rare shall eternize,
And in the heavens write your glorious name.

Where whenas death shall all the world subdue,
Our love shall live, and later life renew."

◆ *Annotations* （原诗注释）

1. strand: *n.* （poetic/literary） the shore of a sea, lake, or large river （诗/文用法）海滨；海滩；湖滨；河岸 （e.g. A heron glided to rest on a pebbly strand. 一只鹭滑过天空，栖息在布满鹅卵石的岸边。）

2. tide: *n.* the alternate rising and falling of the sea, usually twice in each lunar day at a particular place, due to the attraction of the moon and sun 潮（汐）（e.g. They were driven on by wind and tide. 他们被风和潮水驱使着前进。）

3. pain: *n.* （pains） careful effort; great care or trouble 辛苦；努力；苦心；操心 （e.g. She took pains to see that everyone ate well. 她煞费苦心，确保每个人都吃得好。）

4. prey: *n.* an animal that is hunted and killed by another for food 被捕食的动物；捕获物 （e.g. The kestrel is ready to pounce on unsuspecting prey. 红隼准备扑向毫无戒备的猎物。）

5. vain: *adj.* having no meaning or likelihood of fulfilment 徒劳的；无意义的（e.g. a vain boast 徒劳的自夸）

6. dost = does

7. in vain: without success or a result 徒劳地 （e.g. They waited in vain for a response. 他们白等回音。）

8. assay: *n.* （archaic） an attempt; an essay （古旧用法）企图；尝试

essay: *n.* （formal） an attempt or effort （正式用法）企图；尝试

9. mortal: *adj.* （of a living human being, often in contrast to a divine being） subject to death （常指相对于神的人）总有一死的（e.g. All men are mortal. 人总有一死。）

10. immortalize: *v.* （usu. as "be immortalized in"） confer enduring fame upon 使不朽 （e.g. He will be forever immortalized in the history books. 他会永垂史册。）

11. decay: *n.* the state or process of rotting or decomposition 腐败；腐坏；腐烂 （e.g. Hardwood is more resistant to decay than softwood. 硬木材比软木材耐腐。）

12. eke: *v.* （eke something out） make an amount or supply of something last longer by using or consuming it frugally 尽量节省以延长；尽量维持 （e.g. The remains of yesterday's stew could be eked out to make another meal. 昨天剩的炖肉可以再顶一顿饭吃。）

13. likewise: *adv.* in a like manner; similarly 以相似的方式；类似地（e.g. I stuck out my tongue and Frankie did likewise. 我伸出舌头，弗朗基也这样做。）

14. quoth: *v.* （archaic or humorous） said （used only in first and third person singular before the subject）（古旧用法或幽默用法）（仅用于第一和第三人称单数的主语之前）说 （e.g. "Ah," quoth he, as soon as the bike started, "a blown cylinder head gasket." 摩托车一启动，他就说："啊，汽缸盖垫圈压碎了。"）

15. base: *adj.* （archaic） denoting or befitting a person of low social class （古旧用法）卑下的；卑贱的

16. rare: *adj.* unusually good or remarkable 极好的；非凡的 （e.g. He plays with rare strength and sensitivity. 他的演奏有力而细腻。）

17. eternize: *v.* （poetic/literary） make eternal; cause to live or last forever （诗/文用法）使永恒；使不朽

18. heavens: *n.* （poetic/literary） the sky, especially perceived as a vault in which the sun, moon, stars, and planets are situated （诗/文用法）天空 （e.g. Galileo used a telescope to observe the heavens. 伽利略用望远镜来观察天空。）

19. whenas: *conj.* whereas; although 然而；尽管

20. subdue: *v.* bring （a country or people） under control by force 制服；使屈服；征服；使顺从 （e.g. Charles went on a campaign to subdue the Saxons. 查理大帝发起了征服撒克逊人的战役。）

21. renew: *v.* resume （an activity） after an interruption （中断之后）重新开始；继续进行 （e.g. The parents renewed their campaign to save the school. 家长们重新开始了拯救学校的运动。）

◆ *A Lead-in Note* （简明导读）

这首商籁体诗编号为“75”，是斯宾塞最知名的一首商籁体诗歌，即十四行诗。此诗关乎大海、天空、爱情及永恒，更关乎不朽之诗的伟大力量。诗人将自己一位心仪女子的名字写在沙滩上，海浪冲上来洗掉名字。诗人再次写上这位女子的名字，海浪再次冲上来洗掉名字。这实属常情，无须大惊小怪，就连女子本人也认为那样做纯属徒劳。但是，诗人斯宾塞却别出心裁，将她的名字变成永恒，写进了诗里：“在那里，死亡将令整个世界都停息，而我们的爱将永生，以后生活再续。”这种富有诗意的做法该有多么浪漫和甜蜜！

◆ 有一天，我在沙滩上写下她的名字（商籁体第75首）

有一天，我在沙滩上写下她的名字，
但海浪冲上来将字洗掉，不留痕迹。
于是，我换了一只手再次写了出来，
但潮起潮落，我的辛苦全都被掠去。

“徒劳一场，”她说，“那样的尝试属徒劳——
将不长久的东西变长久，如此而已。
对我而言，我宁愿这样的东西腐烂，
同样地，我宁愿自己的名字被抹去。”

"并非这样，"我说，"就让更卑贱的事物
死于尘埃，而你将活下来，满载荣誉：
我写的诗，将使你非凡的美德永恒，
将会把你绚烂的名字，写到天空里。

在那里，死亡将令整个世界都停息，
而我们的爱将永生，以后生活再续。"

008 Henry Austin Dobson
亨利·奥斯汀·多布森

◆ *The Poet's Profile* （诗人小档案）

亨利·奥斯汀·多布森，常用名奥斯丁·多布森（1840—1921）：英国诗人和散文家。多布森的行政职业生涯波澜不惊，但作为一名诗人和传记作家，他却声名显赫。研究他作品的人，惊叹他笔法的娴熟和老道。约在1864年，他将注意力投向原创散文和诗歌。多布森早期的一些作品堪称佳作。

◆ *A Kiss*

Rose kissed me to-day.
Will she kiss me tomorrow?
Let it be as it may,
Rose kissed me today.
But the pleasure gives way
To a savour of sorrow; —
Rose kissed me to-day, —
Will she kiss me tomorrow?

◆ *Annotations* （原诗注释）

1. let it / one be: to not interact with or bother someone or interfere with something; to leave someone or something alone 随它去；莫管它

2. give way to someone or something: to yield to someone or something; to give preference to someone or something 被替代；让步于

3. savour: *n.* a specific taste or smell 味道；风味

◆ *A Lead-in Note*（简明导读）

英文中大写的“Rose”是女子名，音译为“罗丝”。同时，小写的“rose”还有象征着爱情的“玫瑰”之意，可谓一语双关。译诗中勉为其难，增词补译成“玫瑰般的罗丝”，庶几可通。不管怎样，罗丝今天吻了我，也许这是爱情的征兆，也许意味着就此而别。“明日，她是否会吻我?”这也许不是那么重要了，也许可以用“但求一朝拥有，不求天长地久”来自我安慰了。

◆ 一个吻

玫瑰般的罗丝吻了我，就在今天。
明日，她是否会吻我?
不管那么多，顺其自然，
反正罗丝今天将我吻过。
可是，喜悦的滋味感受完，
就要品尝随后的苦涩——
玫瑰般的罗丝吻了我，就在今天。
明日，她是否会吻我?

009 Dante Gabriel Rossetti 丹蒂·加布里埃尔·罗塞蒂

◆ *The Poet's Profile* （诗人小档案）

丹蒂·加布里埃尔·罗塞蒂，全名丹蒂·加布里埃尔·查尔斯·罗塞蒂（1828—1882）：英国画家和诗人。罗塞蒂是“前拉斐尔派兄弟会”的创建人之一。他以画理想化的妇女形象著名，代表作品有《贝塔·比阿特丽斯》和《神女》等。他是克里斯蒂娜·乔治娜·罗塞蒂的哥哥。

◆ *Sudden Light*

I have been here before,
But when or how I cannot tell:
I know the grass beyond the door,
The sweet keen smell,
The sighing sound, the lights around the shore.

You have been mine before, —
How long ago I may not know:
But just when at that swallow's soar
Your neck turned so,
Some veil did fall, —I knew it all of yore.

Has this been thus before?
And shall not thus time's eddying flight
Still with our lives our love restore

In death's despite,
And day and night yield one delight once more?

◆ *Annotations* (原诗注释)

1. keen: *adj.* (poetic / literary) (of a smell, light, or sound) penetrating; clear (诗/文用法)(气味、光线或声音)尖锐的；穿透的；贯穿的；渗透的；清晰的；清楚的

2. swallow: *n.* a migratory swift-flying songbird with a forked tail and long pointed wings, feeding on insects in flight 燕子

3. soar: *v.* fly or rise high in the air 高飞；翱翔 (e.g. The bird spread its wings and soared into the air. 鸟展开翅膀，飞上高空。)

4. veil: *n.* a piece of fine material worn by women to protect or conceal the face 面纱；面罩 (e.g. a white bridal veil 新娘的白色面纱)

5. yore: *n.* (used in "of yore") (poetic/literary) of long ago or former times (used in unostalgic or mock-nostalgic recollection) (诗/文用法) 昔日；往昔(用于表示怀旧或故作怀旧)(e.g. a great empire in days of yore 昔日的强大帝国)

6. eddy: *v.* (of water, air, or smoke) move in a circular way 起旋涡；旋转 (e.g. The mists from the river eddied round the banks. 河上的雾在堤岸上回旋。)

7. in death's despite = in spite of death

◆ *A Lead-in Note* (简明导读)

此诗具有神秘主义色彩，融确定性和不确定性于一体，让人读后有些无所适从。诗的最后一节也许能更好地解释诗题"顿生之光"：冥冥之中，诗人看到已故爱人的样子。"日夜流转"，也许在另一个世界里，诗人又能与爱人相聚，也许"喜悦会再次展露"。此时，顿生之光就是让人顿悟之光了。据说，罗塞蒂的妻子能诗会画，对罗塞蒂影响很大。但因久病之后的一次用药过量而亡，罗塞蒂悲痛欲绝。后来，罗塞蒂故地重游，怀念妻子的音容笑貌，颇为感慨而写下此诗。

◆ 顿生之光

以前我到过这里，
但何时到或如何到，我记不起。
我熟悉门外的小草，
熟悉清新甜蜜的味道，
熟悉海岸周围的光和叹息的声调。

以前你非我莫属，
多久以前，我记不清楚。
但就在燕子飞起时，
你的玉颈转了过去，
某种面纱脱落——对此我似曾相识。

以前的情景果真如此？
时间就这样飞旋而逝，
抛却死亡的因素，
我们的爱仍然会因生活而恢复？
日夜流转，喜悦会再次展露？

010 Geoffrey Chaucer
杰弗里·乔叟

◆ *The Poet's Profile*（诗人小档案）

杰弗里·乔叟（约1342—1400）：英国诗人。乔叟是英国文学之父，是中世纪最伟大的诗人，也是首位葬在威斯敏斯特教堂“诗人角”的诗人。乔叟的著作有《坎特伯雷故事集》《特罗伊拉斯和克莱西德》。乔叟多才多艺，他的作品语言简练、幽默，人物刻画入木三分。

◆ *A Rondel of Merciless Beauty—the Original*

Written by Geoffrey Chaucer

1.

Your yen two wol slee me sodenly;
I may the beautee of hem not sustene,
So woundeth hit throughout my herte kene.

2.

And but your word wol helen hastily
My hertes wounde, while that hit is grene,
Your yen two wol slee me sodenly;
I may the beautee of hem not sustene.

3.

Upon my trouthe I sey you feithfully
That ye ben of my lyf and deeth the quene;
For with my deeth the trouthe shal be sene.
Your yen two wol slee me sodenly;

I may the beautee of hem not sustene,
So woundeth hit throughout my herte kene.

◆ *A Rondel of Merciless Beauty—Modern English Version*

Written by Geoffrey Chaucer
Tr. into Modern English by NortheasternWolf
1.
Your two eyes will slay me suddenly;
I may their beauty not sustain,
So wounds hit throughout my heart keen.
2.
And but your word will heal hastily
My heart's wound, while that is green,
Your two eyes will slay me suddenly;
I may their beauty not sustain.
3.
Upon my truth, I tell you faithfully
That you've been of my life and death the queen;
For with my death the truth shall be seen.
Your two eyes will slay me suddenly;
I may their beauty not sustain,
So wounds hit throughout my heart keen.

—From Part I of "*Merciless Beauty: A Triple Rondel*" by Geoffrey Chaucer

◆ *Annotations to the Modern English Version* （针对现代英语版的注释）

1. merciless: *adj.* showing no mercy or pity 冷酷无情的；残忍的；毫无仁慈之心的 （e.g. a merciless attack with a blunt instrument 残忍的钝器攻击）

2. slay: *v.* （archaic or poetic / literary） kill （a person or animal） in a violent way （古旧用法或诗/文用法）杀；杀戮；杀害 （e.g. St. George slew

the dragon. 圣乔治杀死了那条龙。）

3. sustain: *v.* undergo or suffer （something unpleasant, especially an injury）忍受；经受（不愉快的事情，尤指伤痛）（e.g. He died after sustaining severe head injuries. 他头部受了重伤以后死了。）

4. keen: *adj.* having or showing eagerness or enthusiasm 热心的；热切的；渴望的；热情的 （e.g. a keen desire to learn一种热切的求知欲望）

5. green: *adj.* （archaic） （of a wound） fresh; not heale d（古旧用法）（伤口）新的；未愈合的

6. triple: *adj.* consisting of or involving three parts, things, or people （有）三个部分的；三件事（或物）的；三件套的；三人的

◆ *A Lead-in Note* （简明导读）

英文的回旋体诗或回旋诗（Rondel）是一种带有叠句或副歌的押韵短诗，也是一种相当新的诗歌形式，由浪漫主义诗人阿尔杰农·查尔斯·斯温伯恩创建。这种形式的英诗是以法国的“两韵叠句短诗”（Rondeau）为基础演变而来，两韵叠句短诗可追溯到公元14世纪。

此诗中，诗人乔叟从男子的角度讨论了女子的外表美。全诗共分三节，每一节都描写了这种美给诗人带来的感受。“你的双眼啊，能一下子置我于死地；它们的美啊，我无法承担。”这两行在每一节都出现一次，这就是“回旋诗”的“回旋”所在。同时，这一回旋式的重复，突出了主题，令诗意更加明确和突出。

◆ 致无情美人的回旋诗

作者：杰弗里·乔叟

现英翻译：东北野狼

一

你的双眼啊，能一下子置我于死地；
它们的美啊，我无法承担。

伤痛抽打着我充满渴望的心坎。

二

我内心的伤痛尚未加重之际，
能加速痊愈的只有你的语言。
你的双眼啊，能一下子置我于死地；
它们的美啊，我无法承担。

三

实情是，我真心真意告诉你，
你已是我的女王，生死相伴，
因我死后，实情将得以显现。
你的双眼啊，能一下子置我于死地；
它们的美啊，我无法承担。
伤痛抽打着我充满渴望的心坎。

——译自杰弗里·乔叟《致无情美人的回旋诗三部曲》的第一部分

011 Frances Cornford
弗朗西丝·康福德

◆ *The Poet's Profile* （诗人小档案）

弗朗西丝·康福德（1886—1960）：英国女诗人，全名为弗朗西丝·克罗夫茨·康福德。康福德是英国博物学家查尔斯·达尔文的孙女。康福德的诗集有《弗朗西丝诗集》《春天的早晨》《秋季的午夜》和《每一天都不一样》等。

◆ *E. W. D.*

The sudden knowledge that you are not there,
That I live on alone,
Seems still too vast and desolate to bear,
My dear, my own.

The merciful slow years, that rend and rob,
But yet restore again,
Are shattered suddenly by one great throb
Of the old pain.

◆ *Annotations* （原诗注释）

1. E. W. D. : 应该是一个人名字的首字母缩略词，具体指谁，无法考证。

2. vast: *adj.* of very great extent or quantity; immense 广阔的；广大的 （e.g. a vast plain full of orchards 到处是苹果园的大平原）

3. desolate: *adj.* feeling or showing misery, unhappiness, or loneliness 痛苦的；不幸的；孤独的（e.g. I suddenly felt desolate and bereft. 我突然产生了一种凄苦落寞的感觉。）

4. merciful: *adj.*（of an event） coming as a mercy; bringing someone relief from something unpleasant（事件）带来幸运的；给人解脱的（e.g. Her death was a merciful release. 她的死是幸运的解脱。）

5. rend: *v.*（poetic/literary） cause great emotional pain to（a person or their heart）(诗/文用法）使心碎（e.g. You tell me this in order to make me able to betray you without rending my heart. 你告诉我这事是为了不让我因为背叛你而被痛苦折磨。）

6. throb: *n.* a feeling of pain in a series of regular beats 抽痛

◆ *A Lead-in Note*（简明导读）

这个神秘的"E. W. D."姓甚名谁，不得而知。我们只知道，此人的离去令诗人康福德肝肠寸断，哀痛不已。此诗短短八行，但从中可以触摸到诗人的伤痛，可以感受到诗人真诚的情感流露。都说时间是治愈一切的良药，"但旧痛一阵突发"，将长时间治愈的效果化为泡影："将劫后好时光碾成碎片——片片细小"。

◆ 致某E. W. D.

你已不在，只剩下我一个人生活。
突然得知这一结果，
一切似乎太渺茫，太凄凉。
我挚爱的人啊，我失魂落魄。

时光缓缓流淌，虽仍心碎容憔，
一切却再次转好。
但旧痛一阵突发，将劫后好时光
碾成碎片——片片细小。

012 William Blake
威廉·布莱克

◆ *The Poet's Profile* （诗人小档案）

威廉·布莱克（1757—1827）：英国艺术家和诗人，是英国浪漫主义文学的先驱。他的水彩画和版画作品如同其文学作品一样，直到他去世后才完全为世人所赏识。布莱克的代表诗集有《天真之歌》和《经验之歌》等。

◆ *Love's Secret*

Never seek to tell thy love,
Love that never told can be;
For the gentle wind doth move
Silently, invisibly.

I told my love, I told my love,
I told her all my heart,
Trembling, cold, in ghastly fears.
Ah! she did depart!

Soon after she was gone from me,
A traveller came by,
Silently, invisibly:
He took her with a sigh.

◆ *Annotations* （原诗注释）

1. thy: （also “thine” before a vowel） archaic or dialect form of your（元音前亦作“thine”）（古旧用法或方言用法）你（您）的（同“your”）

2. doth = does

3. ghastly: *adj.* causing great horror or fear; frightful or macabre 可怕的；可怖的；令人毛骨悚然的 （e. g. She was overcome with horror at the ghastly spectacle. 她被眼前可怕的景象吓倒了。）

4. sigh: *n.* a long, deep, audible exhalation expressing sadness, relief, tiredness, or similar 叹气；叹息；叹息声 （e. g. She let out a long sigh of despair. 她失望地长叹一口气。）

◆ *A Lead-in Note* （简明导读）

要保守爱的秘密，尤其是对对方怀有的、得不到回应的爱的秘密。一旦说出来，结果可想而知：“哎呀！她却走开，毅然决然。”由此可见，“爱藏在心中永固”。此诗的最后一节带有神秘色彩。那位远行客是诗人的情敌，是死亡的化身，还是其他什么意象，只有留给读者去思考了。

◆ 爱的秘密

永远不要把心中的爱说出，
爱藏在心中永固。
因轻柔的风，总是
不见踪迹，默默无语。

我心中的爱，我说了，我说了，
向她说出我所有情感：
声音颤抖，浑身发冷，怕得要死。
哎呀！她却走开，毅然决然。

一位远行客路过她的身旁，
就在她离开我之后——
不见踪迹，默默不语：
一声叹息，将她带走。

013 Sir John Suckling
约翰·萨克林爵士

◆ *The Poet's Profile* （诗人小档案）

约翰·萨克林爵士（1609—1642）：英国诗人、戏剧家和保皇党领袖。萨克林的诗《婚礼歌谣》，发表在他的诗集《黄金片段》里。作为一名戏剧家，他的显著成就是将制作假面娱乐剧所使用的那套技巧应用到戏剧创作之中。1639年，萨克林辅佐查理国王一世发动了第一次对苏格兰的战争。

◆ *Why So Pale and Wan, Fond Lover?*

Why so pale and wan, fond lover?
Prithee, why so pale? —
Will, when looking well can't move her,
Looking ail prevail?
Prithee, why so pale?

Why so dull and mute, young sinner?
Prithee, why so mute? —
Will, when speaking well can't win her,
Saying nothing do't?
Prithee, why so mute?

Quit, quit, for shame! this will not move,
This cannot take her—
If of herself she will not love,

Nothing can make her:
The Devil take her!

◆ *Annotations* （原诗注释）

1. wan: *adj.* （of a person's complexion or appearance） pale and giving the impression of illness or exhaustion （人的脸色或外表）苍白的；病态的；疲倦的（e.g. She was looking wan and bleary-eyed. 她看上去脸色苍白，睡眼惺忪。）

2. fond: *adj.* affectionate; loving 深情的；爱慕的 （e.g. I have very fond memories of Oxford. 我对牛津一往情深。）

3. prithee: *interj.* （archaic） please （used to convey a polite request）（古旧用法）（表达礼貌的请求）请 （e.g. Prithee, Jack, answer me honestly. 请吧，杰克，老实回答我。）

4. prevail: *v.* prove more powerful than opposing forces; be victorious 占优势；占上风；获胜 （e.g. It is hard for logic to prevail over emotion. 道理很难战胜感情。）

5. sinner = signior = signor （从发音的角度来考虑的）

signor: *n.* an Italian term of address for a man, equivalent to sir or Mr.

Abbr.: Sig., sig. 先生；绅士

6. do't = do it

7. devil: *n.* （usu. the Devil） （in Christian and Jewish belief） the supreme spirit of evil; Satan （基督教和犹太教中的）魔王；撒旦

◆ *A Lead-in Note* （简明导读）

爱情不能强求，爱情不是一厢情愿，爱情是两个人的事情。让一个女子爱她不爱的人，不亚于让一个失聪的人去听交响乐。爱，确实很难。此诗共三节，每一节都是朋友的劝告，劝告一位多情之人放弃一份无果的爱。否则，多情之人只能自寻烦恼，最后身心俱惫。

◆ 多情的人啊，为何如此疲倦和苍白？

多情的人啊，为何如此疲倦和苍白？
请问，为何如此苍白？
无法打动她的芳心——就算好气色满面，
你一副病态，又怎能赢得她相伴？
请问，为何如此苍白？

年轻的人啊，为何如此沮丧和沉默？
请问，为何如此沉默？
无法赢得她的芳心——就算能言善辩，
你一言不发，又怎能令你如愿？
请问，为何如此沉默？

罢了，罢了，真羞愧！不会令她转变，
无法得到她的爱恋。
如果她不珍爱自己，
无人能与她结缘，
只有魔王撒旦与她爱恋。

014 Emily Bronte
艾米莉·勃朗特

◆ *The Poet's Profile* （诗人小档案）

艾米莉·勃朗特（1818—1848）：英国长篇小说家和诗人。艾米莉最为知名的就是她唯一的长篇小说《呼啸山庄》，这是英国文学的经典之作。在勃朗特家族存活下来的四个兄弟姐妹中，艾米莉排行第三，她上有哥哥布兰韦尔，下有妹妹安妮。艾米莉写作时使用笔名“埃利斯·贝尔”。

◆ *Love and Friendship*

Love is like the wild rose-briar,
Friendship like the holly-tree—
The holly is dark when the rose-briar blooms
But which will bloom most constantly?

The wild rose-briar is sweet in spring,
Its summer blossoms scent the air;
Yet wait till winter comes again
And who will call the wild-briar fair?

Then scorn the silly rose-wreath now
And deck thee with the holly's sheen,
That when December blights thy brow
He may still leave thy garland green.

◆ Annotations （原诗注释）

1. briar: *n.* （also brier） any of a number of prickly scrambling shrubs, especially a wild rose 多刺蔓生灌木（尤指野蔷薇）

2. holly: *n.* a widely distributed evergreen shrub, typically having prickly dark green leaves, small white flowers, and red berries 冬青

3. bloom: *v.* produce flowers; be in flower 开花；在开花；处于花期

6. blossom: *n.* a flower or a mass of flowers, especially on a tree or bush （尤指树上的）花朵；花簇 （e.g. The slopes were ablaze with almond blossom. 山坡上盛开着扁桃树花。）

7. scent: *v.* （usu. be scented with） impart a pleasant scent to 使有香味 （e.g. a glass of tea scented with a local herb 用本地药草使茶带有香味）

8. fair: *adj.* （archaic） beautiful; attractive （古旧用法）美丽的；动人的；有魅力的 （e.g. the fairest of her daughters 她女儿中最漂亮的一位）

9. scorn: *v.* the feeling or belief that someone or something is worthless or despicable; contempt 鄙视；蔑视 （e.g. I do not wish to become the object of scorn. 我不希望成为鄙视的对象。）

10. wreath: *n.* an arrangement of flowers, leaves, or stems fastened in a ring and used for decoration or for laying on a grave 花圈；花环；花冠

11. deck: *v.* （usu. be decked） decorate or adorn brightly or festively 装饰；打扮

12. thee: *pron.* [second person singular] archaic or dialect form of you, as the singular object of a verb or preposition （古英语"thou"的宾格，同"you"）你；汝

13. sheen: *n.* a soft lustre on a surface 光泽；光辉

14. blight: *v.* spoil, harm, or destroy 损坏；伤害；毁坏

15. brow: *n.* a person's forehead 额；脑门子

16. garland: *n.* a wreath of flowers and leaves, worn on the head or hung as a decoration （戴在头上或悬挂起来做装饰的）花冠；花环

◆ *A Lead-in Note* （简明导读）

诗人将爱情和友谊分别比作野蔷薇和冬青树，并对两者在不同情形之下的状态做了对比。通过这样一番对比，诗人最终更倾向友谊，认为友谊如冬青树般长青，而且更为伟大："十二月到来时，你的前额枯萎，但你头戴的冬青树花环，绿色依然。"

◆ 爱情与友谊

爱情像野蔷薇，
友谊似冬青树。
野蔷薇盛开时，冬青树黝黑，
但哪一个花期最为永驻？

春日里，野蔷薇吐露芬芳，
夏日里，花朵令空气飘香。
然而，待冬季再次启幕，
谁还会说野蔷薇娇美无双？

那么，自此蔑视轻佻的野蔷薇花环，
以冬青树的光彩装点你的不凡。
十二月到来时，你的前额枯萎，
但你头戴的冬青树花环，绿色依然。

015 Leigh Hunt
利·亨特

◆ *The Poet's Profile* （诗人小档案）

利·亨特（1784—1859）：英国评论家、散文家、诗人和作家。亨利的全名为詹姆斯·亨利·利·亨特。不管是作为一名作家还是一名编辑，他都是浪漫主义时期英国文学发展中的一个关键性人物。在诗歌方面，他从意大利人那里寻找他所说的“自由的赋诗精神”，而且伊丽莎白时代的作家对他作品的影响也很大。在19世纪前60年时间里，他创作了大量不同形式的诗歌作品，包括叙事诗、讽刺诗、诗剧、颂诗、书信体诗文、商籁体诗、短篇抒情诗，还从希腊语、古罗马语、意大利语及法语作品中翻译了大量诗歌。

◆ *Jenny Kiss'd Me*

Jenny kiss'd me when we met,
Jumping from the chair she sat in;
Time, you thief, who love to get
Sweets into your list, put that in!
Say I'm weary, say I'm sad,
Say that health and wealth have miss'd me,
Say I'm growing old, but add,
Jenny kiss'd me.

◆ *Annotations* （原诗注释）

1. kiss'd= kissed

2. sweet: *n.* （sweets） the pleasures or delights found in something 快乐；乐趣 （e.g. the sweets of office 办公室里的乐趣）

3. weary: *adj.* feeling or showing tiredness, especially as a result of excessive exertion or lack of sleep （尤指过度劳累或睡眠不足）疲劳的；疲倦的 （e.g. He gave a long, weary sigh. 他发出了一声长长的、疲倦的叹息。）

4. miss'd = missed

5. miss: *v.* avoid; escape 避开；逃脱；幸免于 （e.g. Christmas shoppers go out early to miss the crowds. 圣诞节购物者早出家门以避开拥挤人群。）

◆ *A Lead-in Note* （简明导读）

此诗简洁、明快、真挚，给人一种美好的感受，让人读后畅快淋漓，也因此经久不衰。这是一首单节八行"回旋诗"，回旋之处是"珍妮吻了我"。由此，爱情的甜蜜溢于言表，显露无遗。

◆ 珍妮吻了我

珍妮吻了我，就在我们见面时——
她坐在椅子上，一下子跳起……
时间啊，你是贼，喜欢在你清单里
写上乐趣，那就写上此事！
写我很疲倦，写我很难过，
写我的健康和财富都离我而去，
写我正在衰老，但加上一句：
珍妮吻了我。

016 Walter de la Mare
沃尔特·德拉梅尔

◆ *The Poet's Profile* （诗人小档案）

沃尔特·德拉梅尔（1873—1956）：英国诗人和小说家。德拉梅尔尤其以儿童诗而著称。人们记住这位诗人，就是因为他所创作的儿童作品以及诗歌《倾听者》。

◆ *Alone*

The abode of the nightingale is bare,
Flowered frost congeals in the gelid air,
The fox howls from his frozen lair:
Alas, my loved one is gone,
I am alone:
It is winter.

Once the pink cast a winy smell,
The wild bee hung in the hyacinth bell,
Light in effulgence of beauty fell:
I am alone:
It is winter.

My candle a silent fire doth shed,
Starry Orion hunts o'erhead;
Come moth, come shadow, the world is dead:

Alas, my loved one is gone,
I am alone;
It is winter.

◆ Annotations （原诗注释）

1. abode: *n.* （formal or poetic / literary） a place of residence; a house or home （正式用法或诗/文用法）住所；房屋 （e.g. Both defendants were said to be of no fixed abode. 据说，两位被告都没有固定住所。）

2. nightingale: *n.* a small migratory thrush with drab brownish plumage, noted for its rich melodious song which can often be heard at night 夜莺；歌鸲

3. bare: *adj.* without the appropriate or usual contents 空荡荡的 （e.g. a bare cell with just a mattress 一间空荡荡的囚房，里面只有一个床垫）

4. congeal: *v.* become semi-solid, especially on cooling （尤指冷却后）凝结；凝固；冻结 （e.g. The blood had congealed into blobs. 血液已凝成团。）

5. gelid: *adj.* icy; extremely cold （figurative） 冰冷的；极冷的（比喻用意）（e.g. She gave a gelid reply. 她冷冷地答道。）

6. howl: *v.* make a howling sound 嚎叫；怒吼；呼啸 （e.g. The wind howled around the house. 风在房屋周围怒号。）

7. lair: *n.* a wild animal's resting place, especially one which is well hidden （野兽的）窝；巢穴

8. alas: *interj.* （chiefly poetic/literary or humorous） an expression of grief, pity, or concern（主要为诗/文用法或幽默用法）哎呀；唉（表示悲痛、遗憾或关心）（e.g. Alas, my funds have some limitations. 唉，我资金有限。）

9. pink: *n.* a rose wine 粉红色葡萄酒

10. hyacinth: *n.* a bulbous plant of the lily family, with strap-like leaves and a compact spike of bell-shaped fragrant flowers. Native to western Asia, hyacinths are cultivated outdoors and as house plants. 风信子属植物；风信子

11. effulgence: *n.* a brilliant radiance 光辉

12. doth = does

13. Orion: *n.* （Greek Mythology） a giant and hunter who was changed into

a constellation at his death; （Astronomy） a conspicuous constellation （the Hunter）, said to represent a hunter holding a club and shield. It lies on the celestial equator and contains many bright stars, including Rigel, Betelgeuse, and a line of three that form Orion's Belt. （希腊神话）俄里翁（死后化为星座的巨人猎手）;（天文学用语）猎户座

14. o'erhead = overhead

15. moth: *n.* an insect with two pairs of broad wings covered in microscopic scales, typically drably coloured and held flat when at rest. Moths are chiefly nocturnal, and lack the clubbed antennae of butterflies. 蛾；飞蛾

◆ *A Lead-in Note* （简明导读）

此诗颇具中国古典诗歌中以景衬情的特征。这一点在前两节体现得尤为明显。副歌部分“我茕茕孑立，正值寒冬”很好地加深了主题。原来，诗人所爱之人去无踪迹，一切都黯淡下来，一切都已无所谓：“来吧飞蛾，来吧影子，这个世界已死。”

◆ 茕茕孑立

夜莺的巢穴空空，
霜花在空气中冷凝，
冰冷的窝里狐狸哀叫：
唉！我爱的人去无踪，
我茕茕孑立，
正值寒冬。

曾经，粉红色散发出葡萄酒味，
风信子喇叭形花里悬浮着野蜜蜂，
光投下，映出灿烂的美。
我茕茕孑立，

正值寒冬。

我的烛火静燃，发出光明，
上空的猎户座布满星星。
来吧飞蛾，来吧影子，这个世界已死。
唉！我爱的人去无踪，
我茕茕孑立，
正值寒冬。

017 John Clare
约翰·克莱尔

◆ *The Poet's Profile* （诗人小档案）

约翰·克莱尔（1793—1864）：英国诗人。克莱尔是农场苦工的儿子，其诗作以颂扬的方式再现了英国乡村而闻名，也以哀叹乡村的彻底改变而闻名。克莱尔是19世纪最为重要的诗人之一。1837年，他被确诊患有精神疾病，在精神病院度过了余生。克莱尔的代表作品有《描述乡村生活和风景的诗篇》和《乡村缪斯》等。

◆ *First Love*

I ne'er was struck before that hour
With love so sudden and so sweet,
Her face it bloomed like a sweet flower
And stole my heart away complete.

My face turned pale, a deadly pale,
My legs refused to walk away,
And when she looked, what could I ail?
My life and all seemed turned to clay.

And then my blood rushed to my face
And took my eyesight quite away,
The trees and bushes round the place
Seemed midnight at noonday.

I could not see a single thing,
Words from my eyes did start—
They spoke as chords do from the string,
And blood burnt round my heart.

Are flowers the winter's choice?
Is love's bed always snow?
She seemed to hear my silent voice,
Not love's appeals to know.

I never saw so sweet a face
As that I stood before.
My heart has left its dwelling-place
And can return no more.

◆ *Annotations* （原诗注释）

1. ne'er = never

2. bloom: *v.* （of fire, colour, or light） become radiant and glowing （火、色彩或光）发亮；发光 （e.g. Colour bloomed in her cheeks. 她的面颊透出光泽。）

3. ail: *v.* to cause physical or mental pain or uneasiness to 生病；感到不舒服

4. clay: *n.* a stiff, sticky fine-grained earth, typically yellow, red, or bluish-grey in colour and often forming an impermeable layer in the soil. It can be moulded when wet, and is dried and baked to make bricks, pottery, and ceramics. 黏土；泥土；陶土

5. chord: *n.* a group of （typically three or more） notes sounded together, as a basis of harmony 和弦；和音

6. string: *n.* a length of catgut or wire on a musical instrument, producing a note by vibration （乐器的）弦

7. appeal: *n.* an address to a principle or quality in anticipation of a favourable

response （敦请某人恪守某一原则或发扬某种品质的）呼吁 （e.g. The debate was to be an appeal to homophobia. 辩论将要唤起人们对同性恋的恐惧。）

◆ *A Lead-in Note* （简明导读）

诗人克莱尔对一名女子一见钟情，这是他的初恋。从此诗整体上来看，克莱尔的初恋并不成功，没有得到回报："她恍若听到我无声的表达，却不明了爱的呼吁。"但是，诗人却深陷其中不能自拔："我的心离开其寓所，一去无归期。"据说，克莱尔的初恋是玛丽·乔伊斯。克莱尔对她一见钟情，但遭到女孩父亲的反对，她父亲不同意女儿跟一个穷小子交往。

◆ 初　恋

就在那一刻，爱令我窒息：
那么突然，那么甜蜜。
她的脸如甜蜜的花绽放，
彻底将我的心偷去。

我的脸变得苍白，死一般苍白；
双腿无法挪移。
她看着我时，我患上什么病？
我的生命及一切似乎变成陶泥。

随后，血液涌到了脸上，
迷幻了视力；
正午时，周围的树和灌木
看起来恍若半夜已至。

我什么都看不见，

但双眼却流露出话语——
如弦上和音，阵阵弹出。
心中血液像烈火燃起。

花选择在冬天绽放？
爱的花床总是铺满雪粒？
她恍若听到我无声的表达，
却不明了爱的呼吁。

我从未见过如此甜蜜的脸，
看到这样的脸是我人生第一次。
我的心离开其寓所，
一去无归期。

018 Thomas Hardy
托马斯·哈代

◆ *The Poet's Profile* （诗人小档案）

托马斯·哈代（1840—1928）：英国小说家和诗人。哈代的作品多涉及对苦难生活和命运捉弄的抗争。哈代的代表作品有长篇小说《卡斯特桥市长》《德伯家的苔丝》和《无名的裘德》等。

◆ *Shut Out That Moon*

Close up the casement, draw the blind,
Shut out that stealing moon,
She wears too much the guise she wore
Before our lutes were strewn
With years-deep dust, and names we read
On a white stone were hewn.

Step not forth on the dew-dashed lawn
To view the Lady's Chair,
Immense Orion's glittering form,
The Less and Greater Bear:
Stay in; to such sights we were drawn
When faded ones were fair.

Brush not the bough for midnight scents
That come forth lingeringly,

And wake the same sweet sentiments
They breathed to you and me
When living seemed a laugh, and love
All it was said to be.

Within the common lamp-lit room
Prison my eyes and thought;
Let dingy details crudely loom,
Mechanic speech be wrought:
Too fragrant was Life's early bloom,
Too tart the fruit it brought!

◆ *Annotations* （原诗注释）

1. shut sb./sth. out or shut sb./sth. out of sth: to stop sb./sth. from entering a place 使……不能进入（某处）；挡住；遮住 （e.g. I drew the curtains to shut out the light. 我拉上窗帘遮挡光线。）

2. casement: *n.* （chiefly poetic/literary） a window （主要为诗/文用法）窗户

3. blind: *n.* a screen for a window, especially one on a roller or made of slats 窗帘（尤指卷帘或百叶窗）（e.g. She pulled down the blinds. 她拉下窗帘。）

4. stealing: *adj.* avoiding detection by moving carefully 潜行；偷偷摸摸地移动

5. guise: *n.* an external form, appearance, or manner of presentation, typically concealing the true nature of something （尤指掩饰本性的）外观；外表；表现形式；伪装

6. lute: *n.* a plucked stringed instrument with a long neck bearing frets and a rounded body with a flat front, rather like a halved egg in shape 诗琴；琉特琴

7. strew: *v.* （past participle strewn or strewed）（usu. as "be strewn with"） cover （a surface or area） with untidily scattered things 乱盖；乱铺 （e.g. The table was strewn with books and papers. 桌上乱放着书和文件。）

8. hew: *v.* （past participle hewn or hewed） （usu. as "be hewn"） make or shape （something） by cutting or chopping a material such as wood or stone （把木头或石头等原材料）砍成；劈成；削成 （e.g. a seat hewn out of a fallen tree trunk从倒下的树干上砍出一个座椅）

9. Lady's Chair: It refers to Cassiopeia, a beautiful circumpolar constellation. In Greek mythology, Cassiopeia the Queen once was known as the Lady of the Chair, which was supposed to represent the wife of Cepheus seated in a chair and holding up both arms. 这里指的是仙后座，一个漂亮的围绕天极的星座。希腊神话中，卡西俄珀亚王后曾以"椅子上的女士"而著称。人们认为"椅子上的女士"代表的是克普斯的妻子，她两只胳膊举起，坐在椅子上。

10. Orion: *n.* （Greek Mythology） a giant and hunter who was changed into a constellation at his death; （Astronomy） a conspicuous constellation （the Hunter）, said to represent a hunter holding a club and shield. It lies on the celestial equator and contains many bright stars, including Rigel, Betelgeuse, and a line of three that form Orion's Belt. （希腊神话）俄里翁（死后化为星座的巨人猎手)；(天文学）猎户座

11. Less and Greater Bear: also known as the Little Bear and the Great Bear, here they refer to the Ursa Minor and the Ursa Major

Ursa Minor: *n.* a northern constellation （the Little Bear）, which contains the north celestial pole and the pole star Polaris （天文学）小熊座

Ursa Major: *n.* one of the largest and most prominent northern constellations （the Great Bear） （天文学）大熊座

12. glittering: *adj.* shining with a shimmering or sparkling light 发出微光的；闪烁的

13. brush: *v.* push （something） away with a quick movement of the hand 推开；拂开 （e.g. She brushed a wisp of hair away from her face. 她把垂在脸上的一绺头发拂开。）

14. bough: *n.* a main branch of a tree 树枝；大树枝 （e.g. apple boughs laden with blossom 开满了花的苹果树枝）

15. scent: *n.* a distinctive smell, especially one that is pleasant 气味；香味

16. lingering: *adj.* lasting for a long time or slow to end 犹存的；苟延残喘的 （e.g. There are still some lingering doubts in my mind. 我心中仍存疑虑。）

17. sentiment: *n.* a feeling or emotion 感觉；情感 （e.g. an intense sentiment of horror 强烈的恐惧感）

18. common: *adj.* ordinary; of ordinary qualities; without special rank or position 普通的；平凡的；平民的；无特殊级别（或地位）的 （e.g. the dwellings of common people 平民住宅）

19. prison: *v.* （poetic/literary） imprison （诗/文用法）禁锢；限制 （e.g. the young man prisoned behind the doors 被关在家里的年轻人）

20. dingy: *adj.* gloomy and drab 阴暗的；单调的 （e.g. a dingy room 一个昏暗的房间）

21. loom: *v.* appear as a shadowy form, especially one that is large or threatening （尤指大型、可怕之物）阴森地逼近

22. mechanic: *adj.* resembling the action of a machine 机械的；老一套的

23. wrought: *adj.* [in combination] made or fashioned in the specified way 用特定方式制作的；有特定风格的 （e.g. well-wrought pop 制作精良的流行乐）

24. fragrant: *adj.* having a pleasant or sweet smell 芬芳的；香的

25. bloom: *n.* a flower, especially one cultivated for its beauty （尤指供观赏的）花

26. tart: *adj.* sharp or acid in taste 酸的 （e.g. a tart apple 一个酸苹果）

◆ A Lead-in Note （简明导读）

随着时间的推移，一切都会发生改变，包括人的情感。爱情也是如此。托马斯·哈代在此诗中探索的也是这方面的主题。前三节是对过去美好爱情时光的反思，流露出昔日美好时光不再的悲观情绪。最后一节则具劝慰和反省之意。的确如此，时过境迁，过去的一切很难再现，正如唐代诗人崔护所言："去年今日此门中，人面桃花相映红。人面不知何处去，桃花依旧笑春风。"（崔护《题都城南庄》）

◆ 将那月亮隔到外边

关上窗户，拉下窗帘，
将那偷摸夜行的月亮隔到外边。
月亮日渐憔悴后，
我们的诗琴才因岁月的久远
铺满了灰尘，而我们熟知的名字
也被刻到了白石头上面。

莫踏上洒满露珠的草坪
去把仙后座观看，
莫仰望猎户座那闪烁的外形，
大小熊座也莫尽收眼前。
待在屋内吧——如此景物我们曾共赏，
可如今，褪去的当时正娇艳。

莫在午夜拂弄树枝，触发
余留的香气而令其飘散，
唤醒曾吹向我和你
那些同样甜蜜的情感。
彼时，生活似乎是欢笑一场，爱情
据说也是欢笑不断。

这普普通通的屋子被灯照亮，
禁锢了我的思想和双眼。
让单调的琐事残酷地逼近吧，
不假思索地去加工语言。
人生早绽之花过于芬芳，
其果实又太酸、太酸。

019 George Eliot
乔治·艾略特

◆ *The Poet's Profile* （诗人小档案）

乔治·艾略特（1819—1880）：英国女记者、小说家和翻译家。艾略特是维多利亚时代最重要的作家之一。乔治·艾略特是她的笔名，她的原名为玛丽·安·埃文斯。她用了一个男性化的笔名，据她说，是为了她的作品能够得到认真对待。在艾略特生活的时代，女性作者都用真名出版作品，可是她想逃脱人们对女性的成见，即女性只能写出轻松愉快的浪漫之作。艾略特的小说的特点是对道德问题加以探索并运用心理分析法加以展开，而心理分析法则是现代小说的标志。她的代表作品有《亚当·比德》《弗罗斯河上的磨坊》和《米德尔马契》等。

◆ *Sweet Endings Come and Go, Love*

Sweet evenings come and go, love,
They came and went of yore:
This evening of our life, love,
Shall go and come no more.

When we have passed away, love,
All things will keep their name;
But yet no life on earth, love,
With ours will be the same.

The daisies will be there, love,

The stars in heaven will shine:
I shall not feel thy wish, love,
Nor thou my hand in thine.

A better time will come, love,
And better souls be born:
I would not be the best, love,
To leave thee now forlorn.

◆ *Annotations*（原诗注释）

1. sweet: *adj.* pleasing in general; delightful 快乐的；愉快的（e.g. It was the sweet life he had always craved. 他一直渴求的就是快乐的生活。）

2. of yore:（old use or literary） long ago（旧用法或文学用法）很久以前

3. daisy: *n.* a small European grassland plant which has flowers with a yellow disc and white rays. It has given rise to many ornamental garden varieties. 雏菊

4. thy: *adj.*（also "thine" before a vowel） archaic or dialect form of your（元音前亦作"thine"）（古旧用法或方言用法）你（您）的（同"your"）

5. thou: *pron.* [second person singular] archaic or dialect form of you, as the singular subject of a verb（古旧用法或方言用法）（作动词的单数主语）你（同"you"）

6. thine: *pron.*（form of "thy" used before a vowel） archaic form of yours; the thing or things belonging to or associated with thee（元音之前同"thy"）（古旧用法）你的（同"yours"）；（"thou"的物主代词）你（您）的东西

7. thee: *pron.* [second person singular] archaic or dialect form of you, as the singular object of a verb or preposition（古英语"thou"的宾格，同"you"）你；汝

8. forlorn: *adj.* pitifully sad and abandoned or lonely 被遗弃的；孤苦伶仃的；可怜的（e.g. forlorn figures at bus stops 汽车站旁孤零零的几个人）

◆ *A Lead-in Note*（简明导读）

爱就是忠贞不渝，爱就是生死相守。我们的爱是唯一的，与他人的不同。尽管“爱人啊，要是我们死去，所有一切都不会更其名称”，我们要是死去，地球上的一切照旧，该恋爱的恋爱，但他们的爱情无法与我们的相比：“爱人啊，地球上没有谁的生活轨迹会与我们的相同。”此诗最后一节表达了诗人对爱的执着：更佳的时光尚未到来或更好的人尚未出现，所以我不能离开你。现在离开你的人，不会是我，因为我不是最佳的人选。我要与你长相厮守，白头偕老，直至来世。

◆ 爱人啊，愉快的结局来又去

爱人啊，愉快的夜晚来又去；
它们到来又离去，就在很久前。
爱人啊，我们人生的这个夜晚将离去
而不会再回还。

爱人啊，要是我们死去，
所有一切都不会更其名称。
爱人啊，地球上没有谁的生活轨迹
会与我们的相同。

爱人啊，雏菊依旧在，
天空中的星星闪烁依然。
爱人啊，我将感受不到你的愿望何在，
你也感受不到我的手放在你的手里边。

爱人啊，更佳的时光还未到来，

更佳的人选还未降生。
爱人啊，我不愿成为最佳的人选
而置现在的你于孤苦伶仃之中。

020 Robert Burns
罗伯特·彭斯

◆ *The Poet's Profile* （诗人小档案）

罗伯特·彭斯（1759—1796）：苏格兰诗人，英国浪漫主义文学的先锋。彭斯最有名的诗篇包括《快乐的乞丐》《汤姆·奥桑特》以及他所收集的苏格兰老歌，其中包括《友谊天长地久》。他被公认为苏格兰的民族诗人，在世界范围内也得到了推崇。每年1月25日，苏格兰和其他地方都举行“彭斯之夜”纪念活动。彭斯也用标准的英语写作。在其作品中，他直言不讳地表达自己的政治言论。

◆ *A Red, Red Rose*

O my Luve's like a red, red rose
That's newly sprung in June;
O my Luve's like the melodie
That's sweetly play'd in tune.

As fair art thou, my bonnie lass,
So deep in luve am I:
And I will luve thee still, my dear,
Till a' the seas gang dry:

Till a' the seas gang dry, my dear,
And the rocks melt wi' the sun:
I will luve thee still, my dear,

While the sands o' life shall run.

And fare thee well, my only Luve,
And fare thee well, a while!
And I will come again, my Luve,
Tho' it were ten thousand mile.

◆ *Annotations*（原诗注释）

1. luve= love

2. melodie: *n.* the accompanied French art song of the 19th and 20th centuries（法国）小旋律歌曲

3. play'd = played

4. in （or out of） tune: with correct （or incorrect） pitch or intonation 合（或不合）调

5. art thou = are you

6. bonnie: *adj.* good or beautiful 好样的；漂亮的

7. lass: *n.* （chiefly Scottish & N. English） a girl or young woman （主要为苏格兰或北英格兰用法）女孩；少女 （e.g. He married a lass from Yorkshire. 他娶了一个约克夏女孩。）

8. thee: *pron.* [second person singular] archaic or dialect form of you, as the singular object of a verb or preposition （古英语"thou"的宾格，同"you"）你；汝

9. a' = all

10. gang = go

11. wi' = with

12. sands: *n.* moments of allotted time or duration; the sand in an hourglass 生涯；期限；寿命；（沙漏里的）沙子 （e.g. "The sands are numb'red that makes up my life." —Shakespeare "我人生的沙漏里，沙子屈指可数了。"——莎士比亚）

sands of time: （Fig.） the accumulated tiny amounts of time; time represented by the sand in an hourglass（比喻用法）累计的微量时间；沙漏里的沙子代表时间（e.g. The sands of time will make you grow old like everyone else. 岁月推移，你会跟大家一样老去。）

Sands are running out: The allotted time is nearly at an end; there is a limited amount of time before something happens. 所剩时间不多了；时间有限（The phrase refers to an hourglass, in which sand trickles from the top of the hourglass to the bottom through an opening until it has run out. 这一表达与沙漏有关。沙漏里的沙子从沙漏的顶部穿过中间的一个空隙向底部流淌，直至流淌完毕。）

13. o' = of

14. tho' = though

◆ *A Lead-in Note*（简明导读）

此诗有多个标题，《一朵红红的玫瑰》只是其中的一个。彭斯以旅途中所听到的一首民歌为素材，于1794年用苏格兰方言写就此诗。此诗直抒胸臆，颇具中国汉乐府诗歌风范，抒发了诗人对心目中年轻女子的爱。这种爱无法度量，这种爱超越一切。同时，诗人通过运用形象化的比喻和夸张的手法，表达了心中这种无与伦比的爱，极具浪漫主义色彩。

◆ 一朵红红的玫瑰

啊，我的爱人像一朵红红的玫瑰，
在六月里初绽花蕾；
啊，我的爱人像一首小曲儿，
和谐奏出，旋律甜美。

我漂亮的女孩儿，你魅力四射，
你让我深深沉醉；
亲爱的，我会一直爱你，
爱到海枯水乏匮。

爱到海枯水乏匮啊，亲爱的，
爱到岩石都被太阳熔化成灰；
亲爱的，我会一直爱你，
趁人生沙漏之沙仍下坠。

跟你道别吧，我唯一的爱人，
暂别短暂时光，再与你相会！
我的爱人，我将归来，
就算走上十万八千里，也不累。

021 Alfred Edward Housman
艾尔弗雷德·爱德华·豪斯曼

◆ *The Poet's Profile* （诗人小档案）

艾尔弗雷德·爱德华·豪斯曼，亦作A.E.豪斯曼（1859—1936）：英国诗人和古典文学学者。豪斯曼是他所处那个时代最突出的一位古典文学学者，被尊奉为当时最伟大的学者之一。他主要以诗集《什普罗郡一少年》为人们所知。该诗集由系列怀旧诗组成，多以民谣形式写成。

◆ *Oh, When I Was in Love with You ...*

Oh, when I was in love with you,
Then I was clean and brave,
And miles around the wonder grew
How well did I behave.

And now the fancy passes by,
And nothing will remain,
And miles around they'll say that I
Am quite myself again.

◆ *Annotations* （原诗注释）

1. clean: *adj.* morally uncontaminated; pure; innocent 清白的；纯洁的；天真的；无邪的

2. fancy: *n.* a feeling of liking or attraction, typically one that is superficial or

transient （浮泛或短暂的）爱好；迷恋 （e.g. This was no passing fancy, but a feeling he would live by. 这不是转瞬即逝的幻想，而是一种他将保持一生的情感。）

◆ *A Lead-in Note* （简明导读）

曾经与你相恋，我爱得疯狂，爱得彻底，且“那时，我纯净而勇敢”，表现出色。也许是命运捉弄人，你我不能在一起，爱的温度消失，一切归于平常。我也回到了原始状态：“方圆数里，人人都会说，从前的我得以还原。”我还是我，只是爱已走，好像未曾来过。

◆ 啊，我曾与你相恋……

啊，我曾与你相恋。
那时，我纯净而勇敢。
方圆数里，奇迹发生，
我有多么出色的表现。

如今，迷恋渐逝，
一切都将消散。
方圆数里，人人都会说，
从前的我得以还原。

022 Robert Louis Stevenson
罗伯特·路易斯·史蒂文森

◆ *The Poet's Profile* （诗人小档案）

罗伯特・路易斯・史蒂文森（1850—1894）：苏格兰小说家、诗人、散文家和游记作家。史蒂文森的成名作是冒险小说《金银岛》，其他代表作品有《化身博士》和《绑架》等。

◆ *Love, What Is Love?*

Love—what is love? A great and aching heart;
Wrung hands; and silence; and a long despair.
Life—what is life? Upon a moorland bare
To see love coming and see love depart.

◆ *Annotations* （原诗注释）

1. wring: *v.* squeeze and twist （something） to force liquid from it 绞；拧
2. moorland: *n.* （also as "moorlands"） an extensive area of moor 高沼地；广袤的荒野

◆ *A Lead-in Note* （简明导读）

短短的四行诗中，诗人自问自答，揭示出爱情的真谛。爱情是折磨人的。人生中少不了爱情，爱情就是人生中上演的一场又一场悲欢离合之戏。

爱情贯穿人生，“是在光秃的原野上看爱情到来，看爱人离分”。

◆ 爱情，爱情是什么？

爱情——爱情是什么？是一颗伟大而疼痛的心，
是拧疼的手，是沉默，是绝望之情深深。
人生——人生是什么？是在光秃的原野上
看爱情到来，看爱人离分。

023 Michael Drayton 迈克尔·德雷顿

◆ *The Poet's Profile* （诗人小档案）

迈克尔·德雷顿（1563—1631）：英国诗人。德雷顿在伊丽莎白时代声望卓著，可是到了詹姆斯一世时代,. 他就无缘赢得青睐了。这从两方面可以看出来：一方面，他写给新国王的奉承诗受到了奚落；另一方面，他想效力宫廷，却被拒之门外。1631年12月，德雷顿在伦敦去世，葬于威斯敏斯特教堂的一个墓碑下，碑文由本·琼森撰写。本·琼森是英国著名的戏剧家，也是德雷顿的一位好友。

◆ *Love's Farewell*

Since there's no help, come let us kiss and part, —
Nay I have done, you get no more of me;
And I am glad, yea, glad with all my heart,
That thus so cleanly I myself can free.

Shake hands for ever, cancel all our vows;
And when we meet at any time again,
Be it not seen in either of our brows
That we one jot of former love retain.

Now at the last gasp of love's latest breath,
When his pulse failing, passion speechless lies,
When faith is kneeling by his bed of death,

And innocence is closing up his eyes,

Now if thou would'st, when all have given him over,
From death to life thou might'st him yet recover!

◆ *Annotations* （原诗注释）

1. farewell: *n.* an act of parting or of marking someone's departure 道别；告别；辞行；饯行 （e.g. The dinner had been arranged as a farewell. 安排这顿饭是为了饯行。）

2. nay: *n.* a negative answer 否定的回答 （e.g. The cabinet sits to give the final yea or nay to policies. 内阁开会对政策给予最终肯定或否定的回答。）

3. cleanly: *adv.* without difficulty or impediment; smoothly and efficiently 顺利地；干净利落地 （e.g. He vaulted cleanly through the open window. 他干净利落地跃出窗外。）

4. vow: *n.* （vows） a set of such promises committing one to a prescribed role, calling, or course of action, typically to marriage or a monastic career （尤指为婚姻或僧侣生涯立下的）誓约

5. brow: *n.* a person's forehead 额头；脑门子

6. jot: *n.* a very small amount 少量；少额；稍许；些许 （e.g. I have yet to see one jot of evidence. 我还没有见到一点儿证据。）

7. retain: *v.* continue to have （something）; keep possession of 保持；保留 （e.g. Labour retained the seat. 工党保住了这个席位。）

8. gasp: *n.* a convulsive catching of breath （急促的）呼吸 （e.g. His breath was coming in gasps. 他喘得上气不接下气。）

9. passion: *n.* strong and barely controllable emotion 热情；激情 （e.g. a man of impetuous passion 一个极易冲动的人）

10. innocence: *n.* lack of guile or corruption; purity 天真；无邪；纯真 （e.g. The healthy bloom in her cheeks gave her an aura of innocence. 她双颊的健康之色赋予她一种纯真的气息。）

11. thou: *pron.* [second person singular] archaic or dialect form of you, as the singular subject of a verb （古旧用法或方言用法）（作动词的单数主语）你（同“you”）

12. would'st = wouldest （古英语中“would”的第二人称单数形式）

13. might'st = mightiest （古英语中“might”的第二人称单数形式）

◆ *A Lead-in Note* （简明导读）

两个相恋的人，到了分离的边缘，看来一切无可挽回，只有挥手道别；看似潇洒，实则无奈和不舍。还有挽救的余地吗？在此诗的第三节，诗人笔锋一转，将“爱”“激情”“信念”和“天真”拟人化，委婉表达了妥协之意。难道你会见死不救吗？

◆ 爱的别离

既然无可挽回，就让我们亲吻道再见，——
我什么都做不了，你也沾不上我的边。
我很高兴，是啊，我内心真的很高兴：
从此，自由完全来到我的心间。

握手道永别，将所有誓约都放下。
不管何时，若再一次相见，
在我们的眉宇间，一丝一毫
昔日的爱意也不要发现。

现在，**爱**躺下了，奄奄一息。
它的脉搏微弱，**激情**哑口无言，
信念在它的病榻前跪着，

天真也快要合上双眼。

那么，如果你愿意，在它行将就木之时，
你或许能起死回生，让它复原！

024 Margaret Cavendish
玛格丽特·卡文迪什

◆ *The Poet's Profile* （诗人小档案）

玛格丽特·卡文迪什（约1624—1674）：玛格丽特是泰恩河纽卡斯尔公爵夫人，出生时的名字为玛格丽特·卢卡斯。卡文迪什是英国女诗人、哲学家、散文家、剧作家和科学家。在一个多数女性作家匿名发表作品的时代，卡文迪什用的却是真名实姓。1645年，她嫁给了泰恩河纽卡斯尔公爵威廉·卡文迪什（当时他是侯爵），成了他的第二任妻子。卡文迪什写的乌托邦式的浪漫作品《炫目的世界》，是科幻作品的最早典范。在广泛发表自然哲学和早期现代科学作品方面，卡文迪什是绝无仅有的。

◆ *Love and Poetry*

O love, how thou art tired out with rhyme!
Thou art a tree whereon all poets clime;
And from thy branches every one takes some
Of thy sweet fruit, which Fancy feeds upon.
But now thy tree is left so bare and poor,
That they can scarcely gather one plumb more.

◆ *Annotations* （原诗注释）

1. thou art = you are
2. rhyme: *n.* poetry or verse marked by such correspondence of sound 押韵诗；

韵文（e.g. The clues were written in rhyme. 字谜线索是以韵诗形式写成的。）

3. whereon: *adv.* （archaic） on which （古旧用法）在那上面（e.g. the cliff side whereon I walked我走过的悬崖边）

4. clime = climb

5. thy: *adj.* （also "thine" before a vowel） archaic or dialect form of your （元音前亦作"thine"）（古旧用法或方言用法）你（您）的（同"your"）

6. fancy: *n.* a thing that one supposes or imagines, typically an unfounded or tentative belief or idea 想象出来的事物（尤指无根据或不成熟的看法、观点）（e.g. I've a fancy they want to be alone. 我猜他们不想被打扰。）

7. plum: *n.* an oval fleshy fruit which is purple, reddish, or yellow when ripe and contains a flattish pointed stone 李子；梅子

◆ *A Lead-in Note* （简明导读）

此诗是卡文迪什为其丈夫写的一首励志短诗，意在安慰失意中的丈夫：当初你做的事情是多么了不起！诗中，卡文迪什将丈夫比作一棵树，其果实滋养了其他诗人，成了其他诗人创作的灵感和素材，"可如今，你那棵树光秃秃的好可怜，那些诗人几乎连一个李子都摘不下"。可谓牺牲了自己，成全了别人。

◆ 爱与诗

啊，爱人，赋诗押韵多么疲乏！
你是一棵树，所有诗人沿树攀爬。
每个人都能从你的枝条上
摘到果实滋养"想象"而得到升华。
可如今，你那棵树光秃秃的好可怜，
那些诗人几乎连一个李子都摘不下。

025 William Wordsworth
威廉·华兹华斯

◆ *The Poet's Profile* （诗人小档案）

威廉·华兹华斯（1770—1850）：英国诗人。华兹华斯许多作品的灵感来自“湖畔区”。他与柯尔律治共同完成的《抒情歌谣集》是英国浪漫主义诗歌的里程碑，其中包括诗歌《廷滕恩道堂》。华兹华斯的其他代表作品有抒情诗《我好似一朵孤独的流云》（又名《水仙花》）和《序曲》。1843年，他被封为“桂冠诗人”。

◆ *Strange Fits of Passion Have I Known*

Strange fits of passion have I known:
And I will dare to tell,
But in the lover's ear alone,
What once to me befell.

When she I loved looked every day
Fresh as a rose in June,
I to her cottage bent my way,
Beneath an evening-moon.

Upon the moon I fixed my eye,
All over the wide lea;
With quickening pace my horse drew nigh
Those paths so dear to me.

And now we reached the orchard-plot;
And, as we climbed the hill,
The sinking moon to Lucy's cot
Came near, and nearer still.

In one of those sweet dreams I slept,
Kind Nature's gentlest boon!
And all the while my eye I kept
On the descending moon.

My horse moved on; hoof after hoof
He raised, and never stopped:
When down behind the cottage roof,
At once, the bright moon dropped.

What fond and wayward thoughts will slide
Into a Lover's head!
"O mercy!" to myself I cried,
"If Lucy should be dead!"

◆ *Annotations* （原诗注释）

1. fit: *n.* a sudden uncontrollable outbreak of intense emotion, laughter, hysterics, coughing, or other action or activity （强烈的情感、笑声、咳嗽等行为）突然一阵；突发；蓦地爆发 （e.g. in a fit of temper 一时性急）

2. passion: *n.* strong and barely controllable emotion 热情；激情 （e.g. a man of impetuous passion 一个极易冲动的人）

3. befall: *v.* （past befell; past participle befallen） （poetic / literary）（especially of something bad） happen to （someone） （诗/文用法）（尤指不幸的事）发生在（某人）身上；降临于 （e.g. A tragedy befell his daughter. 他

女儿遭遇不幸。)

4. cottage: *n.* a small simple house, typically one in the country （尤指乡村的）小屋；村舍

5. lea: *n.* （poetic/literary） an open area of grassy or arable land （诗/文用法）草地；耕地 （e.g. The lowing herd winds slowly o'er the lea. 发出低沉叫声的牛群在草地上蜿蜒慢行。）

6. nigh: *adv., prep., & adj.* （archaic） near （古旧用法）（靠）近的（地）（e.g. They drew nigh unto the city. 他们朝城市走去。）

7. orchard: *n.* a piece of enclosed land planted with fruit trees （通常指围起来的）果园（e.g. My orchard is bearing well this year. 今年我的果园果实累累。）

8. plot: *n.* a small piece of ground marked out for a purpose such as building or gardening （用于建筑或园林的）小块地；苗圃 （e.g. a vegetable plot 菜地）

9. cot: *n.* a type of bed, in particular （尤指一种类型的）床

10. boon: *n.* a thing that is helpful or beneficia 恩惠；裨益 （e.g. The route will be a boon to many travellers. 这条通道将方便许多游客。）

11. hoof: *n.* the horny part of the foot of an ungulate animal, especially a horse （有蹄动物，尤指马的）蹄 （e.g. There was a clatter of hoofs as a rider came up to them. 当一位骑手向他们骑来时，传来马蹄的得得声。）

12. fond: *adj.* affectionate; loving 深情的；爱慕的 （e.g. I have very fond memories of Oxford. 我对牛津一往情深。）

13. wayward: *adj.* difficult to control or predict because of unusual or perverse behavior 任性的；难以捉摸的；反复无常的 （e.g. her wayward, difficult sister 她那个任性的、难于相处的妹妹）

14. o: *interj.* used to express surprise or strong emotion 哦；哟；啊；唉；哎呀（表示惊讶或强烈的情感）

15. mercy: *excl.* （archaic） used in expressions of surprise or fear （古旧用法）（表示惊愕或恐惧）哎呀 （e.g. "Mercy me!" uttered Mrs Diggory. 迪戈里太太叫了一声："哎呀！"）

◆ *A Lead-in Note*（简明导读）

此诗是诗人《露西组诗》（共5首）中的一首，这组诗收录在《抒情歌谣集》中。此诗是诗人前往露西住处时，个人情感与现实情境的交融。诗的最后，诗人突然想到露西的死而感到悲痛和压抑。

露西的身份是个谜，也存在歧义。有人认为露西代表诗人华兹华斯的妹妹多萝西。可以说，诗人跟妹妹相依为命，他很爱这个妹妹。但不幸的是，多萝西于1829年患了重病，自此余生一直疾病缠身。也有人认为，露西指的是诗人所爱的某位神秘女子。这位神秘女子单纯且拥有天仙般美貌，却不幸英年早逝。

◆ 我所熟悉的奇特之情阵阵闪现

我所熟悉的奇特之情阵阵闪现，
我要说出来，我有这个胆。
可是，只对着情人的耳朵，
道出我曾经遭遇过的体验。

爱她的季节里，每日她都
像六月里的玫瑰一样新鲜。
我弯身策马赶往她的小屋，
那是月亮照耀下的一个夜晚。

我凝视着月亮，
在一片宽阔的草地上面。
我策马加快了速度，
接近了那些小路，如此亲切之感。

现在，我策马抵达果园所在地。

于是，我骑着马开始爬山，
此时，月下沉，沉向露西的小床，
越沉越近，一直沉向小床近前。

我入睡，沉入某个甜美的梦境，
这最温馨的恩惠，来自仁慈的大自然。
但自始至终，我盯着
持续下沉的月亮，一直看。

我继续策马前行，马蹄从未
停歇，抬起又落下，往复循环。
明亮的月沉到小屋后面之时，
一下子跌落，消失不见。

啊，何等深情、微妙的念头会滑进
一个情人的脑袋里面！
“噢，天呐！”我冲自己喊道，
“要是露西死了，可怎么办！”

026 Algernon Charles Swinburne
阿尔杰农·查尔斯·斯温伯恩

◆ *The Poet's Profile* （诗人小档案）

阿尔杰农·查尔斯·斯温伯恩（1837—1909）：英国诗人、剧作家、长篇小说家和评论家。斯温伯恩完成了多部长篇小说，为第11版《大英百科全书》（亦译作《大不列颠百科全书》）做出了贡献。从1903年到1907年，他连续获得诺贝尔文学奖的提名，又于1909年获得诺贝尔文学奖提名。斯温伯恩是前拉斐尔派诗人，他为伊丽莎白和詹姆士一世时期戏剧研究的复兴做出了重大贡献，还写了诸多研究威廉·布莱克和勃朗特姐妹的颇具影响力的作品。

◆ *Dead Love*

Dead love, by treason slain, lies stark,
White as a dead stark-stricken dove:
None that pass by him pause to mark
Dead love.

His heart, that strained and yearned and strove
As toward the sundawn strives the lark,
Is cold as all the old joy thereof.

Dead men, re-risen from dust, may hark
When rings the trumpet blown above:
It will not raise from out the dark
Dead love.

◆ *Annotations* （原诗注释）

1. treason: *n.* the action of betraying someone or something 背叛；不忠；背信（e.g. Doubt is the ultimate treason against faith. 怀疑是对信念的根本背叛。）

2. slay: *v.* （archaic or poetic / literary） kill （a person or animal） in a violent way （古旧用法或诗/文用法）杀；杀戮；杀害（e.g. St. George slew the dragon. 圣乔治杀死了那条龙。）

3. stark: *adj.* （archaic or poetic / literary） stiff, rigid, or incapable of movement （古旧用法或诗/文用法）僵直的；僵硬的（e.g. A human body lying stiff and stark by the stream. 溪边直挺挺地躺着一具僵硬的人尸。）

4. strive: *v.* （past strove or strived; past participle striven or strived） make great efforts to achieve or obtain something 努力；奋斗；力求

5. lark: *n.* a small ground-dwelling songbird with elongated hind claws and a song that is delivered on the wing, typically crested and with brown streaky plumage 百灵鸟；云雀

6. thereof: *adv.* （formal） of the thing just mentioned; of that （正式用法）在其中；其（e.g. the member state or a part thereof 会员国或其一部分）

7. hark: *v.* （poetic/literary） listen （诗/文用法）听；听啊（e.g. Hark! He knocks. 听啊，他在敲门。）

8. trumpet: *n.* a brass musical instrument with a flared bell and a bright, penetrating tone. The modern instrument has the tubing looped to form a straight-sided coil, with three valves. 喇叭；小号

◆ *A Lead-in Note* （简明导读）

这是一首三节十一行“回旋诗”。回旋的部分是“爱已死”。爱已死，“路过的，没有一个驻足观望”。爱的离世是一件根本无法挽回的事情。“死去的人，从尘土中再度起身”，那等于死而复生了，但是“爱，不会从黑暗中站起来，爱已死”。爱已死，无法挽回。

◆ 爱已死

爱已死，死于背叛，尸体僵硬
惨白，如一只直挺挺死去的鸽子：
路过的，没有一个驻足观望，
爱已死。

爱的心，如同云雀竭力飞向黎明，
充满了渴望，用尽了气力去奋争，
却冷了下来，就像昔日的喜悦般冰冷。

死去的人，从尘土中再度起身，
或许会听到上方的号角吹起：
爱，不会从黑暗中站起来，
爱已死。

027 Thomas Campion
托马斯·坎皮恩

◆ *The Poet's Profile* （诗人小档案）

托马斯·坎皮恩（1567—1620）：英国作曲家、诗人和内科医生。坎皮恩写过许多诗歌、假面舞蹈剧和音乐专著。坎皮恩在英国文艺复兴时期非戏剧性文学上的重要性，在于他在作品中对音乐和诗歌独特的驾驭能力。其他诗人和音乐家大谈诗歌和音乐艺术联盟之际，唯独坎皮恩写出了完整的歌曲——完全由自己谱曲的歌曲，唯独坎皮恩写出了文学价值经久不衰的抒情诗篇——将诗人对音乐的思考融入诗中。

◆ *Cherry-Ripe*

There is a garden in her face
Where roses and white lilies blow;
A heavenly paradise is that place,
Wherein all pleasant fruits do flow:
There cherries grow which none may buy
Till "Cherry-ripe" themselves do cry.

Those cherries fairly do enclose
Of orient pearl a double row,
Which when her lovely laughter shows,
They look like rose-buds fill'd with snow;
Yet them nor peer nor prince can buy
Till "Cherry-ripe" themselves do cry.

Her eyes like angels watch them still;
Her brows like bended bows do stand,
Threat'ning with piercing frowns to kill
All that attempt with eye or hand
Those sacred cherries to come nigh,
Till "Cherry-ripe" themselves do cry.

◆ *Annotations*（原诗注释）

1. cherry: *n.* a small, soft round stone fruit that is typically bright or dark red 樱桃

2. ripe: *adj.* （of fruit or grain） developed to the point of readiness for harvesting and eating （果实或谷物）成熟的

3. lily: *n.* a bulbous plant with large trumpet-shaped, typically fragrant, flowers on a tall, slender stem. Lilies have long been cultivated, some kinds being of symbolic importance and some used in perfumery. 百合花

4. blow: *v.* produce flowers or be in flower 开花；在开花 （e.g. I know a bank where the wild thyme blows. 我知道一个堤岸，那里野生百里香正在开花。）

5. paradise: *n.* （in some religions） heaven as the ultimate abode of the just （某些宗教中的）天堂；天国

6. wherein: *adv.* in which 在那里；在那方面；在那时；在那种情况下

7. fairly: *adv.* actually （used to emphasize something surprising or extreme） 实际上；简直是（强调令人吃惊或极端之事）（e.g. He fairly snarled at her. 他简直就是在向她大吼大叫。）

8. bud: *n.* a compact knob-like growth on a plant which develops into a leaf, flower, or shoot 芽；蓓蕾

9. fill'd = filled

10. peer: *n.* a member of the nobility in Britain or Ireland, comprising the ranks of duke, marquess, earl, viscount, and baron （英国或爱尔兰）有爵位的

贵族

11. brow: *n.* （usu. as “brows”） an eyebrow 眉毛 （e.g. His brows lifted in surprise. 他惊讶地扬起眉毛。）

12. threat'ning = threatening

13. piercing: *adj.* （of eyes or a look） appearing to see through someone; searching（眼睛或眼神）锐利的；敏锐的；有洞察力的

14. frown: *n.* a facial expression or look characterized by such a furrowing of one's brows 皱眉；蹙额

◆ *A Lead-in Note* （简明导读）

年轻女孩儿的脸是一座花园，面颊如玫瑰，双唇似红樱桃，牙齿则是东方珍珠。她笑起来时，珍珠与樱桃形成了强烈的对比。但是，她要是不吆喝“樱桃熟了”，没有哪个男子可以买到樱桃——亲吻她。少女等着如意郎君前来摘取樱桃。看不到如意郎君，少女绝不会吆喝：“樱桃熟了！”即使樱桃已经成熟。

◆ 樱桃熟了

她的脸是一座花园，
红玫瑰和白百合盛开在上面。
那是一个圣洁天堂之所，
那里的各种果实讨人喜欢。
樱桃结在那儿，无人可买到——
“樱桃熟了”，除非樱桃这样呼喊。

那些樱桃完全将两排
东方珍珠围到了中间，
她可爱的笑容将珍珠露出时，
看起来像白雪将玫瑰花蕾填满。

可那些樱桃，贵族和王子都买不到——
“樱桃熟了”，除非樱桃这样呼喊。

她的眼如天使般守候着樱桃；
她的眉静静挺立如弯弓一般，
敏锐地皱起观察，将他人眼或手
做出的各种企图扼杀于摇篮。
休想企图靠近那些樱桃——
“樱桃熟了”，除非樱桃这样呼喊。

028 Matthew Prior
马修·普赖尔

◆ *The Poet's Profile* （诗人小档案）

马修·普赖尔（1664—1721）：英国诗人和外交家。普赖尔的诗的风格丰富多彩、讨人喜欢，显示出他对文字极大的驾驭能力。入狱期间，他完成了《阿尔玛》（又名《思想的进步》）。这是一首持怀疑论调的幽默诗，普赖尔因此而扬名至今。普赖尔达到巅峰期的时候，他的作品跟斯威夫特的作品不相上下，萨缪尔·约翰逊和威廉·柯珀也羡慕过他。他被葬于威斯敏斯特教堂的“诗人角”。

◆ *A True Maid*

No, no; for my virginity,
When I lose that, says Rose, I'll die:
Behind the elms last night, cried Dick,
Rose, were you not extremely sick?

◆ *Annotations* （原诗注释）

1. maid: *n.* （archaic or poetic/literary） a virgin （古旧用法或者诗/文用法）处女

2. virginity: *n.* the state of never having had sexual intercourse 处女身份；童贞（e.g. I lost my virginity. 我失去了童贞。）

3. elm: *n.* a tall deciduous tree which typically has rough serrated leaves and propagates from root suckers 榆树

◆ *A Lead-in Note* （简明导读）

关于“罗丝”（Rose）这个名字的含义，读者可参阅本书第008首中“简明导读”部分。此诗前两行中，罗丝对处女贞洁的说法，迪克（应该是罗丝的男朋友）并不认同：“罗丝，难道你深受疾病折磨？”谁了解事情的真相呢？也许，罗丝是在委婉地谢绝男子的追求。

◆ 名副其实的处女

不要这样，不要这样，贞洁不可夺。
少女罗丝继续说，失贞洁我无以活。
昨晚在榆树后，男子迪克大叫：
罗丝，难道你深受疾病折磨？

029 Thomas Carew
托马斯·卡鲁

◆ *The Poet's Profile* （诗人小档案）

托马斯·卡鲁（约1595—1640）：英国诗人。卡鲁的诗在他活着的时候没有发表过，而是以手抄本的形式在朋友中流传。传看的朋友中有本·琼森和约翰·多恩，这两个人对卡鲁的诗歌创作产生了极大的影响。尽管卡鲁从未达到多恩和琼森的高度，但作为一个文雅的作者，他对文学的贡献在于他那典型的骑士派诗风。他死后不久，他的一本诗集才问世。

◆ *The Primrose*

Ask me why I send you here
The firstling of the infant year;
Ask me why I send to you
This primrose all bepearled with dew:
I straight will whisper in your ears,
The sweets of love are washed with tears.

Ask me why this flower doth show
So yellow, green, and sickly too;
Ask me why the stalk is weak
And bending, yet it doth not break:
I must tell you, these discover
What doubts and fears are in a lover.

◆ *Annotations* （原诗注释）

1. primrose: *n.* a European plant of woodland and hedgerows, which produces pale yellow flowers in the early spring 报春花；樱草

2. firstling: *n.* （archaic） the first agricultural produce or animal offspring of a season （古旧用法）（某个季节的）首茬农产品；头生仔

3. infant: *n.* denoting something in an early stage of its development 初期的；摇篮期的 （e.g. the infant Labour Party 初创阶段的工党）

4. dew: *n.* tiny drops of water that form on cool surfaces at night, when atmospheric vapour condenses 露；露滴；露水 （e.g. The grass was wet with dew. 草地被露水打湿了。）

5. doth = does

6. sickly: *adj.* often ill; in poor health 多病的；体弱的 （e.g. She was a thin, sickly child. 她是一个体弱多病的孩子。）

7. stalk: *n.* the main stem of a herbaceous plant （草本植物的）茎；秆

8. discover: *v.* display （a quality or feeling） 流露（品质或感情）（e.g. With what agility did these military men discover their skill in feats of war. 这些军人们是以何等的机敏在战争中展示了他们的技能。）

◆ *A Lead-in Note* （简明导读）

春天里的第一抹金黄就是报春花。送给你报春花，“花上满是珍珠状露滴闪烁”，那是苦尽甘来的爱。你“问我为何花茎弯曲脆弱却不会断折”，那意味着爱还要经历不知多少考验和磨砺。所以，花茎弯曲但不会折断，也不能折断——爱要经得住考验。

◆ 报春花

问我为何给你送出
一年伊始最早绽放的花朵。

问我为何送给你报春花——
花上满是珍珠状露滴闪烁。
我会径直对你低声耳语：
甜蜜的爱以泪洗过。

问我这束花为何
如此金黄、嫩绿、娇弱。
问我为何花茎弯曲
脆弱却不会断折。
我必须告诉你：这些揭示出
爱你之人的心多么忧虑和疑惑。

030 Christopher Marlowe 克里斯托弗·马洛

◆ *The Poet's Profile* （诗人小档案）

克里斯托弗·马洛（1564—1593）：英国戏剧家和诗人。马洛极大地影响了莎士比亚。莎士比亚跟马洛同年出生，莎士比亚一举成为伊丽莎白时代一流的戏剧家，而马洛却过早死去，死因不明。马洛的戏剧作品以无韵诗体和塑造以奸诈取胜的主人公而著名。作为戏剧家，马洛给无韵诗体带来了新的力量和生命。他的作品对莎士比亚早期的历史剧产生了影响。马洛的代表作品有《浮士德》和《马耳他的犹太人》等。

◆ *Who Ever Loved, That Loved Not at First Sight?*

It lies not in our power to love or hate,
For will in us is overruled by fate.

When two are stripped, long ere the course begin,
We wish that one should lose, the other win;

And one especially do we affect
Of two gold ingots like in each respect:
The reason no man knows; let it suffice
What we behold is censured by our eyes.

Where both deliberate, the love is slight:
Who ever loved, that loved not at first sight?

—A fragment of "*Hero and Leander: The First Sestiad*" by Christopher Marlowe

◆ Annotations（原诗注释）

1. will: *n.* a deliberate or fixed desire or intention 意愿；心愿；目的（e.g. Jane had not wanted them to stay against their will. 简并不希望他们违背自己的心愿留下来。）

2. overrule: *v.* to prevail over, dominate, or influence 压倒；统治；制服；影响

3. ere: *prep. & conj.*（poetic/literary or archaic） before （in time） （诗/文用法或古旧用法）在……之前（在时间上）(e.g. We hope you will return ere long. 我们希望你很快回来。）

4. affect: *v.* to have or show a liking for; to fancy or love 喜欢；喜爱；钟情

5. ingot: *n.* a block of steel, gold, silver, or other metal, typically oblong in shape（钢、金、银等金属的）铸块；锭（尤呈长方形或长椭圆形）

6. suffice: *v.* be enough or adequate 足够；合适 （e.g. A quick look should suffice. 迅速看一下就行了。）

7. behold: *v.* （past and past participle beheld）（archaic or poetic/literary） see or observe （someone or something, especially of remarkable or impressive nature）（古旧用法或诗/文用法）看；观看（尤指看非凡的或感人的人或事物）

8. censure: *v.* （often as "be censured"） express severe disapproval of（someone or something）, typically in a formal statement （尤指在正式声明中）严厉指责；谴责；申斥

9. deliberate: *adj.* fully considered; not impulsive 深思熟虑的；非一时冲动的（e.g. a deliberate decision 深思熟虑的决定）

10. Hero and Leander: （Greek Mythology） Hero is a priestess of Aphrodite at Sestos on the European shore of the Hellespont, whose lover Leander, a youth of Abydos on the opposite shore, swam the strait nightly to visit her. One stormy night he was drowned and Hero in grief threw herself into the sea. （希腊神话）海洛与利安得：海洛是阿佛洛狄特的女祭司，住在赫勒斯滂海峡欧洲海岸一边的塞斯特斯。海洛的情人利安得是一位住在对岸阿比杜斯地区的青年，他每晚游过海峡与她会面。一个暴风雨的夜晚，他溺水身亡，痛苦万分的海洛也投海自尽。

11. sestiad: *n.* Here, it refers to Marlowe's unfinished narrative poem "*Hero and Leander*". 这个词在这里指的是马洛未完成的叙事长诗《女祭司海洛与情人利安得》。

◆ *A Lead-in Note* （简明导读）

此诗正好验证了汉语中的一个说法：一见钟情。如果“两个人赤裸裸，远在应有的进程之初——”则行不通，此时“我们希望：一个赢，另一个输”。此诗结尾的两句则紧扣主题，从而说明：爱具有情感性——“曾经爱过的人，谁不一见钟情？”

◆ 曾经爱过的人，谁不一见钟情？

爱或恨，我们无权决定，
因内心的意愿由命运统领。

两个人赤裸裸，远在应有的进程之初——
我们希望：一个赢，另一个输。

两块金锭，其中一块我们特别喜欢——
尽管相似，无论从哪一个方面来看。
原因没人清楚，但足够清楚的是：
我们所见，由眼睛评判。

两个人谨慎行事，爱会轻如风。
曾经爱过的人，谁不一见钟情？
——克里斯托弗·马洛《女祭司海洛与情人利安得：第一部叙事长诗》片段

031 Walter Savage Landor
沃尔特·萨维奇·兰多

◆ *The Poet's Profile* （诗人小档案）

沃尔特·萨维奇·兰多（1775—1864）：英国诗人和评论家。在兰多漫长而活跃的89年的人生旅途中，他创作了大量题材各异的作品，它们可以分成四大类型：散文、抒情诗、政论文（包括讽刺诗）和拉丁文作品。他写过政论短文、散文和300多首拉丁文诗歌，但这样的作品在他的文集中普遍受到了冷落。兰多的代表作品有东方英雄史诗《格比尔》和散文《文人与政治家的假想对话》等。

◆ *Twenty Years Hence*

Twenty years hence my eyes may grow
If not quite dim, yet rather so,
Still yours from others they shall know
Twenty years hence.

Twenty years hence though it may hap
That I be called to take a nap
In a cool cell where thunderclap
Was never heard,

There breathe but o'er my arch of grass
A not too sadly sighed Alas,
And I shall catch, ere you can pass,
That winged word.

◆ Annotations （原诗注释）

1. hence: *adv.* in the future （used after a period of time） （用于一段时间之后）……之后；今后…… （e.g. Two years hence they might say something quite different. 两年之后他们也许就有不同的说法。）

2. dim: *adj.* （of the eyes） not able to see clearly （眼睛）昏花的；看不清楚的 （e.g. His eyes became dim. 他的视力开始模糊。）

3. know: *v.* （know someone/thing from） be able to distinguish one person or thing from （another） 能区分；能识别 （e.g. You are convinced you know your own baby from any other in the world. 你确信能够把自己的孩子和世界上别的小孩区分开来。）

4. hap: *v.* come about by chance 偶然发生 （e.g. What can hap to him worthy to be deemed evil? 他能遇到什么可以称得上邪恶的事情?）

5. nap: *n.* a short sleep, especially during the day （尤指白天的）小睡；打盹 （e.g. Excuse me, I'll just take a little nap. 对不起，我要小睡一会。）

6. thunderclap: *n.* a crash of thunder （often used to refer to something startling or unexpected） 雷声；霹雳；晴天霹雳；突发的意外事件 （e.g. The door opened like a thunderclap. “咣”的一声巨响，门开了。）

7. breathe: *v.* say something with quiet intensity （低声细气地）说出；吐露

8. o'er = over

9. arch: *n.* a curved symmetrical structure spanning an opening and typically supporting the weight of a bridge, roof, or wall above it 拱形结构

10. alas: *interj.* （chiefly poetic、literary or humorous） an expression of grief, pity, or concern （主要为诗/文用法或幽默用法）哎呀；唉 （表示悲痛、遗憾或关心）（e.g. Alas, my funds have some limitations. 唉，我资金有限。）

11. ere: *prep. & conj.* （poetic/literary or archaic） before （as conjunction） （诗/文用法或古旧用法）在……之前 （e.g. I was driven for some half mile ere we stopped. 我们驱车半英里之后才停下来。）

◆ *A Lead-in Note* （简明导读）

二十年之后，谁知道会发生什么事情呢？衰老是肯定的，比如视力开始模糊。但不管怎么模糊，看到你我还是那么熟悉。“二十年之后，说不定有人会让我打个盹儿而把我召唤”，那是死神的召唤。“打个盹儿”说起来轻巧，其实是长眠不醒。诗的结尾颇具神秘色彩：谁发出一声叹息，诗人又为什么不让心爱的人听到这声叹息，只有靠读者插上想象的翅膀去体悟了。

◆ 二十年之后

二十年之后，我的双眼
定会模糊起来，睹物昏暗；
二十年之后，却仍可将
你的眼与他人的眼来分辨。

二十年之后，说不定有人
会让我打个盹儿而把我召唤。
睡在一间凉爽的小屋，
霹雳声我再也听不见。

就在我那长了草的拱门上方，
发出一声“唉”的叹息，不太伤感。
在你有可能路过之前，我要截住
那振翅疾飞的字眼。

032 Amy Levy
埃米·利维

◆ *The Poet's Profile* （诗人小档案）

埃米·利维（1861—1889）：英国女诗人、散文家及长篇小说家。利维最令人称道的是她的文学天赋。1881年，她的第一部诗集《〈粘西比〉及其他诗集》出版，其中，《粘西比》（粘西比为苏格拉底的妻子），是一首以苏格拉底的妻子的口气写的诗。在利维人生的末期，她的精神状况每况愈下。1889年9月10日，她把自己关进了房间，点燃木炭。母亲和妹妹后来发现她死在房间里，她当时年仅28岁。

◆ *A Farewell*

(*After Heine*)
The sad rain falls from Heaven,
A sad bird pipes and sings;
I am sitting here at my window
And watching the spires of "King's."

O fairest of all fair places,
Sweetest of all sweet towns!
With the birds, and the greyness and greenness,
And the men in caps and gowns.

All they that dwell within thee,
To leave are ever loth,

For one man gets friends, and another
Gets honour, and one gets both.

The sad rain falls from Heaven;
My heart is great with woe—
I have neither a friend nor honour,
Yet I am sorry to go.

◆ *Annotations*（原诗注释）

1. farewell: *n.* an act of parting or of marking someone's departure 道别；告别；辞行；饯行（e.g. The dinner had been arranged as a farewell. 安排这顿饭是为了饯行。）

2. pipe: *v.*（of a bird）sing in a high or shrill voice（鸟）尖声叫；尖声唱

3. spire: *n.* a tapering conical or pyramidal structure on the top of a building, typically a church tower（尤指教堂塔楼的）尖顶

4. o: *interj.* used to express surprise or strong emotion 哦；哟；啊；唉；哎呀（表示惊讶或强烈的情感）

5. King's = King's College

注：这里的"King's College"指的是英国剑桥大学的国王学院。国王学院是剑桥大学内最有名的学院之一，成立于1441年，由当时的英国国王亨利六世设立，因而得名"国王学院"。另外，这行诗中的"spires"则指国王学院内的"国王学院礼拜堂"(King's College Chapel)，是剑桥古建筑的典型代表，由亨利六世亲自设计，耗时近100年，于1547年建成完工。礼拜堂上面的尖顶尤其突出和醒目，成为一种标志。

6. thee: *pron.* [second person singular] archaic or dialect form of you, as the singular object of a verb or preposition（古英语"thou"的宾格，同"you"）你；汝

7. loth = loath

loath: *adj.* reluctant; unwilling 不情愿的（e.g. I was loath to leave. 我不愿离开。）

8. woe: *n.* （often humorous） great sorrow or distress （常用于幽默用法）悲哀；悲苦；苦恼 （e.g. The Everton tale of woe continued. 埃弗顿的悲哀故事还在延续。）

◆ *A Lead-in Note* （简明导读）

这是一首伤感的诗，关乎友情，很多人也把此诗当作一首关乎爱情的诗。“那些都不愿意离去，都常驻你心房”，那么，我还是离去吧，尽管这里让我留恋，尽管这是一个“最为美丽的地方”！

◆ 道　别

（仿海涅的诗而作）
伤感的雨落下，源自天堂，
一只鸟儿在尖声鸣唱，歌声忧伤。
我坐在这里的窗户前，
朝着国王学院的尖顶观望。

啊，最为温馨的城镇，
最为美丽的地方！
有鸟儿，有灰色，有绿意，
还有男子，都是戴帽穿袍的模样。

那些都不愿意离去，
都常驻你心房。
因有的获友谊，有的得荣耀，
还有的，两者都如愿以偿。

伤感的雨落下，源自天堂，

我的心极度痛苦凄凉。
我未获友谊，亦未得荣耀，
还是离开，心怀遗憾和感伤。

033 William Cowper
威廉·柯珀

◆ *The Poet's Profile* （诗人小档案）

威廉·柯珀（1731—1800）：英国诗人和赞美诗作者。作为那个时代最受欢迎的诗人之一，柯珀通过书写日常生活和英国乡村的场景而改变了18世纪自然诗的走向。无论从哪一个方面来说，柯珀都是浪漫主义诗歌的先驱者之一。他的代表作品有长诗《任务》和妙趣横生的民谣《约翰·吉尔平趣史》。1779年，他与福音派新教会牧师约翰·牛顿合作，完成了《奥尔尼赞美诗》，里面有这样的诗句："噢！愿与上帝走得更近。"

◆ *To a Young Lady*

Sweet stream that winds through yonder glade,
Apt emblem of a virtuous maid
Silent and chaste she steals along,
Far from the world's gay busy throng:
With gentle yet prevailing force,
Intent upon her destined course;
Graceful and useful all she does,
Blessing and blest where'er she goes;
Pure-bosom'd as that watery glass,
And Heaven reflected in her face.

◆ Annotations （原诗注释）

1. wind: *v.* move in or take a twisting or spiral course 弯曲前进；蜿蜒而行（e.g. The path wound among olive trees. 这条小道在橄榄树丛中蜿蜒。）

2. yonder: *det.* （archaic or dialect） that or those （used to refer to something situated at a distance）（古旧用法或方言用法）（用于指称一定距离以外的东西）那个；那些 （e.g. What light through yonder window breaks? 从那边的那个窗子里透出来的是什么光?）

3. glade: *n.* an open space in a wood or forest 林中空地

4. apt: *adj.* exactly suitable; appropriate 恰当的；适宜的 （e.g. The remark was most apt. 那评论很恰当。）

5. emblem: *n.* （emblem of） a thing serving as a symbolic representation of a particular quality or concept 象征；标志 （e.g. Our child would be a dazzling emblem of our love. 孩子将是我们引以为豪的爱情象征。）

6. virtuous: *adj.* （archaic）（especially of a woman） chaste （古旧用法）（尤指妇女）贞洁的

7. maid: *n.* （archaic or poetic/literary） a girl or young woman, especially an unmarried one （古旧用法或诗/文用法）少女；（尤指未婚的）年轻妇女

8. chaste: *adj.* abstaining from extramarital, or from all, sexual intercourse （对婚姻）忠贞的；禁欲的；贞洁的

9. steal: *v.* move somewhere quietly or surreptitiously 偷偷地向……移动；秘密地向……移动 （e.g. He stole down to the kitchen. 他偷偷地走向厨房。）

10. throng: *n.* a large, densely packed crowd of people or animals 聚集的人群；一大群；众多 （e.g. He pushed his way through the throng. 他艰难地穿过一大群人。）

11. prevailing: *adj.* having superior power or influence 有力的；有影响的

12. intent: *adj.* attentively occupied with 专心致志于；专注于 （e.g. Gill was intent on her gardening magazine. 吉尔专心于她的园艺杂志。）

13. where'er = wherever

14. bosom'd = bosomed

15. reflect: *v.* （of a mirror or shiny surface） show an image of （镜子或光

洁表面）照出；映出 （e.g. He could see himself reflected in Keith's mirrored glasses. 他可看到自己映在基思的反光墨镜上。）

◆ *A Lead-in Note* （简明导读）

诗人将自己对一位年轻女子的爱慕之情融入对一条清澈小溪的描写之中。诗人将这位女子比作清澈的小溪，女子与小溪相互映衬，突出了这位女子的外表和内心。诗的最后，这位年轻的女子与清澈的小溪达到了完美的融合："心胸清纯，如剔透的玻璃水杯，天堂映上了她的脸。"

◆ 致一位年轻女子

清澈的小溪蜿蜒于远处的林间，
那是纯情少女恰当的体现：
她默默前行，纯真无瑕，
远离世俗的喧闹和人群的忙乱。
她温柔却坚定执着，
专注于命中注定的路线。
所到之处，受人保佑或护佑他人，
她举止优雅，与人为善。
心胸清纯，如剔透的玻璃水杯，
天堂映上了她的脸。

034 Samuel Daniel 塞缪尔·丹尼尔

◆ *The Poet's Profile* （诗人小档案）

塞缪尔·丹尼尔（1562—1619）：英国诗人和历史学家。丹尼尔是韵体诗的创新之人。1911年版的《大不列颠百科全书》是这样描述他的："他的文风饱满、通俗、庄严，却不很栩栩如生或壮丽辉煌；他的文风维持在水平飞行状态，并无大起大落。从好用格言警句这方面来说，丹尼尔接近查普曼，但丹尼尔的文风更加具有音乐性，一气呵成、前后贯通。他虽缺乏火热和激情，但具备学者的风度和亲切、忧伤的遐想。"

◆ *Love is a Sickness*

Love is a sickness full of woes,
All remedies refusing;
A plant that with most cutting grows,
Most barren with best using.
Why so?

More we enjoy it, more it dies;
If not enjoy'd, it sighing cries—
Heigh ho!

Love is a torment of the mind,
A tempest everlasting;
And Jove hath made it of a kind

Not well, nor full nor fasting.
Why so?

More we enjoy it, more it dies;
If not enjoy'd, it sighing cries—
Heigh ho!

◆ *Annotations* （原诗注释）

1. woe: *n.* （often humorous） great sorrow or distress （常含幽默之意）悲哀；悲苦；苦恼 （e.g. The Everton tale of woe continued. 埃弗顿的悲哀故事还在延续。）

2. remedy: *n.* a medicine or treatment for a disease or injury 治疗；治疗法；药品（e.g. herbal remedies for aches and pains 疼痛的草药疗法）

3. barren: *adj.* （of land） too poor to produce much or any vegetation （土地）贫瘠的；荒芜的

4. enjoy'd = enjoyed

5. heigh: *interj.* （archaic） expressing encouragement or enquiry （古旧用法）（表示鼓励或询问）嗨

6. ho: *interj.* used as the second element of various exclamations （用在感叹词后）嗨；嗬；嘞 （e.g. What ho! 嗨，什么！）

7. tempest: *n.* a violent windy storm 大风暴；暴风雨；暴风雪

8. Jove: *n.* another name for Jupiter 朱庇特主神（同"Jupiter"）

9. fasting: *adj.* abstaining from food 禁食的

◆ *A Lead-in Note* （简明导读）

什么是爱？答案千千万。诗人丹尼尔认为，爱是一种"病"。诗人以生动形象的说法，对其症状加以描述，从而说明爱的本质。爱这种"病"，虽说不是什么绝症，却也没有什么良药可医治。

◆ 爱是一种病

爱是一种病，悲苦满腹，
无良方可医。
切口最多的植物能生长；
使用充分的，会变得最为贫瘠。
为何如此？

我们愈是喜爱的东西，它就愈加消亡；
要是不喜欢，它就叹气嚷嚷——
哎呀！哎！

爱是对心灵的折磨，
是经久不息的暴风雨。
朱庇特主神令爱变得
不令人舒服：没吃饱，也没禁食。
为何如此？

我们愈是喜爱的东西，它就愈加消亡。
要是不喜欢，它就叹气嚷嚷——
哎呀！哎！

035 Sir Philip Sidney 菲利浦·锡德尼爵士

◆ *The Poet's Profile* （诗人小档案）

菲利浦·锡德尼爵士（1554—1586）：英国诗人、政治家和战士。为避免作品商业化，锡德尼一生中没出版过作品。他到荷兰与西班牙人作战时负伤，最终因伤牺牲，年仅32岁。英格兰举国哀悼这位政治家和战士，他成了伊丽莎白时代美德的典范。锡德尼最著名的作品是《阿卡迪亚》。这是一部田园浪漫散体文集，收录了各种押韵形式写就的诗歌，于1590年出版。

◆ *To the Sad Moon* （*Sonnet 31*）

With how sad steps, O Moon, thou climb'st the skies!
How silently, and with how wan a face!
What! May it be that even in heavenly place
That busy archer his sharp arrows tries?
Sure, if that long-with-love-acquainted eyes
Can judge of love, thou feel'st a lover's case:
I read it in thy looks; thy languished grace
To me, that feel the like, thy state descries.

Then, even of fellowship, O Moon, tell me,
Is constant love deemed there but want of wit?
Are beauties there as proud as here they be?
Do they above love to be loved, and yet
Those lovers scorn whom that love doth possess?
Do they call "virtue" there—ungratefulness?

◆ *Annotations* （原诗注释）

1. thou: *pron.* [second person singular] archaic or dialect form of you, as the singular subject of a verb （古旧用法或方言用法）（作动词的单数主语）你（同“you”）

2. climb'st = climbest = climbs

3. wan: *adj.* （of a person's complexion or appearance） pale and giving the impression of illness or exhaustion （人的脸色或外表）苍白的；病态的；疲倦的（e.g. She was looking wan and bleary-eyed. 她看上去脸色苍白，睡眼惺忪。）

4. heavenly: *adj.* of heaven; divine 天国的；神圣的

5. archer: *n.* a person who shoots with a bow and arrows, especially at a target as a sport 弓箭手；射箭运动员

注：这里的“archer”指的是罗马神话中的爱神丘比特（Cupid）。

6. acquaint: *v.* （acquaint someone with） make someone aware of or familiar with 使认识；使熟悉 （e.g. New staff should be acquainted with fire exit routes. 新员工应熟悉火警疏散路线。）

7. feel'st = feelest = feels

8. thy: *adj.* （also “thine” before a vowel） archaic or dialect form of your （元音前亦作“thine”）（古旧用法或方言用法）你（您）的（同“your”）

9. languish: *v.* be forced to remain in an unpleasant place or situation 受苦；受折磨（e.g. He has been languishing in a Mexican jail since 1974. 自从1974年以来，他一直在墨西哥的一个监狱中受折磨。）

10. descry: *v.* to discover by careful observation or scrutiny; detec 观察出；探查出（e.g. He descried a message of hope in her words. 他从她的话语里觉察出一丝希望。）

11. fellowship: *n.* a group of people meeting to pursue a shared interest or aim （志趣相同的）团体；协会；联谊会

12. o: *interj.* used to express surprise or strong emotion 哦；哟；啊；唉；哎呀（表示惊讶或强烈的情感）

13. deem: *v.* （formal） regard or consider in a specified way （正式用法）认为；视为（e.g. The event was deemed a great success. 大家认为该项活动很

成功。）

14. want of: lacking 缺乏

15. wit: *n.* mental sharpness and inventiveness; keen intelligence 颖悟力；聪颖；机智；才智

16. scorn: *v.* the feeling or belief that someone or something is worthless or despicable; contempt 鄙视；蔑视（e.g. I do not wish to become the object of scorn. 我不希望成为被鄙视的对象。）

17. doth = does

18. virtue: *n.* behaviour showing high moral standards 德行（e.g. paragons of virtue 德行典范）

19. ungrateful: *adj.* not feeling or showing gratitude 不感激的；忘恩负义的；不领情的（e.g. She's so ungrateful for everything we do. 她对我们所做的一切没有丝毫感激之情。）

◆ *A Lead-in Note*（简明导读）

此诗颇具李白“举杯邀明月，对影成三人”的意蕴，都具有一定的“情感共鸣”。诗人爱情受挫，仰望天空，看见了月亮，感觉月亮那副模样跟自己多么相似。最后，诗人问了与自己感情经历相似的月亮很多问题，实质上诗人是向读者交代自己爱情失意的原因所在。

◆ 致伤心的月亮（商籁体第31首）

啊，月亮，你爬上天空，步履多么忧伤！
你默默无语，脸色多么难看似白霜！
什么？那个忙碌的弓箭手竟然朝你
射出利箭，在天空这么神圣的地方？
当然，若弓箭手对爱习以为常的眼
能甄别爱，你感受的就是爱的境况：
你的表情和状态，让我了解了一切；

你优雅却受煎熬，因你我感受相像。

即使你我相像，啊，月亮，还得告诉我：
永恒之爱在那里，但无法如愿以偿？
那儿的美人是否跟这儿的一样傲慢？
给予她们的爱是否真的要至高无上？
那些美人是否蔑视想拥有真爱之人？
“不领情”难道真是她们所谓的“善良”？

036 Alfred Tennyson
艾尔弗雷德·丁尼生

◆ *The Poet's Profile* （诗人小档案）

艾尔弗雷德·丁尼生（1809—1892）：英国诗人。1850年，丁尼生被封为"桂冠诗人"。他的长诗《悼念》为他赢得了声誉，这首长诗是关于永生、变化和演变的。丁尼生的其他代表作品有《轻旅之冲锋》和《国王的叙事诗》等。

◆ *The Song of Love and Death*

Sweet is true love, tho' given in vain, in vain;
And sweet is death, who puts an end to pain;
I know not which is sweeter, no, not I.

Love, art thou sweet? then bitter death must be;
Love, thou art bitter; sweet is death to me.
O Love, if death be sweeter, let me die.

Sweet love, that seems not made to fade away,
Sweet death, that seems to make us loveless clay,
I know not which is sweeter, no, not I.

I fain would follow love, if that could be;
I needs must follow death, who calls for me:
Call and I follow, I follow! let me die!

◆ *Annotations*（原诗注释）

1. tho' = though

2. in vain: without success or a result 徒劳地 （e.g. They waited in vain for a response. 他们白等回音。）

3. art: *v.* archaic or dialect second person singular present of be （古旧用法及诗歌中用法）"be" 的第二人称、单数、现在时形式

4. thou: *pron.* [second person singular] archaic or dialect form of you, as the singular subject of a verb （古旧用法或方言用法）（作动词的单数主语）你（同 "you"）

5. o: *interj.* used to express surprise or strong emotion 哦；哟；啊；唉；哎呀（表示惊讶或强烈的情感）

6. clay: *n.* （poetic/literary） the substance of the human body （诗/文用法）肉体；人体 （e.g. this lifeless clay 这毫无生气的躯体）

7. fain: *adv.* with pleasure; gladly 乐意地；欣然地 （e.g. I am weary and would fain get a little rest. 我累坏了，很乐意休息一小会儿。）

8. must needs （or needs must） do something: cannot avoid or help doing something 必须；不得不 （e.g. They must needs depart. 他们不得不离开。）

◆ *A Lead-in Note*（简明导读）

爱与死之歌，经久不衰。爱与死皆甜蜜，各具内涵，令诗人疑惑："我不知道哪个更甜蜜。不，我不知道。" 爱与死又是一对矛盾体，"甜蜜的爱，其产生似乎不是要销声匿迹"。但是，一旦死去，"甜蜜的死，其产生似乎要我们变成无爱的躯体"。爱终究抵不过死的呼唤："呼唤我，我跟上，我跟上！让我死掉！"

◆ 爱与死之歌

真爱甜蜜，尽管来之不易，来之不易；
死亡甜蜜，因其结束了痛苦的经历。
我不知道哪个更甜蜜。不，我不知道。

爱，你甜蜜吗？那死一定苦涩不止；
爱，你很苦涩，那死对于我，很甜蜜。
啊，爱神！若死更甜蜜，让我死掉。

甜蜜的爱，其产生似乎不是要销声匿迹；
甜蜜的死，其产生似乎要我们变成无爱的躯体。
我不知道哪个更甜蜜。不，我不知道。

我会欣然跟随爱，若能在一起；
我不得不跟上死，死呼唤我同去。
呼唤我，我跟上，我跟上！让我死掉！

037 John Wilmot 约翰·威尔莫特

◆ *The Poet's Profile* （诗人小档案）

约翰·威尔莫特（1647—1680）：英国诗人和查理二世复位时期的朝臣。威尔莫特在世时，他的诗是以手稿的形式流传的，大多数诗歌作品在他死后才以他的名字公开出版。查理二世在位时，威尔莫特因生活放荡而臭名昭著，曾写过十分露骨的色情诗，还写过讽刺诗。

◆ *Love and Life*

All my past life is mine no more,
The flying hours are gone,
Like transitory dreams giv'n o'er,
Whose images are kept in store
By memory alone.

The time that is to come is not;
How can it then be mine?
The present moment's all my lot;
And that, as fast as it is got,
Phyllis, is only thine.

Then talk not of inconstancy,
False hearts, and broken vows;
If I, by miracle, can be

This live-long minute true to thee,
'Tis all that Heav'n allows.

◆ *Annotations* （原诗注释）

1. transitory: *adj.* not permanent 短暂的 （e.g. transitory periods of medieval greatness 昙花一现的中世纪辉煌时期）

2. giv'n o'er = given over

give over: to cause an activity to stop 使停止

3. in store: in a safe place while not being used or displayed 储藏着；准备着（e.g. items held in store 储藏的物品）

4. lot: *n.* （the lot or the whole lot） （chiefly Brit.） the whole number or quantity that is involved or implied （主要为英国用法）所有；一切 （e.g. You might as well take the whole lot. 你可以带走一切。）

5. thine: *pron.* （form of "thy" used before a vowel） archaic form of yours; the thing or things belonging to or associated with thee （元音之前同"thy"）（古旧用法）你的（同"yours"）；（"thou"的物主代词）你（您）的东西

6. inconstancy: *n.* the state or quality of being eccentrically variable or fickle 反复无常；易变性

7. live-long or livelong: *adj.* （poetic/literary） （of a period of time） entire （诗/文用法）整段（时间）的 （e.g. All this livelong day I lay in the sun. 这一整天里，我一直躺着晒太阳。）

8. minute: *n.* an instant or a point of time 瞬间；很短的时间

9. thee: *pron.* [second person singular] archaic or dialect form of you, as the singular object of a verb or preposition （古英语"thou"的宾格，同"you"）你；汝

10. 'Tis = It is

11. heav'n = heaven

◆ *A Lead-in Note* （简明导读）

此诗是对“活在当下”这一说法的诠释。不要说什么过去和未来，“目前”是最真实的人生，而且“目前时刻是我的全部，却快速消失”。目前的人生、爱情也最为真实。于是，诗人对爱人菲利斯说：“菲利斯，它非你莫属。”诗的最后一节将这一主题推向了高潮，大有“今朝有酒今朝醉”之意。其实，诗人的人生大致如此：饮酒过度，多次遭朝廷放逐，且其一生多有“劣迹”出现。

◆ 爱情与人生

我过去的所有生活不再属于我，
时光都是一闪而过，
恰似短暂的梦戛然而止。
唯有记忆
将梦中形象保存到一起。

未来时光已不再有，
又怎能为了我而不溜走？
目前时刻是我的全部，
却快速消失；
菲利斯，它非你莫属。

那么，不要说变幻频繁，
不要说虚情假意和空许诺言。
要是有奇迹，在这完整的瞬间里
我能做到真心真意对你，
那就是老天的旨意。

038 Sarah Flower Adams
萨拉·弗劳尔·亚当斯

◆ *The Poet's Profile* （诗人小档案）

萨拉·弗劳尔·亚当斯（1805—1848）：英国女诗人。萨拉是上帝一位论者，写过多部圣歌，包括《我的上帝，靠你更近些》和《上帝赐予太阳，上帝赐予雨露》。她的女权思想、职业行为、作品的性质以及非常规的生活方式都根植于上帝一位论。

◆ *Love*

O Love! thou makest all things even
In earth or heaven;
Finding thy way through prison-bars
Up to the stars;
Or, true to the Almighty plan,
That out of dust created man,
Thou lookest in a grave, —to see
Thine immortality!

◆ *Annotations* （原诗注释）

1. thou: *pron.* [second person singular] archaic or dialect form of you, as the singular subject of a verb （古旧用法或方言用法）（作动词的单数主语）你（同“you”）

2. makest = makes

3. thy: *adj.* （also “thine” before a vowel） archaic or dialect form of your（元音前亦作 “thine” ）（古旧用法或方言用法）你（您）的（同 “your” ）

4. almighty: *n.*（the Almighty）a name or title for God 上帝（名字或称谓）

5. lookest = looks

6. grave: *n.* a place of burial for a dead body, typically a hole dug in the ground and marked by a stone or mound 墓穴；坟墓

7. thine: *pron.* （form of “thy” used before a vowel） archaic form of yours; the thing or things belonging to or associated with thee （元音之前同 “thy” ）（古旧用法）你的（同 “yours” ）;（ “thou” 的物主代词）你（您）的东西

8. immortality: *n.* endless life or existence 永恒；不朽

◆ *A Lead-in Note* （简明导读）

诗人萨拉用宗教里的一些意象对爱加以讴歌。爱神代表爱。上帝造人，造出亚当和夏娃，偷吃伊甸园禁果，产生了爱。从此后，爱具有了伟大的力量，成为生命中的永恒。

◆ 爱　神

啊，爱神！不论地上或天空，
你让一切得以平衡；
你设法越出监狱的栏杆，
升到众星之间；
或者，遵循上帝的安排——
从尘土中造出人来。
你看向坟墓里头，
看到了你的不朽！

039 Ernest Christopher Dowson 欧内斯特·克里斯托弗·道森

◆ *The Poet's Profile* （诗人小档案）

欧内斯特·克里斯托弗·道森（1867—1900）：英国诗人和小说家。道森经常跟“颓废”派成员中的奥斯卡·王尔德和奥布里·比尔兹利保持联络。他的两本诗集：《道森韵体诗集》和《装饰》，是有关无聊倦怠和厌烦人世方面的。道森死后，奥斯卡·王尔德这样写道：“可怜的家伙虽受了伤，却本质非凡。他是所有悲剧性诗歌中的一个悲剧性复制，如同一个象征或者一个场景。我希望有月桂树叶撒在他的坟墓上，也希望有芸香和桃金娘放在他的坟墓上，因为他知道爱为何物。”

◆ *What Is Love?*

What is Love?
Is it a folly,
Is it mirth, or melancholy?
Joys above,
Are there many, or not any?
What is Love?

If you please,
A most sweet folly!
Full of mirth and melancholy:
Both of these!
In its sadness worth all gladness,

If you please!

Prithee where,
Goes Love a-hiding?
Is he long in his abiding
Anywhere?
Can you bind him when you find him;
Prithee, where?

With spring days
Love comes and dallies:
Upon the mountains, through the valleys
Lie Love's ways.
Then he leaves you and deceives you
In spring days.

◆ *Annotations* （原诗注释）

1. folly: *n.* a foolish act, idea, or practice 蠢行；傻念头；蠢事 （e.g. the follies of youth 青年人的傻事）

2. mirth: *n.* amusement, especially as expressed in laughter 欢乐；欢笑（e.g. His six-foot frame shook with mirth. 他那六英尺身躯乐得直抖。）

3. melancholy: *n.* a deep, pensive, and long-lasting sadness 忧思；愁思

4. if you please: used as an exclamation expressing astonishment, indignation, etc. 你看多奇怪；竟然 （e.g. The missing letter was in his pocket, if you please! 丢失的信竟然在他的口袋里，你看怪不怪！）

5. prithee: *interj.* （archaic） please （used to convey a polite request） （古旧用法）（表达礼貌的请求）请 （e.g. Prithee, Jack, answer me honestly. 请吧，杰克，老实回答我。）

6. abide: *v.* （archaic） live; dwell （古旧用法）生活；居住

7. bind: *v.* restrain （someone） by tying their hands and feet 捆绑……的手

和脚

8. dally: *v*. act or move slowly 磨蹭；动作慢吞吞

◆ *A Lead-in Note* （简明导读）

什么是爱？爱有方方面面，爱也有疑问重重。爱神象征着爱。爱神随着春天到来，却到处闲荡，“接着，他离开你，欺骗了你——在春天里”。

◆ 什么是爱？

什么是爱？
爱是犯傻，
是欢笑，或是悲哀？
欢乐为佳，
那么，欢乐多多，或欢乐不再？
什么是爱？

你看多神奇，
爱是最为甜蜜的犯傻！
满溢着欢笑和悲戚，
两者都不缺乏！
其伤感性令一切喜悦有价值，
你看多神奇！

请问，在哪里
爱神隐藏？
他是否会长久居于
任何一个地方？
找到后，你可否将他捆起？

请问，在哪里？

紧随着春天
爱神来到，随即闲荡。
群山之巅、峡谷之上，
他都前往。
接着，他离开你，欺骗了你——
在春天里。

040 David Herbert Lawrence
大卫·赫伯特·劳伦斯

◆ *The Poet's Profile* （诗人小档案）

大卫·赫伯特·劳伦斯（1885—1930）：英国小说家、诗人和散文家。劳伦斯的作品以抨击工业社会和对性关系不加掩饰的探索为特征，如《查特莱夫人的情人》。这部作品于1928年首先在意大利出版，其未删节版本直到1960年才在英国面世。劳伦斯的代表作品还有《儿子和情人》。

◆ *A Winter's Tale*

Yesterday the fields were only grey with scattered snow,
And now the longest grass-leaves hardly emerge;
Yet her deep footsteps mark the snow, and go
On towards the pines at the hills' white verge.

I cannot see her, since the mist's white scarf
Obscures the dark wood and the dull orange sky;
But she's waiting, I know, impatient and cold, half
Sobs struggling into her frosty sigh.

Why does she come so promptly, when she must know
That she's only the nearer to the inevitable farewell;
The hill is steep, on the snow my steps are slow—
Why does she come, when she knows what I have to tell?

◆ Annotations （原诗注释）

1. tale: *n.* a fictitious or true narrative or story, especially one that is imaginatively recounted 故事

2. emerge: *v.* move out of or away from something and come into view 浮现；显露 （e.g. Black ravens emerged from the fog. 黑色的渡鸦从雾中飞了出来。）

3. verge: *n.* an edge or border 边；边沿 （e.g. They came down to the verge of the lake. 他们来到湖边。）

4. mist: *n.* a cloud of tiny water droplets suspended in the atmosphere at or near the earth's surface limiting visibility （to a lesser extent than fog; strictly, with visibility remaining above 1 km） （能见度大于1千米的）薄雾；轻雾；霭 （e.g. The peaks were shrouded in mist. 山峰笼罩在雾霭中。）

5. scarf: *n.* a length or square of fabric worn around the neck or head 头巾；围巾；披肩

6. sigh: *n.* a long, deep, audible exhalation expressing sadness, relief, tiredness, or similar 叹气；叹息；叹息声 （e.g. She let out a long sigh of despair. 她失望地长叹一口气。）

7. farewell: *n.* an act of parting or of marking someone's departure 道别；告别；辞行；饯行 （e.g. The dinner had been arranged as a farewell. 安排这顿饭是为了饯行。）

8. steep: *adj.* （of a slope, flight of stairs, or angle） rising or falling sharply; almost perpendicular （斜面、楼梯或角度）陡的；陡峭的；陡直的 （e.g. She pushed the bike up the steep hill. 她把自行车推上陡峭的山坡。）

◆ A Lead-in Note （简明导读）

冬天的故事是一个凄惨的故事，预示着结局的寒凉。两个恋人即将分手，约定在一个昏暗冬日的树林中见面。昨天还零星飘着雪花，今天已经白雪皑皑，淹没了最长的草叶，模糊了天际，“可她的足迹深深印在雪中，通向松林——位于群山的白色边缘”。于是，诗人知道她已经到来，可“她为何来得如此迅速”？诗人爱着她，有些不舍，但又不得不分手。冬天的故事，

其结局有所预示，但却是不明确的。

◆ 冬天的故事

昨天，田野灰蒙，白雪零星分散。
而眼下，连最长的草叶几乎都看不见，
可她的足迹深深印在雪中，通向
松林——位于群山的白色边缘。

我看不见她，因白色的雪雾
模糊了幽暗的树林和橘黄的阴天。
可我知道，她在等待，在寒冷中急切等待，
几乎开始抽泣，叹息凝霜，竭力御寒。

她为何来得如此迅速？可她必须知道，
她正一步步靠近必然要分别的边缘。
山很陡峭，雪中的我缓慢迈步。
她为何要来？而她知道，我要说的有何内涵。

041 Hartley Coleridge
哈特利·柯尔律治

◆ *The Poet's Profile* （诗人小档案）

哈特利·柯尔律治（1796—1849）：英国诗人、传记作家和散文家。哈特利是以哲学家大卫·哈特利的名字来命名的。柯尔律治的声名主要建立在他的批评类作品、《普罗米修斯》（一部未完成的抒情诗剧）以及商籁体诗歌（一种特别适合他的创作技能的文学形式）上。他是诗人塞缪尔·泰勒·柯尔律治的大儿子。

◆ *She Is Not Fair to Outward View*

She is not fair to outward view,
As many maidens be;
Her loveliness I never knew
Until she smiled on me.
O, then I saw her eye was bright, —
A well of love, a spring of light.

But now her looks are coy and cold;
To mine they ne'er reply;
And, yet, I cease not to behold
The love-light in her eye.
Her very frowns are better far
Than smiles of other maidens are!

◆ Annotations （原诗注释）

1. fair: *adj.* （archaic） beautiful; attractive （古旧用法）美丽的；动人的；有魅力的 （e.g. the fairest of her daughters 她女儿中最漂亮的一位）

2. outward: *adj.* relating to the external appearance of something rather than its true nature or substance 外表的；表面的 （e.g. an outward display of friendliness 表面上的友好）

3. maiden: *n.* （archaic or poetic/literary） a girl or young woman, especially an unmarried one （古旧用法或诗/文用法）少女；（尤指未婚的）年轻妇女

4. o: *interj.* used to express surprise or strong emotion 哦；哟；啊；唉；哎呀（表示惊讶或强烈的情感）

5. well: *n.* a plentiful source or supply （大量）来源；源泉 （e.g. She could feel a deep well of sympathy and compassion. 她可以感受到极大的同情。）
（archaic） a water spring or fountain （古旧用法）泉水；喷泉

6. coy: *adj.* （especially of a woman） making a pretence of shyness or modesty which is intended to be alluring but is often regarded as irritating （尤指女性）忸怩作态的；卖弄风情的 （e.g. She treated him to a coy smile of invitation. 她对他忸怩一笑，以示邀请。）

7. frown: *n.* a facial expression or look characterized by such a furrowing of one's brows 皱眉；蹙额

◆ A Lead-in Note （简明导读）

俗话说，情人眼里出西施。但是，西施眼中不一定有这个情人。此诗中，诗人抛开诸多模样漂亮、笑容喜悦的玉女，偏偏喜欢这位外表看来并不漂亮的女子。“可如今，她忸怩而冷漠，从不回应我示意的神情”，但诗人还是喜欢目不转睛地看她，这也许就是爱的魔力，可惜是单向的爱。

◆ 外表看来她并不漂亮

外表看来她并不漂亮，
如诸多玉女那样。
若她未朝我微露笑容，
我永远看不到她俊俏的形象。
啊，我看到她明亮的眼睛——
爱之源泉，春之光亮。

可如今，她忸怩而冷漠，
从不回应我示意的神情。
然而，我不断看见
爱之光闪烁在她的眼中。
她每一次皱眉都远胜过
所有玉女喜悦的笑容！

042 Robert Browning
罗伯特・布朗宁

◆ *The Poet's Profile* （诗人小档案）

罗伯特・布朗宁（1812—1889）：英国诗人和剧作家。1842年，布朗宁因《戏剧抒情诗》一举成名。《戏剧抒情诗》包括《哈默尔恩的派德・派珀》（亦译作《哈默尔恩的花衣魔笛手》）和《我已故的公爵夫人》等诗歌。1846年，布朗宁迎娶了比他年长的诗人伊丽莎白・巴雷特，成就了历史上最为著名的文学婚姻之一。伊丽莎白当时比他更为知名。婚后他们定居意大利，布朗宁把这个国家称作“我的大学”，它经常成为布朗宁作品中的重头戏。截至1861年他妻子去世时，他出版了关键性的一部作品集《男与女》。他的诗因讽刺手法、对人物的刻画、黑色幽默、社会评论等而著名。

◆ *Meeting at Night*

I

The grey sea and the long black land;
And the yellow half-moon large and low;
And the startled little waves that leap
In fiery ringlets from their sleep,
As I gain the cove with pushing prow,
And quench its speed i' the slushy sand.

II

Then a mile of warm sea-scented beach;
Three fields to cross till a farm appears;
A tap at the pane, the quick sharp scratch

And blue spurt of a lighted match,
And a voice less loud, thro' its joys and fears,
Than the two hearts beating each to each!

◆ *Annotations* （原诗注释）

1. startled: *adj.* excited by sudden surprise or alarm and making a quick involuntary movement 受惊吓的；感到吃惊的；惊跳起来的 （e.g. There was a startled look on his face when the flash bulb went off. 闪光灯灭时，他脸上露出一副惊愕的表情。）

2. fiery: *adj.* （of behaviour or words） passionately angry and deeply felt （言行）激烈的；怒气冲冲的

3. ringlet: *n.* a lock of hair hanging in a corkscrew-shaped curl 下垂长螺旋形卷发

4. cove: *n.* a small sheltered bay 小湾；小海湾

5. prow: *n.* the pointed front part of a ship; the bow 船首；船头

6. quench: *v.* stifle or suppress （a feeling） 抑制；压制（感情）（e.g. Fury rose in him, but he quenched it. 他心中燃起怒火，但他压制着没发作。）

7. i' = in

8. slushy: *adj.* resembling, consisting of, or covered with slush 似雪泥的；多雪泥的；由雪泥覆盖的

9. tap: *n.* a quick light blow or the sound of such a blow 轻敲；轻轻敲击声

10. pane: *n.* a single sheet of glass in a window or door 窗玻璃片；框格玻璃

11. scratch: *n.* a rasping or grating noise produced by something rubbing against a hard surface 划擦声 （e.g. the scratch of a match lighting a cigarette 划着火柴点烟的声响）

12. spurt: *n.* a sudden gushing stream 喷射流 （e.g. A sudden spurt of blood gushed into her eyes. 一股血喷进她的眼里。）

13. thro' = through

◆ *A Lead-in Note*（简明导读）

诗人航海归来，归心似箭，急于想见到朝思暮想的情人。尽管相会的愿望如饥似渴，诗人还需一步一步行动：越过大海，跨过巨浪，停靠海湾，走过海滩，最后“穿越三片田野，一座农场映入眼帘”。最终，夜晚喜悦的相会开始，但是诗歌本身却戛然而止，将想象留给了读者。

◆ 夜晚相会

一

大海灰灰，长陆黑黑，
黄黄的半轮巨盘低垂。
细浪从睡梦中惊醒，
怒气冲冲，卷动、跳跃、翻飞。
此时，我破浪驶入小小的海湾，
沙子似雪泥，将船速减退。

二

接着，走过一段暖湿的海滩，
穿越三片田野，一座农场映入眼帘。
轻敲窗玻璃，尖锐划擦之声随即响起，
火柴点燃，蹿起火苗蓝蓝。
细语传来，透着不安和喜悦，
声音轻得彼此心跳都听得见。

043 Richard Lovelace 理查德·洛夫莱斯

◆ *The Poet's Profile* （诗人小档案）

理查德·洛夫莱斯（1618—1657）：英国诗人。洛夫莱斯英俊潇洒、风流倜傥、幽默风趣，是追求者的偶像。身为保皇党成员，洛夫莱斯于1642年被打入监牢。或许就是那时在狱中，他写下了广为人知的诗篇《狱中致奥尔西娅》，其中包含这样的名句："石墙构不成监狱，铁栏围不出牢笼。"

◆ *To Lucasta, Going to the Wars*

Tell me not （Sweet） I am unkind,
That from the nunnery
Of thy chaste breast and quiet mind
To war and arms I fly.

True, a new mistress now I chase,
The first foe in the field;
And with a stronger faith embrace
A sword, a horse, a shield.

Yet this inconstancy is such
As you too shall adore;
I could not love thee （Dear） so much,
Lov'd I not Honour more.

◆ *Annotations* （原诗注释）

1. nunnery: *n.* a building or group of buildings in which nuns live as a religious community; a convent 修女聚居点；女修道院；尼姑庵

2. thy: *adj.* （also “thine” before a vowel） archaic or dialect form of your（元音前亦作“thine”）（古旧用法或方言用法）你（您）的（同“your”）

3. chaste: *adj.* abstaining from extramarital, or from all, sexual intercourse（对婚姻）忠贞的；禁欲的；贞洁的

4. foe: *n.* （poetic/literary or formal） an enemy or opponent （诗/文用法或正式用法）敌人；对手 （e.g. Join forces against the common foe. 联合力量对付共同的敌人。）

5. embrace: *v.* hold （someone） closely in one's arms, especially as a sign of affection 拥抱；怀抱 （e.g. The two embraced, holding each other tightly. 两人紧紧地拥抱在一起。）

6. shield: *n.* a broad piece of metal or another suitable material, held by straps or a handle attached on one side, used as a protection against blows or missiles 盾；盾牌

7. inconstancy: *n.* the state or quality of being eccentrically variable or fickle 反复无常；易变性

8. adore: *v.* love and respect （someone） deeply 敬爱；崇敬（某人）（e.g. He adored his mother. 他对母亲十分敬爱。）

9. lov'd = loved

◆ *A Lead-in Note* （简明导读）

此诗直抒胸臆，简单明了，是诗人仗剑奔向战场前对其情人卢卡丝塔心存不满的回应。卢卡丝塔是一个虚构的女子名，这个名字来自拉丁文“lux casta”，意为“纯洁之光”。卢卡丝塔这位女子可能基于现实中的露西·萨谢弗雷尔而设。诗人跟她有过浪漫的恋情，但最终她嫁给了别人。据说，令人伤感的原委是她接到误报，说洛夫莱斯战死疆场。

◆ 征战前致卢卡丝塔

不要说，（亲爱的，）我不仁慈：
飞奔战场，拿起武器，
我脱离了港湾——
你圣洁的心灵和娴静的举止。

的确，我有新欢要去追求——
战场上的第一个敌手。
我信念更加坚定，握住
刀剑、马匹和护盾。

然而，我如此善变，
你仍要爱恋。
若非我更爱荣誉，（亲爱的，）
便无以与你长久缠绵。

044 Robert Herrick
罗伯特·赫里克

◆ *The Poet's Profile* （诗人小档案）

罗伯特·赫里克（1591—1674）：英国抒情诗人和牧师。赫里克最出名的作品是诗集《金苹果园》，其中包含世俗和宗教诗。他写过2500多首诗，大多收录在《金苹果园》里。赫里克以自己独特的诗风而闻名，早期作品经常提及男女交欢之事和女性的身体，晚期作品则更具哲理性特征。

◆ *To the Virgins, Make Much of Time*

Gather ye rose-buds while ye may:
Old Time is still a-flying;
And this same flower that smiles to-day,
To-morrow will be dying.

The glorious lamp of heaven, the Sun,
The higher he's a-getting,
The sooner will his race be run,
And nearer he's to setting.

That age is best, which is the first,
When youth and blood are warmer;
But being spent, the worse, and worst
Times, still succeed the former.

—Then be not coy, but use your time,
And while ye may, go marry;
For having lost but once your prime,
You may for ever tarry.

◆ *Annotations* （原诗注释）

1. virgin: *n.* a person, typically a woman, who has never had sexual intercourse 处女；童男

2. ye: *pron.* [second person plural] （archaic or dialect） plural form of thou （古旧用法或方言用法）你们（“thou”的复数形式）

3. rosebud or rose-bud: *n.* an unopened flower of a rose 玫瑰花苞

4. race: *n.* （archaic） the course of the sun or moon through the heavens （古旧用法）（日或月的）行程；历程

5. coy: *adj.* reluctant to give details, especially about something regarded as sensitive （尤指对敏感问题）含糊其词的；不愿表态的 （e.g. He is coy about his age. 他避而不谈他的年龄。）

6. succeed: *v.* take over a throne, inheritance, office, or other position from 接替；继承 （e.g. He would succeed Hawke as Prime Minister. 他将接替霍克成为首相。）

7. prime: *n.* a state or time of greatest strength, vigour, or success in a person's life 青春；青年；壮年；全盛时期 （e.g. You're in the prime of life. 你正值青春年华。）

8. tarry: *v.* （tarries, tarried） （dated） stay longer than intended; delay leaving a place （过时用法）拖延；逗留 （e.g. She could tarry a bit and not get home until four. 她可以再逗留一会直到四点再回家。）

◆ *A Lead-in Note* （简明导读）

此诗与本书第037首《爱情与人生》有着近乎相同的“及时行乐”的思想，只不过此诗的对象是那些处于青春年华中的少男少女。这不禁让人联想

到唐代诗人李白某些诗的主题，例如“人生得意须尽欢，莫使金樽空对月”和“暂伴月将影，行乐须及春”等。

◆ 致少男少女

有能力之时，玫瑰花苞你要尽力收集，
欢乐旧时光依然飞逝。
同样一朵花，今日露出微笑，
明日就会奄奄一息。

太阳，天空中辉煌的一盏灯，
越是高高挂起，
其行程就会越快结束，
也就越接近落幕之际。

起初的年龄时段为最佳，
青春飞扬而愈发热血满溢。
但会渐渐耗尽，愈来愈糟的
时段仍然会前来接替。

那就别含糊，利用好时间，
趁你有能力，步入婚姻殿堂里。
因哪怕只一次失去青春，
你或许永远逗留原地。

045 Elizabeth Barrett Browning
伊丽莎白·巴雷特·布朗宁

◆ *The Poet's Profile*（诗人小档案）

伊丽莎白·巴雷特·布朗宁（1806—1861）：英国女诗人。出生时的名字为伊丽莎白·巴雷特。伊丽莎白是维多利亚时代最具声望的英国诗人之一。在她生活的时代，她的诗无论在英国还是美国都广受欢迎。《巴雷特诗集》为她赢得了声誉。1846年，她跟罗伯特·布朗宁私奔。

◆ *How Do I Love Thee?*（*Sonnet 43*）

How do I love thee? Let me count the ways.
I love thee to the depth and breadth and height
My soul can reach, when feeling out of sight
For the ends of being and ideal grace.
I love thee to the level of every day's
Most quiet need, by sun and candle-light.
I love thee freely, as men strive for right.
I love thee purely, as they turn from praise.
I love thee with the passion put to use
In my old griefs, and with my childhood's faith.
I love thee with a love I seemed to lose
With my lost saints. I love thee with the breath,
Smiles, tears, of all my life; and, if God choose,
I shall but love thee better after death.

◆ Annotations （原诗注释）

1. thee: *pron.* [second person singular] archaic or dialect form of you, as the singular object of a verb or preposition （古英语"thou"的宾格，同"you"）你；汝

2. grace: *n.* （graces） an attractively polite manner of behaving 风度；魅力（e.g. She has all the social graces. 她很有社交风度。）

3. passion: *n.* strong and barely controllable emotion 热情；激情 （e.g. a man of impetuous passion 一个极易冲动的人）

◆ A Lead-in Note （简明导读）

此诗表达了诗人对丈夫罗伯特·布朗宁强烈的爱意："我爱你所能达到的深度、宽度、高度，受制于心灵所及，而心灵会跃出视线，去探寻生命的意义和绝佳的风度。"她甚至将这种强烈的爱意延续到来生："来生我会加倍爱你，若上帝允许。"诗人对丈夫的爱胜于一切，但此诗中只是简单列举了不同情况下对他爱的程度。

◆ 我要怎样爱你呢？（商籁体第43首）

我要怎样爱你呢？让我把答案数一数。
我爱你所能达到的深度、宽度、高度，
受制于心灵所及，而心灵会跃出视线，
去探寻生命的意义和绝佳的风度。
我爱你所能达到的水平，能使阳光里
和烛光下最基本的日常所需得到满足；
我爱你心甘情愿，如同人为自由奉献；
我爱你不掺杂念，如同做事不求夸赞；
我爱你激情不变，如历经苦难意志坚，

又如同孩提时代恪守信仰而心无杂念；
我爱你，所有的爱都倾注于你，
如同随年龄增长，我所有纯真的失去；
我爱你，耗尽此生的呼吸、笑容、眼泪，
来生我会加倍爱你，若上帝允许。

046 Charlotte Mary Mew
夏洛特·玛丽·缪

◆ *The Poet's Profile* （诗人小档案）

夏洛特·玛丽·缪（1869—1928）：英国维多利亚及现代主义时期的女诗人。缪一生中主要以短篇抒情诗而为人所知，同时她还得到同时代诗人如埃兹拉·庞德、托马斯·哈代等的欣赏。缪的第一部诗集《农夫的新娘》于1916年出版。在美国，这部诗集以《周六集市》为书名，由麦克米伦出版公司于1921年出版。这部诗集吸引了众人的眼球，使她成为一名大众喜爱的诗人。

◆ *I So Liked Spring*

I so liked Spring last year
Because you were here; —
The thrushes too —
Because it was these you so liked to hear —
I so liked you.

This year's a different thing, —
I'll not think of you.
But I'll like the Spring because it is simply Spring
As the thrushes do.

◆ *Annotations*（原诗注释）

thrush: *n.* a small or medium-sized songbird, typically having a brown back, spotted breast, and loud song 鸫；歌鸫

◆ *A Lead-in Note*（简明导读）

去年的春天和今年的春天都如约而至，歌鸫鸟也按时歌唱。不同的是，去年春天有你相伴，今年春天你我互不相干。跟歌鸫鸟一样，没有你的春天我也喜欢，只是“我不会想到你”。由此可见，这个世界少了谁，地球还是一样地旋转。也许今年的春天里，内心波澜起伏，但外表仍是一副不以为意的神态。去年春天鸟语花香，今年春天也是如此，但也许内心增添了些许苦涩。

◆ 我如此喜爱春天

我如此喜爱去年的春天，
因为你是那里的一员。
歌鸫鸟也在那里，
其歌声你如此喜欢——
我如此喜欢你。

今年情况迥异——
我不会想到你。
但我只会因为春天到来而喜爱春天，
如歌鸫鸟对春天的喜爱之意。

047 Alfred Austin
艾尔弗雷德·奥斯汀

◆ *The Poet's Profile* （诗人小档案）

艾尔弗雷德·奥斯汀（1835—1913）：英国诗人、批评家、小说家和政治新闻工作者。尽管奥斯汀接受的是法律教育，但他的专业生涯却主要集中在文学方面。半个世纪以来，奥斯汀隔一段时间就有作品问世。1896年，继艾尔弗雷德·丁尼生男爵之后，奥斯汀被封为“桂冠诗人”。奥斯汀唯一的一部畅销书是《我热爱的花园》，这是一部描写田园生活的散文集，被公认为奥斯汀的最佳作品，深得当时大众的喜爱。但是，奥斯汀的诗歌至今很少有人记得。他的抒情诗缺乏自然情感的流露，没有个性特征。

◆ *Love's Trinity*

Soul, heart, and body, we thus singly name,
Are not in love divisible and distinct,
But each with each inseparably link'd.
One is not honour, and the other shame,
But burn as closely fused as fuel, heat, and flame.

They do not love who give the body and keep
The heart ungiven; nor they who yield the soul,
And guard the body. Love doth give the whole;
Its range being high as heaven, as ocean deep,
Wide as the realms of air or planet's curving sweep.

◆ *Annotations*（原诗注释）

1. trinity: *n.* a group of three people or things （三个人或三件物组成的）三位一体；三合一；三件套；三人组合 （e.g. The wine was the first of a trinity of three excellent vintages. 这酒是上好佳酿三合一的第一种。）

2. distinct: *adj.* recognizably different in nature from something else of a similar type 可辨别的；有区别的；不同的

3. link'd = linked

4. fuse: *v.* join or blend to form a single entity 合并；使融为一体 （e.g. Intermarriage had fused the families into a large unit. 联姻把几个家庭合并为一个大家庭。）

5. yield: *v.* relinquish possession of （something）; give （something） up 泄露；放弃；让出

6. doth = does

7. realm: *n.* a field or domain of activity or interest 界；领域；范围（e.g. It is beyond the realms of possibility. 这超出了可能的范围。）

8. sweep: *n.* （figurative） the range or scope of something （比喻用法）范围

◆ *A Lead-in Note*（简明导读）

爱是灵魂、心灵和身体三者完美融合而成的一个整体，所谓“爱的三位一体”。如同燃烧时，燃料、热量和火焰密不可分。诗人奥斯汀写就此诗，可能是受基督教中上帝是圣父、圣子、圣灵三位一体的启发。同时，爱是倾尽所有的奉献，爱又宽广无边，没有界限。

◆ 爱的三位一体

灵魂、心灵和身体，个体名称莫过如此，
在爱情中不可分立，难辨同异，
但彼此之间不可分割地连在一起。
一个觉得不荣耀，另一个则认为可耻，
如同燃烧时，燃料、热量和火焰紧密融为一体。

给出身体，保留不被原谅的心灵，
则构不成爱；同样，让出灵魂而保住身体，
也构不成爱——爱就是给出全部。
爱的范围高至天顶，深达洋底，
宽到大气的边界或者这个星球弯曲的长度。

048 Thomas Hood 托马斯·胡德

◆ *The Poet's Profile* （诗人小档案）

托马斯·胡德（1799—1845）：英国诗人和幽默作家。胡德就很多社会问题写出了幽默之作。在他那个时代最大的社会问题就是盗墓。盗墓者盗完墓，将尸体卖给解剖学家。胡德写过很多幽默的诗篇，但主要以严肃的诗歌如《衬衫之歌》而流传后世。胡德身体状况一直不佳，去世时年仅45岁。威廉·迈克尔·罗塞蒂称他是雪莱时代和丁尼生时代之间“最优秀的英国诗人”。托马斯·胡德是剧作家和幽默作家汤姆·胡德的父亲。

◆ *I Love Thee*

I love thee—I love thee!
'Tis all that I can say; —
It is my vision in the night,
My dreaming in the day;
The very echo of my heart,
The blessing when I pray:
I love thee—I love thee!
Is all that I can say.

I love thee—I love thee!
Is ever on my tongue;
In all my proudest poesy
That chorus still is sung;

It is the verdict of my eyes,
Amidst the gay and young:
I love thee—I love thee!
A thousand maids among.

I love thee—I love thee!
Thy bright hazel glance,
The mellow lute upon those lips,
Whose tender tones entrance;
But most, dear heart of hearts, thy proofs
That still these words enhance,
I love thee—I love thee!
Whatever be thy chance.

◆ *Annotations* （原诗注释）

1. thee: *pron.* [second person singular] archaic or dialect form of you, as the singular object of a verb or preposition （古英语“thou”的宾格，同“you”）你；汝

2. 'Tis = It is

3. blessing: *n.* God's favour and protection 上帝的祝福；上帝的保佑；天恩（e.g. May God continue to give us his blessing. 愿上帝继续保佑我们。）

4. poesy: *n.* （archaic or poetic/literary） poetry （古旧用法或诗/文用法）诗歌

5. chorus: *n.* a part of a song which is repeated after each verse, typically by more than one singer 副歌；叠歌（尤指合唱句）

6. verdict: *n.* an opinion or judgement 意见；判断

7. amidst = amid

8. thy: *adj.* （also “thine” before a vowel） archaic or dialect form of your （元音前亦作“thine”）（古旧用法或方言用法）你（您）的（同“your”）

9. hazel: *n.* a reddish-brown or greenish-brown colour, especially of

someone's eyes （尤指某人的眼睛）棕红色（或棕绿色）

10. mellow: *adj.* （especially of sound, taste, and colour） pleasantly smooth or soft; free from harshness （尤指音、色）柔和的；（味道）可口的；松软的（e.g. She was hypnotized by the mellow tone of his voice. 她对他那柔和的嗓音着了迷。）

11. lute: *n.* a plucked stringed instrument with a long neck bearing frets and a rounded body with a flat front, rather like a halved egg in shape 诗琴；琉特琴

12. entrance: *v.* （often be entranced） fill （someone） with wonder and delight, holding their entire attention 使狂喜；使着迷

13. proof: *n.* （archaic） a test or trial （古旧用法）测试；选拔

14. chance: *n.* an opportunity to do or achieve something 机会 （e.g. I gave her a chance to answer. 我给了她作答的机会。）

◆ *A Lead-in Note* （简明导读）

纵有千言万语，无一能抵得上"我爱你"这三字构成的一句话。此诗中，诗人认为这一句具有无尽的力量。可以说，有了这句话，走遍天下都不怕。"在我所有最得意的诗篇中"，这一句如同一首歌中不断重复的部分，即副歌，而且"这句副歌一直吟唱不止"。

◆ 我爱你

我爱你——我爱你！
我能说的仅此一句——
是我白昼的梦乡，
是我夜晚的视力；
是我内心的回音，
是我祈祷时上帝的恩赐：

我爱你——我爱你！

是我唯一能说的一句。

我爱你——我爱你！
是永远挂在我嘴边的一句。
在我所有最得意的诗篇中
这句副歌一直吟唱不止。
在年轻欢快的人群中，
这句话让我双眼有了判断力：
我爱你——我爱你！
纵然有三千玫瑰般少女。

我爱你——我爱你！
爱你棕红明眸惊鸿一瞥际。
柔和的琴音飘浮唇间，
音调温柔让人着迷狂喜。
最心爱的人，所有考验表明
这三个字日益强大有力：
我爱你——我爱你！
不管你给的机会有几许。

049 Matthew Arnold 马修·阿诺德

◆ *The Poet's Profile* （诗人小档案）

马修·阿诺德（1822—1888）：英国诗人、散文家和社会批评家，曾当过学校督查员。阿诺德的职业生涯始于写诗，早年在拉格比公学上学时他写的诗就得到了认可。当时，他的父亲托马斯·阿诺德任拉格比公学的校长，严厉且具创新精神，知名度很高。给阿诺德带来诗人声望的是戏剧诗《埃特纳火山上的恩培多克勒》和《阿诺德诗集》。

◆ *Longing*

Come to me in my dreams, and then
By day I shall be well again!
For so the night will more than pay
The hopeless longing of the day.

Come, as thou cam'st a thousand times,
A messenger from radiant climes,
And smile on thy new world, and be
As kind to others as to me!

Or, as thou never cam'st in sooth,
Come now, and let me dream it truth,
And part my hair, and kiss my brow,
And say, My love why sufferest thou?

Come to me in my dreams, and then
By day I shall be well again!
For so the night will more than pay
The hopeless longing of the day.

◆ *Annotations* （原诗注释）

1. longing: *n.* a yearning desire 渴望 （e.g. Miranda felt a wistful longing for the old days. 米兰达十分渴望那过去的日子。）

2. thou: *pron.* [second person singular] archaic or dialect form of you, as the singular subject of a verb （古旧用法或方言用法）（作动词的单数主语）你（同 “you” ）

3. cam'st = came

4. messenger: *n.* a person who carries a message or is employed to carry messages 信使；报信者；信差；通信员

5. radian: *adj.* sending out light; shining or glowing brightly 发光的；明亮的，光辉灿烂的 （e.g. a bird with radiant green and red plumage 红绿相间羽毛鲜亮的鸟）

6. clime: *n.* （chiefly poetic/literary） a region considered with reference to its climate （主要为诗/文用法）气候；地域；地方；风土

7. thy: *adj.* （also “thine” before a vowel） archaic or dialect form of your （元音前亦作 “thine” ）（古旧用法或方言用法）你（您）的（同 “your” ）

8. in sooth: in truth; really 事实上；确实

9. part: *v.* separate （the hair of the head on either side of the parting） with a comb 把（头发）往两边分开梳理

10. sufferest = suffers

◆ *A Lead-in Note* （简明导读）

诗人渴望见到的对象，或者已经逝去，或者已与诗人分离，前者的可能性较大。不管怎样，诗人渴望见到对方，哪怕在夜晚的梦中见到对方，也会“对白天无望的渴望予以偿还”。哪怕对方以前千万次来过，诗人也渴望对方再来一次；要是以前对方一次也没来过，那就初次到来吧：“分开我的头发，吻着我的额头问，我的爱人，你为何痛苦不堪？”这究竟是梦境还是现实？

◆ 渴　望

来我梦里吧，如此这般，
到了白天，我将再次好转！
若这样，黑夜就会加倍
对白天无望的渴望予以偿还。

你是信使，来自明亮的地区；
来吧，如同你千万次来过那般。
在你抵达的新世界里微笑，对我
要跟对他人一样和善！

或者，如同你从未来过那样，
这就来吧，让我梦成现实在眼前：
分开我的头发，吻着我的额头问，
我的爱人，你为何痛苦不堪？

来我梦里吧，如此这般，
到了白天，我将再次好转！
若这样，黑夜就会加倍
对白天无望的渴望予以偿还。

050 Thomas Wyatt
托马斯·怀亚特

◆ *The Poet's Profile* （诗人小档案）

托马斯·怀亚特（1503—1542）：英国外交官和抒情诗人。商籁体诗歌被引进英国文学，怀亚特功不可没。亨利八世在位时的1527年，怀亚特赴意大利任外交官，此行促使他翻译了彼特拉克的作品。怀亚特的作品还包括商籁体诗、回旋诗和诗琴歌等。怀亚特活着的时候，一首诗也没有发表过。第一本能见得到怀亚特诗歌的书是《托特尔杂集》，这本书在他死后整整15年才出版发行。

◆ *What Should I Say?*

What should I say,
Since faith is dead,
And truth away
From you is fled?
Should I be led
With doubleness?
Nay, nay, mistress!

I promised you,
And you promised me,
To be as true
As I would be.
But since I see

Your double heart,
Farewell my part!

Though for to take
It is not my mind;
But to forsake
[One so unkind;]
And as I find,
So will I trust:
Farewell, unjust!

Can ye say nay?
But you said
That I alway
Should be obeyed?
And thus betrayed,
Or that I wiste—
Farewell, unkissed.

◆ *Annotations* （原诗注释）

1. nay: *adv.* （archaic or dialect） no （古旧用法或方言用法）不 （e.g. Nay, I must not think thus. 不，我可不能那样想。）

2. mistress: *n.* （archaic or poetic/literary） a woman loved and courted by a man （古旧用法或诗/文用法）女情人

3. true: *adj.* loyal or faithful 忠实的；忠诚的 （e.g. He was a true friend. 他是个忠实的朋友。）

4. forsake: *v.* （past forsook; past participle forsaken）（chiefly poetic/literary） abandon （someone or something） （主要为诗/文用法）抛弃；遗弃（人或物）

5. unjust: *adj.* not based on or behaving according to what is morally right and fair 非正义的；不公正的；不合理的 （e.g. resistance to unjust laws 对不公正

法律的反抗）

6. ye: *pron.* [second person plural] （archaic or dialect） plural form of thou （古旧用法或方言用法）你们（“thou”的复数形式）

7. alway = always

8. wiste = wiste: past and past participle of wit “wit”的过去式和过去分词 wit: *v.* （wot, witting; past and past participle wist）（archaic） have knowledge （古旧用法）知道

◆ *A Lead-in Note* （简明导读）

是啊，我该说什么呢？我们之间没有了信任，你也不再忠诚。是啊，我该说什么呢？我那么忠诚，而你却三心二意。是啊，我该说什么呢？我有责任感，而你却是“如此的无情无义”。是啊，我该说什么呢？你说的服从却是最终的背叛，让我情何以堪啊。情人之间分手，常常是吻别后分道扬镳，但你我却是“永别，而不是吻别”。

◆ 我该说什么呢？

我该说什么呢？
信任已死，
且忠诚逃离
你那里。
我该遵从
这两者行事？
不，不，亲爱的人！

我对你许过诺，
你也许诺过我
要忠诚，

如我那般忠诚不辍。
可我发现你
三心二意。
永别，我的一部分！

尽管我没打算
索取后一走了之，
但却可抛弃
（如此的无情无义。）
因眼中所见
皆为可信之事。
永别，不公正的待遇！

你能否认吗？
但你说过
自始至终
应该服从我？
也这样背叛了我，
或许我知道——
永别，而不是吻别。

051 Sir Walter Scott
沃尔特·斯科特爵士

◆ *The Poet's Profile* （诗人小档案）

沃尔特·斯科特爵士（1771—1832）：苏格兰历史题材小说家、诗人、剧作家和历史学家。斯科特的很多作品既是英国文学的经典之作，又是苏格兰文学的经典之作。人们记住他主要是因为他那些数量庞大的文学作品以及他在政治上的业绩。尽管如此，他的本职工作却是做辩护律师、法官及法律事务管理者。现在，人们普遍认可斯科特为历史题材小说的创始人。在整个19世纪的欧洲大陆，他的作品被人们广泛地阅读和模仿。斯科特的代表作品有《伊万霍》《罗布·罗伊》《湖上女士》《韦弗利》和《中洛锡安正中心区》等。

◆ *Love*

In peace, Love tunes the shepherd's reed;
In war, he mounts the warrior's steed;
In halls, in gay attire is seen;
In hamlets, dances on the green.
Love rules the court, the camp, the grove,
And men below and saints above;
For love is heaven, and heaven is love.

◆ *Annotations* （原诗注释）

1. tune: *v.* adjust （a musical instrument） to the correct or uniform pitch 给（乐器）调音；定调 （e.g. He tuned the harp for me. 他替我的竖琴调音。）

2. shepherd: *n.* a person who tends and rears sheep 牧羊人

3. reed: *n.* （poetic/literary） a rustic musical pipe made from such plants or from straw （诗/文用法）芦笛

4. mount: *v.* get up on （an animal or bicycle） in order to ride it 骑上（动物或自行车）

5. steed: *n.* （archaic or poetic/literary） a horse being ridden or available for riding （古旧用法或诗/文用法）马；坐骑

6. gay: *adj.* brightly coloured; showy; brilliant 明亮的；绚丽的；灿烂的

7. hall: *n.* the principal living room of a medieval house （中世纪寓所的）主厅；会客厅

8. attire: *n.* clothes, especially fine or formal ones （尤指华丽或正式的）服装；盛装

9. hamlet: *n.* a small settlement, generally one smaller than a village, and strictly （in Britain） one without a church 小村庄；（英国的）没有教堂的小村子

10. grove: *n.* a small wood, orchard, or group of trees 树丛；小树林；果园

◆ *A Lead-in Note* （简明导读）

爱神代表的是爱或爱情。爱具有无比的驱动力。在不同的时期和不同的地点，爱都具有非凡的力量。同时，爱又是至高无上的，甚至是无所不在的，“因为爱就是天，而天就是爱”。

◆ 爱 神

和平期，爱神为牧羊人的芦笛调音；
交战时，他骑上勇士的马打拼。
在会客大厅，他身着艳丽服装露面；
在小山村，他起舞，脚下绿草如茵。
爱神统治着宫廷、营房、林地，
还有下方百姓，以及上方圣人，
因为爱就是天，而天就是爱。

052 Phillip Edward Thomas
菲利普·爱德华·托马斯

◆ *The Poet's Profile* （诗人小档案）

菲利普·爱德华·托马斯（1878—1917）：英国诗人、散文家和小说家。尽管爱德华的诗没有几首与其战争经历直接相关，但人们一般都把他看成战争诗人。爱德华的诗歌生涯起步之时，他已经是一位成功的作家和文学评论家了。1915年，他加入英国陆军，在第一次世界大战中作战。1917年阿拉斯战役爆发时，他赴法作战，不久身亡。

◆ *The Sorrow of True Love*

The sorrow of true love is a great sorrow
And true love parting blackens a bright morrow:
Yet almost they equal joys, since their despair
Is but hope blinded by its tears, and clear
Above the storm the heavens wait to be seen.
But greater sorrow from less love has been
That can mistake lack of despair for hope
And knows not tempest and the perfect scope
Of summer, but a frozen drizzle perpetual
Of drops that from remorse and pity fall
And cannot ever shine in the sun or thaw,
Removed eternally from the sun's law.

◆ *Annotations* （原诗注释）

1. parting: *n.* the action of leaving or being separated from someone 离别；分别 （e.g. They exchanged a few words on parting. 他们在分别时互相说了几句话。）

2. morrow: *n.* （the morrow） （archaic or poetic/literary） the following day （古旧用法或诗/文用法）翌日 （e.g. On the morrow they attacked the city. 次日，他们进攻了城市。）

3. equal: *v.* be equivalent to 与……相当；等同于 （e.g. His work is concerned with why private property equals exploitation. 他的著作是关于私有财产之所以等于剥削的原因的。）

4. despair: *n.* the complete loss or absence of hope 绝望；无望 （e.g. Driven to despair, he throws himself under a train. 他陷入绝望，一头撞到了火车底下。）

5. tempest: *n.* a violent windy storm 大风暴；暴风雨；暴风雪

6. drizzle: *n.* light rain falling in very fine drops 毛毛雨；细雨 （e.g. Scotland will be cloudy with patchy drizzle. 苏格兰的天气将是多云，局部地区有小雨。）

7. perpetual: *adj.* occurring repeatedly; so frequent as to seem endless and uninterrupted 连续不断的；重复不停的

8. remorse: *n.* deep regret or guilt for a wrong committed 痛悔；悔恨；内疚 （e.g. They were filled with remorse and shame. 他们心中满是悔恨和羞愧。）

9. thaw: *v.* （of ice, snow, or another frozen substance, such as food） become liquid or soft as a result of warming up （冰、雪等）融化；融解；（冷冻食品等）解冻；化冻 （e.g. The river thawed and barges of food began to reach the capital. 河流解冻后，一船船的食品开始运抵首都。）

◆ *A Lead-in Note* （简明导读）

真爱带来的苦痛，别离带来的绝望，的确都不小。但是，这种苦痛与绝望孕育的却是希望之种，如同“暴风雨上方有晴空，却有待发现”。缺少爱或者没有真爱是彻底的绝望，如细雨成冰而“滴滴坠落——落自悔恨，落自同情”。无爱之冰“永远无法在太阳下闪耀或者融化，永永远远无法落入太阳的掌控中”，那就意味着没有爱或者缺少爱，将会遭受更大的苦痛，其苦痛远远大于真爱所带来的苦痛。所以，享受真爱的苦痛吧。

◆ 真爱的苦痛

真爱的苦痛是极大的苦痛，
真爱的别离，遮蔽了明日灿烂之景。
但苦与别近乎喜悦，苦与别的绝望
正是绝望之泪遮掩下的希望之种。
暴风雨上方有晴空，却有待发现，
可缺爱的苦痛更大，将绝望之净
误作希望之存，甚至不知风暴为何物，
不知完美之夏何时起始，何时止停。
只知细雨冻成了冰，连绵无绝期，
滴滴坠落——落自悔恨，落自同情。
永远无法在太阳下闪耀或者融化，
永永远远无法落入太阳的掌控中。

053 Richard Crashaw
理查德·克拉肖

◆ *The Poet's Profile* （诗人小档案）

理查德·克拉肖（1613—1649）：英国诗人、教师、英格兰圣公会牧师和罗马天主教皈依者。在17世纪英国文学领域，很多重要人物与玄学派诗人有交往，克拉肖就是其中的一位。尽管克拉肖的诗经常与当时的英国玄学派诗人的诗归为一类，但他的诗却展示出与巴洛克式艺术风格诗人作品的相似性。他的诗受到意大利及西班牙神秘主义作品的影响。

◆ *On Marriage*

I would be married, but I'd have no wife;
I would be married to a single life.

◆ *Annotations* （原诗注释）

1. marriage: *n.* the formal union of a man and a woman, typically recognized by law, by which they become husband and wife 结婚

2. marry: *v.* take （someone） as one's wife or husband in marriage 嫁；娶

3. single: *adj.* unmarried or not involved in a stable sexual relationship 未婚的；单身的 （e.g. a single mother 单亲妈妈）

◆ *A Lead-in Note*（简明导读）

此诗只有短短两行，被称为“双行偶合体诗（Couplet）”，每行为五音步抑扬格（Iambic Pentameter）。诗人在每行词数不多的情况下，在每行的开头采用了副歌形式的表达“I would be married”（我愿意结婚成家），如同在汉语古诗五绝中采用叠音字的处理手法。但是，这并不影响诗人以幽默的手法写出他对婚姻关系的看法和感触。

◆ 论结婚

我愿意结婚成家，但不应娶老婆；
我愿意结婚成家而过上单身生活。

054 Abraham Cowley
亚伯拉罕·考利

◆ *The Poet's Profile* （诗人小档案）

亚伯拉罕·考利（1618—1667）：英国诗人，是17世纪英国主要的诗人之一。其诗富于幻想，端庄得体。考利的父亲是书商，考利是遗腹子。考利在威斯敏斯特学校及剑桥的三一学院接受过教育。他很早就展露出诗人的才能，年仅15岁就出版了第一部诗集《诗之花》，这部作品使他成为闻名遐迩的早慧天才。1647年，考利的爱情诗集《情人》出版，这部诗集是当时最受欢迎的诗歌读物，而今却成为考利诸多作品中最受冷落的读物。考利极受敬重，死后被葬在英国的名人墓地威斯敏斯特教堂，紧挨着乔叟和斯宾塞。

◆ *Thisbe's Song*

Come, love, why stay'st thou? The night
Will vanish ere wee taste delight.
The moone obscures her selfe from sight,
Thou absent, whose eyes give her light.

Come quickly deare, be briefe as time,
Or we by morne shall be o'retane,
Love's Joy's thing owne as well as mine,
Spend not therefore, time in vaine.

◆ Annotations （原诗注释）

1. Thisbe: *n.* （Roman Mythology） a Babylonian girl, lover of Pyramus. Pyramus and Thisbe are a pair of star-crossed lovers whose story forms part of Ovid's *Metamorphoses*. The story has since been retold by many authors. （罗马神话）西斯贝（巴比伦少女，皮拉摩斯的情人。他们两个是一对不幸的情人，其故事构成了古罗马诗人奥维德长篇叙事诗《变形记》的一部分。自奥维德之后，很多作者复述过这个故事。）

2. stay'st = stayest = stays

3. thou: *pron.* [second person singular] archaic or dialect form of you, as the singular subject of a verb （古旧用法或方言用法）（作动词的单数主语）你（同"you"）

4. ere: *prep. & conj.* （poetic/literary or archaic） before （in time） （诗/文用法或古旧用法）在……之前（在时间上）(e.g. We hope you will return ere long. 我们希望你很快回来。)

5. wee = we

6. moone = moon

7. obscure: *v.* keep from being seen; conceal 隐藏；遮蔽 （e.g. Grey clouds obscure the sun. 乌云蔽日。）

8. selfe = self

9. deare = dear

10. breife = brief

11. morne = morn = morning

12. o'retane = of retain or on retain

注：其实，按照英语语法要求，此处应为"retained"，但出于音步和押韵考虑，诗人用了这样非标准的形式。

13. Joy: *n.* goddess of joy 欢乐女神

14. owne = own

15. vaine = vain

16. in vain: without success or a result 徒劳地 （e.g. They waited in vain for a response. 他们白等回音。）

◆ *A Lead-in Note* （简明导读）

此诗基于古希腊罗马神话中巴比伦少女西斯贝和情人皮拉摩斯的感人故事而写。这个故事经过古罗马诗人奥维德在其长篇叙事诗《变形记》中的演绎而在西方世界变得家喻户晓。此诗表现了少女西斯贝对爱情的大胆追求。西斯贝为了爱情而去付诸行动，勇敢追求，高声歌唱：活在当下，珍惜眼前；为了爱情，赶快行动，“莫将时间浪费而徒悲叹”。

◆ 西斯贝之歌

爱人，来吧！你为何不动身？今晚
将消失，我们却没有品尝欢乐而如愿。
月儿把自己隐藏了起来，
你若不来，谁的眼睛让月儿光明再现？

亲爱的，快些来！要快如时间之箭，
否则早晨到来，我们将彼此分离不得见。
爱是欢乐女神的事情，也是我的事情，
因此，莫将时间浪费而徒悲叹。

055 Robert Seymour Bridges
罗伯特·西摩·布里奇斯

◆ *The Poet's Profile* （诗人小档案）

罗伯特·西摩·布里奇斯（1844—1930）：英国诗人。布里奇斯因对韵律的娴熟掌握而著称，也因其对友人杰拉尔德·曼利·霍普金斯的诗提供赞助而知名。尽管布里奇斯发表过几首长诗和数部诗剧，但他的名声有赖于他《更短诗歌集》中那些抒情诗。1913—1930年，布里奇斯一直稳坐“桂冠诗人”的宝座。

◆ *So Sweet Love Seemed That April Morn*

So sweet love seemed that April morn,
When first we kissed beside the thorn,
So strangely sweet, it was not strange
We thought that love could never change.

But I can tell—let truth be told—
That love will change in growing old;
Though day by day is naught to see,
So delicate his motions be.

And in the end 'twill come to pass
Quite to forget what once he was,
Nor even in fancy to recall
The pleasure that was all in all.

His little spring, that sweet we found,
So deep in summer floods is drowned,
I wonder, bathed in joy complete,
How love so young could be so sweet.

◆ *Annotations* （原诗注释）

1. morn = morning

2. thorn: *n.* （also thorn bush or thorn tree） a thorny bush, shrub, or tree, especially a hawthorn 带刺小灌木；荆棘；山楂树

3. naught: *pron.* （archaic） nothing （古旧用法）无；没有什么 （e.g. He's naught but a worthless fool. 他是一个不中用的笨蛋。）

4. 'twill = it will

5. fancy: *n.* the faculty of imagination 想象力 （e.g. My research assistant is prone to flights of fancy. 我的研究助手时有古怪想法。）

◆ *A Lead-in Note* （简明导读）

"四月那个早晨"所代表的正是我们浪漫无邪的青春岁月。那个时候，我们感觉"爱似乎如此甜蜜"。不仅如此，"如此奇特的甜蜜，不奇特的地方在于当时我们认为：爱，永不渝"。那仅仅是"似乎"而已，因"爱会改变，会日益老去"。但是，我们看不到量的积累，只见证了质的飞跃。无论爱最终会达到一个什么样"质的飞跃"，我们仍然怀念，怀念曾经那个四月的早晨。当时我们认为：爱，永不渝——"如此年轻的爱，怎么竟能如此甜蜜！"

◆ 四月那个早晨爱似乎如此甜蜜

四月那个早晨爱似乎如此甜蜜，
荆棘丛旁我们亲吻，这是首次。

如此奇特的甜蜜，不奇特的地方
在于当时我们认为：爱，永不渝。

但我断定——拨开迷雾见实情：
爱会改变，会日益老去。
尽管日复一日不见任何变更，
可如此细微的是其移动的痕迹。

爱最终会经过，失去踪迹，
一干二净忘掉曾经的样子。
甚至在意念中也回忆不出
曾经拥有的所有欢乐之事。

那微小的四月之春，那我们曾找到的甜蜜，
都如此之深地淹没在夏日的洪水里。
完全沐浴欢快之河时，不禁惊奇起来：
如此年轻的爱，怎么竟能如此甜蜜！

056 Sir Edward Dyer
爱德华·戴尔爵士

◆ *The Poet's Profile* （诗人小档案）

爱德华·戴尔爵士（1543—1607）：英国诗人。戴尔就读于牛津大学，之后承蒙莱斯特伯爵的栽培，入朝任职。戴尔跟菲利浦·锡德尼爵士是朋友，锡德尼爵士去世时戴尔为他写了挽歌。在当时，戴尔的诗人声望很高，他的作品或者匿名发表，或者以其名字的首字母缩略形式（S. E. D.）发表。他最知名的一首诗是《对我而言，我的心灵即是一个王国》。

◆ *The Lowest Trees Have Tops*

The lowest trees have tops, the ant her gall,
The fly her spleen, the little sparks their heat;
The slender hairs cast shadows, though but small,
And bees have stings, although they be not great;
Seas have their source, and so have shallow springs;
And love is love, in beggars as in kings.

Where rivers smoothest run, deep are the fords;
The dial stirs, yet none perceives it move;
The firmest faith is in the fewest words;
The turtles cannot sing, and yet they love:
True hearts have eyes and ears, no tongues to speak;
They hear and see, and sigh, and then they break.

◆ Annotations （原诗注释）

1. gall: *n.* an animal's gall bladder （动物的）胆囊

2. spleen: *n.* （Anatomy） an abdominal organ involved in the production and removal of blood cells in most vertebrates and forming part of the immune system （解剖学）脾

3. slender: *adj.* （especially of a rod or stem） of small girth or breadth （尤指杆或茎）细长的

4. but: *adv.* no more than; only 仅仅；只 （e.g. He is but a shadow of his former self. 他瘦得不成人形了。）

5. sting: *n.* a small sharp-pointed organ at the end of the abdomen of bees, wasps, ants, and scorpions, capable of inflicting a painful or dangerous wound by injecting poison （蜜蜂、黄蜂、蚂蚁、蝎子的）螯针；螯刺

6. ford: *n.* a shallow place in a river or stream allowing one to walk or drive across 浅滩；可涉水而过的地方

7. dial: *n.* a sundial 日晷

8. turtle: *n.* （also sea turtle） a large marine reptile with a bony or leathery shell and flippers, coming ashore annually on sandy beaches to lay eggs 海龟

◆ A Lead-in Note （简明导读）

此诗以类推的手法，写出了爱的无所不在。只要你靠近观察，你就会发现，爱存在于任何事物中。第一节中，诗人经过一番观察和列举后，得出结论："爱无彼此之分，不管是乞丐还是国王。"这说明爱无所不在，且没有贫富之分。第二节中，诗人以"河流""日晷""海龟"等意象说明爱的实质以及爱的过程。爱不张扬，爱很适度，爱不偏不倚。同时，爱也会经历"心听心看心还叹，然后心碎于心房"这样的过程。

◆ 最矮小的树木也有树梢

最矮小的树木也有树梢，蚂蚁有胆囊，
苍蝇有脾脏，小火花也发热和光。
细毛照样投下阴影，虽然阴影细小；
蜜蜂长有螫刺，尽管螫刺不长。
深海有源头，浅泉也如此；
爱无彼此之分，不管是乞丐还是国王。

河水流淌最为平缓之处，浅滩不浅；
日晷移动，但无人觉察其动了地方。
最坚定的信念不用言辞表现；
海龟不会唱情歌，却知爱要结对成双。
真诚的心有眼有耳，但无舌说话语；
心听心看心还叹，然后心碎于心房。

057 William Congreve
威廉·康格里夫

◆ *The Poet's Profile* （诗人小档案）

威廉·康格里夫（1670—1729）：英国复辟时期的诗人和剧作家。康格里夫23岁时完成了他人生的第一部戏剧《老光棍》，并获得了极大的成功。康格里夫的戏剧以睿智的、讽刺性的对话而著称。他或许是唯一一位可以与法国剧作家莫里哀相提并论的英国剧作家。

◆ *False Though She Be*

False though she be to me and love,
I'll ne'er pursue revenge;
For still the charmer I approve,
Though I deplore her change.

In hours of bliss we oft have met:
They could not always last;
And though the present I regret,
I'm grateful for the past.

◆ *Annotations* （原诗注释）

1. false: *adj.* treacherous; unfaithful 背信弃义的；不忠的 （e.g. a false lover 背信弃义的情人）

2. ne'er = never

3. pursue: *v.* engage in （an activity or course of action） 从事；忙于（活

动）；实行；采取（行动路线）（e. g. Andrew was determined to pursue a computer career. 安德鲁决心从事计算机行业。）

4. charmer: *n.* a person with an attractive, engaging personality 可爱迷人的人；尤物

5. approve: *v.* （archaic） prove; show （古旧用法）证明；显示 （e.g. He approved himself ripe for military command. 他证明自己已成熟，足以胜任军事指挥的工作。）

6. deplore: *v.* feel or express strong disapproval of （something） 强烈反对；谴责

7. bliss: *n.* perfect happiness; great joy 完美的愉悦感；福分；欣喜 （e.g. She gave a sigh of bliss. 她幸福地长舒了一口气。）

8. oft = often

◆ *A Lead-in Note* （简明导读）

有些爱情半路而终，这样的爱情往往残留心中，无法抹去。此诗中，诗人描述的正是这样的爱情。诗人怀恋过去的美好时光，厌弃她的不义之举，但挥不去对她的爱："尽管现在我痛惜在心，但对过去，我感激不已。"

◆ 她虽背信弃义

对我对爱情，她虽背信弃义，
但对她我永不会有报复之举。
因我仍坚信她迷人如初，
但她的改变，令我厌弃。

我们那时常相见——幸福时光，
但幸福时光不能一直持续。
尽管现在我痛惜在心，
但对过去，我感激不已。

Chapter 02

Short Love Verse by Poets from the United States of America

第二章

美国诗人的韵体爱情短诗

058 Edna St. Vincent Millay
埃德娜・圣文森特・米莱

◆ *The Poet's Profile* （诗人小档案）

埃德娜・圣文森特・米莱（1892—1950）：美国抒情女诗人和剧作家，笔名是南希・博伊德。1923年，米莱获普利策诗歌奖，是第三位获此奖项的女性。她以女权激进主义而闻名。诗人理查德・威尔伯这样说道："她写出了这个世纪里一些最好的商籁体诗歌。"米莱的代表作品有《〈复活〉及其他诗集》《米莱商籁体诗集》和《米莱抒情诗集》等。

◆ *Time Does Not Bring Relief* （*Sonnet 2*）

Time does not bring relief; you all have lied
Who told me time would ease me of my pain!
I miss him in the weeping of the rain;
I want him at the shrinking of the tide;
The old snows melt from every mountain-side,
And last year's leaves are smoke in every lane;
But last year's bitter loving must remain
Heaped on my heart, and my old thoughts abide!

There are a hundred places where I fear
To go, —so with his memory they brim!
And entering with relief some quiet place
Where never fell his foot or shone his face
I say, "There is no memory of him here!"
And so stand stricken, so remembering him!

◆ *Annotations*（原诗注释）

1. relief: *n.* a feeling of reassurance and relaxation following release from anxiety or distress （忧虑或痛苦消除后感到的）宽慰；欣慰；放心（e.g. Much to her relief, she saw the door open. 使她大感欣慰的是，她看到门开了。）

2. ease: *v.* make （something unpleasant, painful, or intense） less serious or severe 减轻；舒缓；缓解（e. g. a huge road-building programme to ease congestion 一项宏大的缓解交通阻塞的道路建设计划）

3. weep: *v.* shed tears 流泪；哭泣（e.g. A grieving mother wept over the body of her daughter. 悲痛的母亲对着她女儿的遗体哭泣。）

4. shrink: *v.* become or make smaller in size or amount; contract or cause to contract 变小；减少；收缩；使收缩

5. heap: *v.* put in a pile or mound 堆积（e.g. She heaped logs on the fire. 她往火上堆了些木柴。）

6. abide: *v.* （of a feeling or a memory） continue without fading or being lost （感情或记忆）始终不渝

7. brim: *v.* （figurative） be full of a particular quality, feeling, etc. （比喻用法）充满（e.g. He is brimming with ideas. 他满脑子的点子。）

◆ *A Lead-in Note*（简明导读）

此诗为意大利式商籁体诗。译诗偶数行押韵，但平仄通押。考虑到原诗抒情意味较浓，为求得情感充分释放，译诗的每一行没有严格限定字数。此诗前八行，诗人米莱述说了对他（也许离开了人世）极度的思念之情。“每个山坡上的积雪都已消融”，时光荏苒，冬去春来，而且“去年的落叶化作烟，飘在每一条街巷”，大自然变得清净，迎接崭新的季节。但是，诗人内心思念的落叶却层层堆积，无法清空。后六行，诗人力图清空记忆，尝试去他未曾去过的地方，却适得其反：“可站稳后我竟如此悲伤，对他如此难忘！”毕竟，他竟没来得及跟她一起到这些新的地方来。自己独来，又有何用？可谓“才下眉头，却上心头”。

◆ 时间不能让人解脱（商籁体第2首）

时间不能让人解脱，你们都撒了谎：
告诉我说，时间会止住我的悲伤！
在雨的哭泣声中我思念着他；
潮退时想要他，那是我的渴望。
每个山坡上的积雪都已消融，
去年的落叶化作烟，飘在每一条街巷。
可去年苦痛的爱恋滋味，
却在内心堆积——旧思永驻我心房。

有千百个地方令我心惊胆战，
不敢进入——对他的记忆填满那些地方！
为求解脱只好进入某个安静之所——
那里他从未涉足，从未到场。
我说："这里没有对他的记忆。"
可站稳后我竟如此悲伤，对他如此难忘！

059 Christopher Morley 克里斯托弗·莫利

◆ *The Poet's Profile* （诗人小档案）

克里斯托弗·莫利（1890—1957）：美国诗人、记者、小说家和散文家。莫利写过几年的舞台剧，还在大学讲过课。他写过长篇小说、散文集、诗集等百余部，其中最有名的当属1939年出版的长篇小说《基蒂·福伊尔》（亦译作《女人万岁》）。这部小说被改编成了电影，获得了奥斯卡电影金像奖。他的另一部代表作品是《左边的雷声》。

◆ *Reading Aloud*

Once we read Tennyson aloud
In our great fireside chair;
Between the lines my lips could touch
Her April-scented hair.

How very fond I was, to think
The printed poems fair,
When close within my arms I held
A living lyric there!

◆ *Annotations* （原诗注释）

1. Tennyson: *n.* Alfred Tennyson （1809—1892）, English poet, and Poet Laureate from 1850. His reputation was established by *In Memoriam* , a long poem

concerned with immortality, change, and evolution. Other notable works: *The Charge of the Light Brigade* and *Idylls of the King* . 艾尔弗雷德·丁尼生（1809—1892）：英国诗人。1850年，丁尼生被封为“桂冠诗人”。他的长诗《悼念》（1850年为他赢得了声誉，这首长诗是关于永生、变化和演变的。丁尼生的其他著名作品有《轻旅之冲锋》和《国王的叙事诗》等。

2. fireside: *n.* the area round a fireplace （used especially with reference to a person's home or family life）（壁）炉边（尤其用在指家、家庭生活）

3. fond: *adj.* （fond of） having an affection or liking for 喜爱的；喜欢的

4. lyric: *n.* （usu. lyrics） a lyric poem or verse 抒情诗

◆ *A Lead-in Note* （简明导读）

曾经的那一幕多么令诗人沉醉：“曾经我们坐在壁炉边那把大椅子上一起朗读丁尼生的诗。”如此浪漫的一幕，足以让人产生共鸣！她就是优美动人的诗行，就是“一首活生生的抒情诗”。

◆ 朗　读

曾经我们坐在壁炉边那把大椅子上
一起朗读丁尼生的诗。
字里行间，我的双唇能够触摸到
她那散发出四月馨香的发丝。

我多么喜欢这一幕，想到
印刷的诗行多么动人时！
当时当地我双臂中紧紧拥抱
一首活生生的抒情诗。

060 Joyce Kilmer
乔伊斯·吉尔默

◆ *The Poet's Profile* （诗人小档案）

乔伊斯·吉尔默（1886—1918）：美国作家和诗人。出生时的名字为艾尔弗雷德·乔伊斯·吉尔默。他为人们所记住，主要是因为他于1913年写的一首题为《树》的诗。后来，这首诗收录到他的诗集《〈树〉及其他诗集》中。吉尔默是一位多产的诗人，其作品歌颂的是自然界的美以及他作为罗马天主教徒的信仰。此外，吉尔默还是记者、文学评论家、讲师和编辑。吉尔默死于第一次世界大战。他的诗主要收录在《爱的夏季》和《〈树〉及其他诗集》中。

◆ *Love's Lantern*

（*For Aline*）
Because the road was steep and long
And through a dark and lonely land,
God set upon my lips a song
And put a lantern in my hand.

Through miles on weary miles of night
That stretch relentless in my way
My lantern burns serene and white,
An unexhausted cup of day.

O golden lights and lights like wine,

How dim your boasted splendors are.
Behold this little lamp of mine;
It is more starlike than a star!

◆ *Annotations* （原诗注释）

1. lantern: *n.* a lamp with a transparent case protecting the flame or electric bulb, and typically having a handle by which it can be carried or hung 灯笼；提灯（e.g. a paper lantern 纸灯笼）

2. steep: *adj.* （of a slope, flight of stairs, or angle） rising or falling sharply; almost perpendicular （斜面、楼梯、角度）陡的；陡峭的；陡直的 （e.g. She pushed the bike up the steep hill. 她把自行车推上陡峭的山坡。）

3. weary: *adj.* calling for a great amount of energy or endurance; tiring and tedious 使人疲劳的；令人厌烦的；沉闷乏味的 （e.g. The weary journey began again. 令人疲乏的旅程又开始了。）

4. relentless: *adj.* never ending; oppressively constant 不间断的；持续的 （e.g. the relentless heat of the desert 沙漠里持续的高温）

5. serene: *adj.* calm, peaceful, and untroubled; tranquil 安详的；宁静的（e.g. Her eyes were closed and she looked very serene. 她闭着眼，看上去很平静。）

6. unexhausted: *adj.* （especially of resources or reserves） not exhausted （尤指资源或储备）未用完的

7. o: *interj.* used to express surprise or strong emotionn 哦；哟；啊；唉；哎呀（表示惊讶或强烈的情感）

8. splendour or splendor: *n.* （splendours） magnificent features or qualities 壮丽辉煌（的特色，格调）；华贵 （e.g. the splendours of the imperial court 皇家宫廷的壮丽辉煌）

◆ *A Lead-in Note* （简明导读）

艾琳是诗人钟爱的女孩，是上帝送给他的一只爱的灯笼。有了这只灯笼陪伴，前方的路再漫长、再幽暗，诗人也能走过。爱的力量如此强大！“金色之光，如红酒之光”，想必是月亮之光，但跟爱的灯笼一比，则黯淡了许多。

◆ 爱的灯笼

（为艾琳而作）
因道路陡峭且漫长
还通过一段幽暗且孤独的地方，
上帝让我唇间哼出一首歌曲，
还让我提一只灯笼在身旁。

走过一里又一里的疲乏夜路，
路无穷无尽地延伸至前方。
灯火燃得又白又宁静，
那是一团燃烧不尽的时光。

啊，金色之光，如红酒之光，
你拥有多么黯淡的辉光！
看我手提的这只小小灯盏——
不是星星却有着星星的面庞。

061 Oliver Wendell Holmes
奥利弗·温德尔·霍姆斯

◆ *The Poet's Profile* （诗人小档案）

奥利弗·温德尔·霍姆斯（1809—1894）：美国内科医生、诗人和散文家。霍姆斯的职业是内科医生，却因写作获得了声望。他是19世纪美国最受瞩目的诗人之一。霍姆斯最有名的文学作品是被称为“餐桌上谈话”的幽默小品系列，其开篇作品为《早餐桌上的霸主》。

◆ *Too Young for Love*

Too young for love?
Ah, say not so!
Tell reddening rose-buds not to blow!
Wait not for spring to pass away, —
Love's summer months begin with May!
Too young for love?
Ah, say not so!
Too young? Too young?
Ah, no! no! no!

Too young for love?
Ah, say not so,
While daisies bloom and tulips glow!
June soon will come with lengthened day
To practise all love learned in May.

Too young for love?
Ah, say not so!
Too young? Too young?
Ah, no! no! no!

◆ *Annotations* （原诗注释）

1. blow: *v.* produce flowers or be in flower 开花；在开花 （e.g. I know a bank where the wild thyme blows. 我知道一个堤岸，那里野生百里香正在开花。）

2. ah: *interj.* used to express a range of emotions including surprise, pleasure, sympathy, and realization 啊；呀 （用于表示惊讶、喜悦、同情和意识到等一系列情绪）

3. daisy: *n.* a small European grassland plant which has flowers with a yellow disc and white rays. It has given rise to many ornamental garden varieties 雏菊

4. bloom: *v.* produce flowers; be in flower 开花；在开花；处于花期

5. tulip: *n.* a bulbous spring-flowering plant of the lily family, with boldly coloured cup-shaped flowers 郁金香

6. glow: *v.* have an intense colour and a slight shine 因色彩浓烈而微微发光

◆ *A Lead-in Note* （简明导读）

要是认为恋爱太年轻，就等于“告诉渐渐红润的玫瑰花苞莫开放”；要是认为恋爱太年轻，“啊，莫如此声明，因雏菊开了花，郁金香红了脸”！五月正是好时候，正是恋爱好季节，因为“六月很快到来，延长了白昼的光明，以实践五月学到的所有爱恋”。恋爱太年轻？不，五月恋爱正是时候，五月正是青春好年华。

◆ 恋爱太年轻

恋爱太年轻?
啊，莫如此声明!
告诉渐渐红润的玫瑰花苞莫开放!
莫等春天消失无踪——
爱的夏季始于五月!
恋爱太年轻?
啊，莫如此声明!
太年轻了? 太年轻了?
啊，不行! 不行! 不行!

恋爱太年轻?
啊，莫如此声明，
因雏菊开了花，郁金香红了脸!
六月很快到来，延长了白昼的光明，
以实践五月学到的所有爱恋。
恋爱太年轻?
啊，莫如此声明!
太年轻了? 太年轻了?
啊，不行! 不行! 不行!

062 Lizette Woodworth Reese 利泽特·伍德沃思·里斯

◆ *The Poet's Profile* （诗人小档案）

利泽特·伍德沃思·里斯（1856—1935）：美国女诗人和教师。里斯从教长达45年，其中21年是在巴尔的摩的西部高中度过的。她的诗以情感强烈和语言简洁而著称，并与埃米莉·狄更生的诗相提并论。里斯最为知名的诗是商籁体诗《年华》。里斯出版的诗集有《五月的一根枝条》《一把薰衣草》《一条安静之路》《山胡椒树》和《里斯诗选》等。

◆ *Love Came Back at Fall o' Dew*

Love came back at fall o' dew,
Playing his old part;
But I had a word or two
That would break his heart.

"He who comes at candlelight,
That should come before,
Must betake him to the night
From a barred door."

This the word that made us part
In the fall o' dew;
This the word that brake his heart—
Yet it brake mine, too.

◆ *Annotations* （原诗注释）

1. o' = of

2. dew: *n.* tiny drops of water that form on cool surfaces at night, when atmospheric vapour condenses 露；露滴；露水（e.g. The grass was wet with dew. 草地被露水打湿了。）

3. betake: *v.* （past betook; past participle betaken）（betake oneself to）（poetic/literary） go to （诗/文用法）前往 （e.g. I shall betake myself to my lodgings. 我要到我的住所去。）

4. bar: *v.* （barred, barring） fasten （something, especially a door or window） with a bar or bars （用横木）闩（门、窗等）（e.g. She bolts and bars the door. 她用门闩把门闩紧。）

4. brake: *v.* （archaic ） a past tense of break （古旧用法）动词“break”的一个过去式形式

◆ *A Lead-in Note* （简明导读）

靠近地面的水蒸气，夜间遇冷凝结成的小水球，便形成露。虽说露水四季都有，可秋天时节特别多。按照中国人的思维，露降之时爱回归，天已凉，心已冷，爱也就错过了最佳的时节。但此诗中的女主人公认为，他应该在露降之前、夜幕还未降临时而归，“却在烛光亮起后才回”。那么，他只能吃闭门羹悻然而去，“走向夜晚的漆黑”。爱，不能错过；爱，要把握好时机。

◆ 露降之时爱回归

露降之时爱回归，
将旧作用发挥。
可是我的一两句话语
会伤害他的心扉。

“他应早些至此，
却在烛光亮起后才回。
他就必须从紧闭的门口
走向夜晚的漆黑。”

这话语令我们分手
于露降时的氛围。
这话语将他的心伤害，
也令我的心破碎。

063 Edgar Allan Poe
埃德加·爱伦·坡

◆ *The Poet's Profile* （诗人小档案）

埃德加·爱伦·坡（1809—1849）：美国短篇小说家、诗人和评论家。坡的小说和诗歌具有哥特派风格，以探索恐怖和怪诞的题材为特点。他的代表作品有短篇小说《厄舍古屋的倒塌》，侦探小说《莫格街的凶杀案》和诗歌《乌鸦》。

◆ *Eulalie*

I dwelt alone
In a world of moan,
And my soul was a stagnant tide,
Till the fair and gentle Eulalie became my blushing bride—
Till the yellow-haired young Eulalie became my smiling bride.

Ah, less—less bright
The stars of the night
Than the eyes of the radiant girl!
And never a flake
That the vapor can make
With the moon-tints of purple and pearl,
Can vie with the modest Eulalie's most unregarded curl—
Can compare with the bright-eyed Eulalie's most humble and careless curl.

Now Doubt—now Pain
Come never again,
For her soul gives me sigh for sigh,
And all day long
Shines, bright and strong,
Astarte within the sky,
While ever to her dear Eulalie upturns her matron eye—
While ever to her young Eulalie upturns her violet eye.

◆ *Annotations* （原诗注释）

1. stagnant: *adj.* （of a body of water or the atmosphere of a confined space） having no current or flow and often having an unpleasant smell as a consequence （水或封闭空间的空气）停滞的；不流动的；因不流动有难闻气味的 （e.g. a stagnant ditch 一条臭水沟）

2. ah: *interj.* used to express a range of emotions including surprise, pleasure, sympathy, and realization 啊；呀（用于表示惊讶、喜悦、同情和意识到等一系列情绪）

3. radiant: *adj.* （of a person or their expression） clearly emanating great joy, love, or health （人或表情）喜气洋洋的；洋溢着爱的；光华照人的（e.g. She gave him a radiant smile. 他对她粲然一笑。）

4. flake: *n.* a snowflake 雪花；雪片

5. vie: *v.* （vying） compete eagerly with someone in order to do or achieve something 竞争；相争 （e.g. The athletes were vying for a place in the British team. 运动员为了能成为英国队选手在展开竞争。）

6. unregarded: *adj.* not respected or considered; ignored 不被尊重的；不予考虑的；被忽略的 （e.g. Her sarcasm went unregarded. 她的讥讽未引起注意。）

7. curl: *n.* （with reference to a person's hair） a state or condition of being curled （头发）卷曲状态

◆ *A Lead-in Note* （简明导读）

诗人短暂的一生中经历过许多亲人去世的悲剧。其中，母亲1811年去世，爱妻弗吉尼亚1847年去世。此诗发表于1845年，据说是写给他的妻子弗吉尼亚的。诗人以第一人称的视角写了在遇到一个名叫厄拉利的年轻女子后，他的世界所发生的变化。厄拉利的魅力令夜晚的星光黯淡许多，她那一头卷曲的秀发无一可匹敌，就连"整个白天的时间里，她的心灵闪着光，明亮而强烈"，甚至月亮女神白天也一直盯着她，无法无视她的存在。厄拉利到达前后，诗人的生活有着天壤之别。

◆ 厄拉利

我独居于
一个痛苦呻吟的世界里。
我的灵魂是不再涌动的潮水，
直至娇美温柔的厄拉利成为我的新娘，脸庞羞红；
直至一头黄发的年轻厄拉利成为我的新娘，微露笑容。

啊！夜晚的点点星光
越来越不明亮，
比起这位魅力四射女孩的双眼要黯淡许多。
没有任何一朵
水汽凝结成的雪花——
带有月亮的色调：紫白混杂，
能匹敌端庄的厄拉利最为自然卷曲的秀发，
能比得上眼睛闪亮的厄拉利最为朴素和随意的卷发。

时而忧虑重重，时而痛苦不堪——
永不再犯。

因她的心灵让我只为叹息而叹息；
整个白天的时间里，
她的心灵闪着光，明亮而强烈；
空中月亮女神阿斯塔蒂，
抬起其监管一切的眼，一直盯着亲爱的厄拉利，
抬起其紫色的眼，一直盯着年轻的厄拉利。

064 Dorothy Parker 多萝西·帕克

◆ *The Poet's Profile* （诗人小档案）

多萝西·帕克（1893—1967）：美国女诗人、短篇小说家和文学批评家。帕克以其才智、妙语而著称，对20世纪城市怪癖独居慧眼。从1927年起，她开始为《纽约客》杂志撰写书评和短篇小说，成为才智过人的传奇人物之一。

◆ *A Very Short Song*

Once, when I was young and true,
Someone left me sad—
Broke my brittle heart in two;
And that is very bad.

Love is for unlucky folk,
Love is but a curse.
Once there was a heart I broke;
And that, I think, is worse.

◆ *Annotations* （原诗注释）

1. true: *adj.* loyal or faithful 忠实的；忠诚的 （e.g. He was a true friend. 他是个忠实的朋友。）

2. brittle: *adj.* hard but liable to break or shatter easily 脆的；易碎的（e.g.

Her bones became fragile and brittle. 她的骨头变得脆弱而易碎。）

3. folk: *n.* （also as “folks”） （informal） people in general （非正式用法）人们（泛指）

◆ *A Lead-in Note* （简明导读）

爱脆弱，爱也无情。诗人以幽默的笔触道出了爱的真谛。爱离去，人心碎，所以“爱属于倒霉的家伙”；爱的争执和分歧，也许导致“爱只是一阵咒骂之声”。某人离我而去，我心碎不已，可是“一旦我将某颗心弄碎，嗯，我想，那事儿更不幸”。

◆ 一首极短的歌

曾经，我年轻而真诚，
某个人离我而去，令我伤痛，
将我脆弱的心碎成两半儿。
那样的事很不幸。

爱属于倒霉的家伙，
爱只是一阵咒骂之声。
一旦我将某颗心弄碎，
嗯，我想，那事儿更不幸。

065 Robert Frost
罗伯特 · 弗罗斯特

◆ *The Poet's Profile* （诗人小档案）

罗伯特 · 弗罗斯特（1874—1963）：美国诗人。弗罗斯特以其讽刺的笔触和朴实无华的语言风格著称。他的许多诗反映了他对新英格兰的亲密情感，诗集有《波士顿以北》和《新罕布什尔州》等。他先后四次获得普利策诗歌奖。

◆ *Meeting and Passing*

As I went down the hill along the wall
There was a gate I had leaned at for the view
And had just turned from when I first saw you
As you came up the hill. We met. But all
We did that day was mingle great and small
Footprints in summer dust as if we drew
The figure of our being less than two
But more than one as yet. Your parasol

Pointed the decimal off with one deep thrust.
And all the time we talked you seemed to see
Something down there to smile at in the dust.
(Oh, it was without prejudice to me!)
Afterward I went past what you had passed
Before we met and you what I had passed.

◆ Annotations （原诗注释）

1. wall: *n.* a continuous vertical brick or stone structure that encloses or divides an area of land 围墙 （e.g. a garden wall 花园围墙）

2. gate: *n.* a hinged barrier used to close an opening in a wall, fence, or hedge 门；围墙门；篱笆门

3. mingle: *v.* mix or cause to mix together （使）混合；（使）相混 （e.g. The sound of voices mingled with a scraping of chairs. 说话声和椅子刮擦声混杂在一起。）

4. footprint: *n.* the impression left by a foot or shoe on the ground or a surface 脚印；足迹

5. figure: *n.* a numerical symbol, especially any of the ten in Arabic notation （尤指十个阿拉伯数字的）符号；字码

6. as yet: until now or a particular time in the past 直到现在；从过去某一时间

7. parasol: *n.* a light umbrella used to give shade from the sun 太阳伞

8. point off: （Mathematics） to mark off from the right-hand side （a number of decimal places） in a whole number to create a mixed decimal （数学用语）分开；点开；点出（小数位）（e.g. She has forgotten to point off the last two figures of 4235. 她忘了把4235的最后两位用小数点分开了。）

9. decimal: *n.* （also decimal fraction） a fraction whose denominator is a power of ten and whose numerator is expressed by figures placed to the right of a decimal point 小数；十进小数

10. thrust: *n.* a sudden or violent lunge with a pointed weapon or a bodily part 猛推；插；刺 （e.g. He drove the blade upwards with one powerful thrust. 他猛一推，让刀片朝上。）

11. oh: *interj.* used to express a range of emotions including surprise, anger, disappointment, or joy, or when reacting to something that has just been said （表示惊讶、愤怒、失望、高兴等感情）噢；啊；哦；唉；哎呀

12. prejudice: *n.* dislike, hostility, or unjust behaviour formed on such a basis 偏见；歧视；反感

◆ *A Lead-in Note*（简明导读）

此诗为意大利式商籁体诗。诗中，诗人下山途中与一位上山途中的女子相遇，有过短暂的交集后又彼此路过："随后，我走过相遇前你路过的地方，而你，则走过相遇前我经过的路线。"两个人并没有融为一体，化作数字"1"，而是介于"2"和"1"之间，女子那把太阳伞点出的正是这两个数字之间的那个小数点，令他们的相遇值不等于"1"。爱，就这样擦肩而过。

◆ 相遇和路过

沿着围墙，我走下小山；
途中观景，倚在墙门边。
刚一转身，就初次见到了你：
你走上小山，我们相遇山间。
但那日所为，皆是将大小脚印
叠印于夏之尘，像要勾勒一番，
画出你我相融之数——小于二，
但仍大于一。你将你的太阳伞

深深一戳，小数位被清晰点出。
我们一直谈呀谈，你似乎看见
夏之尘里什么可触发微笑的东西。
（哦，那绝不是对我有什么反感！）
随后，我走过相遇前你路过的地方，
而你，则走过相遇前我经过的路线。

066 Witter Bynner
威特·宾纳

◆ *The Poet's Profile* （诗人小档案）

威特·宾纳（1881—1968）：美国诗人、作家和翻译家。宾纳以笔名伊曼纽尔·摩根而为人所知。宾纳也以住在新墨西哥州的圣达菲并与那里的文学人物交往而知名。1907年，他的第一本诗集《哈佛颂》出版（后来书名改为《年轻的哈佛》）。

◆ *Lest I Learn*

Lest I learn, with clearer sight,
Such beauty cannot be—
Tie a bandage, pull it tight,
Blind me, I would not see!

Lest I learn, with clearer will,
Such a wonder cannot be—
Oh, kiss me nearer, nearer still,
And make a fool of me!

◆ *Annotations* （原诗注释）

1. lest: *conj.* （formal） with the intention of preventing （something undesirable）; to avoid the risk of （正式用法）免得；唯恐 （e.g. He spent whole days in his room, headphones on lest he disturb anyone. 他整天待在屋里，

戴着耳机，以免打扰别人。）

2. bandage: *n.* a strip of woven material used to bind up a wound or to protect an injured part of the body （用于包扎伤口或保护受伤部位）绷带（e.g. Her leg was swathed in bandages. 她的腿用绷带裹着。）

◆ *A Lead-in Note* （简明导读）

得不到爱时，向他人寻求慰藉，麻痹自己："用绷带缠上我的眼睛，缠得紧紧，让我什么都看不到！"得到爱后，无法创造奇迹时，向爱人寻求安慰，缓解情绪："啊，吻我吧！靠近再靠近些，就让我傻笑！"也许，这就是诗人要表达的诗意吧。

◆ 免得我知晓

这样的美，无法成真，
尽管我视力更佳。免得我知晓——
用绷带缠上我的眼睛，
缠得紧紧，让我什么都看不到！

这样的奇迹，无法成真，
尽管我意志更坚。免得我知晓——
啊，吻我吧！靠近再靠近些，
就让我傻笑！

067 John Boyle O'Reilly 约翰·博伊尔·奥赖利

◆ *The Poet's Profile* （诗人小档案）

约翰·博伊尔·奥赖利（1844—1890）：爱尔兰裔美国诗人、新闻工作者和活动家。1869年，奥赖利从西澳大利亚流放地逃走后，到了美国波士顿，开始了写作和新闻工作生涯，获得成功。1872年，奥赖利娶了玛丽·墨菲，生有四个女儿。在奥赖利生命的最后四年时光里，他的身体出现了各种问题。1890年，他因一次用药过量去世，死在位于马萨诸塞州赫尔的避暑别墅中。1873年，奥赖利出版了第一部诗集《南部海域之歌》。在随后的15年时间里，他先后出版了三部诗集、一部小说以及一部有关健康与锻炼方面的专著。

◆ *A Disappointment*

Her hair was a waving bronze, and her eyes
Deep wells that might cover a brooding soul;
And who, till he weighed it, could ever surmise
That her heart was a cinder instead of a coal!

◆ *Annotations* （原诗注释）

1. bronze: *n.* a yellowish-brown colour 青铜色；古铜色；黄褐色（e.g. rich, gleaming shades of bronze 鲜艳的闪闪发光的青铜色）

2. brood: *v.* think deeply about something that makes one unhappy 沉思；念

念不忘（尤指不愉快的事）（e.g. He brooded over his dead mother. 他念念不忘已故的母亲。）

3. surmise: *v.* suppose that something is true without having evidence to confirm it 猜想；臆测 （e.g. He surmised that something must be wrong. 他猜想肯定有什么地方不对劲儿。）

4. cinder: *n.* a small piece of partly burnt coal or wood that has stopped giving off flames but still has combustible matter in it 炭渣；煤渣

5. coal: *n.* （Brit.） a piece of coal for burning（英国用法）煤块（e.g. loading coals into a wagon 把煤块装车）

◆ *A Lead-in Note* （简明导读）

她很迷人，长发飘飘，双眸闪亮。都说眼睛是心灵的窗户，但她的双眼如深井，具有魔力，能让他思考迟钝，思考不出她的实质。好在他还有理性去判断，发现了真相："她是一个心如灰渣而非煤块之人。"于是，他感觉到了一种失望之情。

◆ 一种失望之情

她的黄褐色头发飘逸，而她的双眼
是深井，或许能遮蔽他沉思的灵魂。
不经过思考权衡，他不可能猜测到
她是一个心如灰渣而非煤块之人。

068 Henry van Dyke
亨利·凡·戴克

◆ *The Poet's Profile* （诗人小档案）

亨利·凡戴克（1852—1933）：美国作家、教育家和牧师。凡戴克最受欢迎的作品是两篇圣诞小说：《另一智慧之人》和《第一棵圣诞树》。不同类型的宗教主题体现在他的诗歌、圣歌、散文集里，如《小小的河流》和《渔夫的运气》。

◆ *A Lover's Envy*

I envy every flower that blows
Along the meadow where she goes,
And every bird that sings to her,
And every breeze that brings to her
The fragrance of the rose.

I envy every poet's rhyme
That moves her heart at eventime,
And every tree that wears for her
Its brightest bloom, and bears for her
The fruitage of its prime.

I envy every Southern night
That paves her path with moonbeams white,
And silvers all the leaves for her,

And in their shadow weaves for her
A dream of dear delight.

I envy none whose love requires
Of her a gift, a task that tires:
I only long to live to her,
I only ask to give to her
All that her heart desires.

◆ *Annotations* （原诗注释）

1. envy: *n.* a feeling of discontented or resentful longing aroused by someone else's possessions, qualities, or luck 妒忌；羡慕

2. envy: *v.* desire to have a quality, possession, or other desirable attribute belonging to （someone else） 羡慕（或妒忌）（他人）

3. blow: *v.* produce flowers or be in flower 开花；在开花 （e.g. I know a bank where the wild thyme blows. 我知道一个堤岸，那里野生百里香正在开花。）

4. meadow: *n.* a piece of grassland, especially one used for hay 草地；草场；牧场

5. eventime = evening

6. bloom: *n.* a flower, especially one cultivated for its beauty （尤指供观赏的）花

7. fruitage: *n.* （archaic or poetic/literary） fruit collectively （古旧用法或诗/文用法）（总称）果实

8. prime: *n.* a state or time of greatest strength, vigour, or success in a person's life 青春；青年；壮年；全盛时期 （e.g. You're in the prime of life. 你正值青春年华。）

9. silver: *v.* （poetic / literary） （especially of the moon） give a silvery appearance to （诗/文用法）（尤指月光）使呈银色外表 （e.g. The brilliant moon silvered the turf. 明亮的月光使草地披上了银装。）

10. dear: *adj.* endearing; sweet 可爱的；美好的 （e.g. a dear little puppy 可爱的小狗儿）

11. require: *v.* （require something of） regard an action, ability, or quality as due from （someone） by virtue of their position 认为（某人）应做到（或拥有）

◆ *A Lead-in Note* （简明导读）

爱是自私的、排他的。因此，我嫉妒对她好的所有人和物。同时，爱又是无私的奉献，因此“爱她要求她回赠之人，我无一嫉妒；那样做让人疲乏，很辛苦”。嫉妒她，是因为爱慕她，而爱慕她，“我只想与她一同生活，我只求给她快乐，满足她内心所有渴望之物”。

◆ 爱慕者的嫉妒之情

她沿着草地行走，所行之处
鲜花盛开，每一朵花儿我都嫉妒。
还嫉妒每一只为她歌唱的鸟儿，
还嫉妒每一阵微风习习
为她带来玫瑰芳香满腹。

为她做押韵诗表情愫
打动她夜晚芳心的诗人，我都嫉妒。
还嫉妒每一棵为她开绽
最亮丽花朵的树，为她挂满
累累果实，数不胜数。

南方白色月光为她铺路，
每一个这样的夜晚，我都嫉妒。
夜晚将叶子换上银装，为了她；
还在叶子的影子里织梦，为了她。

梦中的她心满意足。

爱她要求她回赠之人，我无一嫉妒；
那样做让人疲乏，很辛苦。
我只想与她一同生活，
我只求给她快乐，
满足她内心所有渴望之物。

069 Paul Laurence Dunbar
保罗·劳伦斯·邓巴

◆ *The Poet's Profile* （诗人小档案）

保罗·劳伦斯·邓巴（1872—1906）：非洲裔美国诗人。邓巴是19世纪末20世纪初具有重大影响力的非洲裔美国诗人。1896年出版的《低微生活抒情诗集》使邓巴得到了认可。邓巴出生于俄亥俄州的代顿市，父母都是出逃的奴隶。邓巴死于肺结核，年仅34岁。他出版过12本诗集、4部短篇小说集、5部长篇小说和1部戏剧。他的散文和诗歌广泛发表在当时的主流期刊上。

◆ *A Golden Day*

I found you and I lost you,
All on a gleaming day.
The day was filled with sunshine,
And the land was full of May.

A golden bird was singing
Its melody divine,
I found you and I loved you,
And all the world was mine.

I found you and I lost you,
All on a golden day,
But when I dream of you, dear,
It is always brimming May.

◆ *Annotations* （原诗注释）

1. gleaming: *adj.* emitting or reflecting light readily or in large amounts 闪闪发光的 （e.g. a gleaming array of vintage cars 一排闪闪发光的老爷车）

2. melody: *n.* a sequence of single notes that is musically satisfying 旋律 （e.g. He picked out an intricate melody on his guitar. 他用吉他慢慢奏出复杂的旋律。）

3. divine: *adj.* devoted to God; sacred 敬神的；神圣的 （e.g. divine liturgy 圣餐仪式）

4. brimming: *adj.* full to the point of flowing over 溢满的；满溢的

◆ *A Lead-in Note* （简明导读）

金色的一天多么美好，我找到了你；金色的一天多么凄惨，我又失去了你。金色的一天是五月里的一天，而五月正是人生好时光，又是爱恋的季节。五月里金色的一天失去你，"可我梦到你，亲爱的，总是在丰实的五月盛季"。

◆ 金色的一天

我找到了你，又失去了你，
都是在闪亮的一天里。
这一天，阳光灿烂，
这片土地正值五月盛季。

一只金色的鸟儿在鸣唱，
曲调美妙神奇。
我发现了你，又把你爱恋，
整个世界都是我的领地。

我发现了你，又失去了你，
都是在金色的一天里。
可我梦到你，亲爱的，
总是在丰实的五月盛季。

070 Anne Bradstreet
安妮·布雷兹特里特

◆ *The Poet's Profile* （诗人小档案）

安妮·布雷兹特里特（1612—1672）：殖民时期的美国女诗人，也是第一位公开发表作品的美国女作家。安妮16岁时嫁给了西蒙·布雷兹特里特。他当时还是一名雇员，却是后来马萨诸塞湾殖民地的州长。1630年，她随丈夫从英格兰迁至马萨诸塞湾殖民地。她的诗歌主题涉及家庭和宗教两方面。1650年，她的作品《新近在美洲出现的第十位缪斯》在伦敦问世。

◆ *To My Dear and Loving Husband*

If ever two were one, then surely we.
If ever man were lov'd by wife, then thee.
If ever wife was happy in a man,
Compare with me, ye women, if you can.
I prize thy love more than whole Mines of gold
Or all the riches that the East doth hold.
My love is such that Rivers cannot quench,
Nor ought but love from thee give recompetence.
Thy love is such I can no way repay.
The heavens reward thee manifold, I pray.
Then while we live, in love let's so persever
That when we live no more, we may live ever.

◆ *Annotations* （原诗注释）

1. lov'd = loved

2. thee: *pron.* [second person singular] archaic or dialect form of you, as the singular object of a verb or preposition （古英语"thou"的宾格，同"you"）你；汝

3. ye: *pron.* [second person plural] （archaic or dialect） plural form of thou （古旧用法或方言用法）你们（"thou"的复数形式）

4. prize: *v.* （often as "be prized"） value extremely highly 重视；珍视 （e.g. The berries were prized for their healing properties. 这些浆果因其疗效备受珍视。）

5. mine: *n.* an excavation in the earth for extracting coal or other minerals 矿；矿山；矿井（e.g. a copper mine 铜矿）

6. thy: *adj.* （also "thine" before a vowel） archaic or dialect form of your （元音前亦作"thine"）（古旧用法或方言用法）你（您）的（同"your"）

7. doth = does

8. quench: *v.* satisfy （one's thirst） by drinking （喝水）止（渴）

9. recompentence = recompense

recompense: *n.* （archaic） restitution made or punishment inflicted for a wrong or injury （古旧用法）赔偿；补偿；惩罚

10. manifold: *adj.* （formal & poetic/literary） many and various （正式用法及诗/文用法）多种多样的；繁多的

11. pray: *v.* wish or hope strongly for a particular outcome or situation 祈望；祈求（e.g. After several days of rain, we were praying for sun. 下了几天雨之后，我们祈望阳光。）

12. persever = persevere

persevere: *v.* continue in a course of action even in the face of difficulty or with little or no indication of success 坚持不懈；锲而不舍 （e.g. His family persevered with his treatment. 他的家人坚持对他进行治疗。）

◆ *A Lead-in Note*（简明导读）

这是17世纪时一位妻子对丈夫的真情告白。此诗中，诗人表达了自己对丈夫深沉而忠贞不渝的爱："若妇幸福，对夫满意，你们诸女有胆，跟我比比。"接着，诗人列举了几种情况下，她对丈夫爱的程度，大有汉乐府诗中痴情女子的架势。最后，诗人表达了对丈夫爱的决心："只要活着，我们爱不放手；一旦死去，我们将活永久。"此诗影响深远，由于其所表达的忠贞且赤诚的爱意，在西方经常被用在婚礼上朗读。

◆ 致我至亲至爱的丈夫

若能合二为一，那非我们莫属；
若夫为妇所爱，那无法将你排除。
若妇幸福，对夫满意，
你们诸女有胆，跟我比比。
我珍视你的爱，胜过全部金矿，
或者胜过东方所有宝藏。
我的爱如斯，竭江河无以止渴；
唯有你以爱补偿，才有理想效果。
你的爱如斯，我无以回报；
我祈愿：上苍加倍给你酬劳。
只要活着，我们爱不放手；
一旦死去，我们将活永久。

071 Louisa May Alcott
路易莎·梅·奥尔科特

◆ *The Poet's Profile* （诗人小档案）

路易莎·梅·奥尔科特（1832—1888）：美国女小说家及诗人。奥尔科特以小说《小妇人》及其续篇《小男人》以及《乔的男孩儿们》而知名。奥尔科特家庭经济困难，她很小的时候就做工来贴补家用，同时寻找机会进行写作。19世纪60年代，奥尔科特的写作获得巨大成功。奥尔科特是一位废奴主义者，也是一位女权主义者，终身未嫁。她的父亲死后两天，即1888年3月6日，她在波士顿死于中风。

◆ *A Little Bird I Am*

"A little bird I am,
Shut from the fields of air,
And in my cage I sit and sing
To Him who placed me there:
Well pleased a prisoner to be,
Because, my God, it pleases Thee!

"Naught have I else to do;
I sing the whole day long;
And He whom most I love to please
Doth listen to my song,
He caught and bound my wandering wing,
But still He bends to hear me sing."

◆ *Annotations* （原诗注释）

1. cage: *n.* a structure of bars or wires in which birds or other animals are confined 鸟笼；兽槛

2. thee: *pron.* [second person singular] archaic or dialect form of you, as the singular object of a verb or preposition （古英语"thou"的宾格，同"you"）你；汝

3. naught: *pron.* （archaic） nothing （古旧用法）无；没有什么 （e.g. He's naught but a worthless fool. 他是一个不中用的笨蛋。）

4. doth: *v.* （archaic） third person singular present of do （古旧用法）"do"的第三人称现在式单数形式

◆ *A Lead-in Note* （简明导读）

此诗的主人公，也就是诗人奥尔科特将自己描述成一只笼中之鸟。以笼外人的角度来看，她喜爱在笼子里唱歌给他——捕捉她入笼的人听。但是，从诗人在第二节中所创造出的看似矛盾的意象可以看出，诗人在字里行间所隐藏的具有讽刺意义的笔调：爱情犹在，自由不再。

◆ 我是一只小鸟儿

"我是一只小鸟儿，
被关离了原野和新鲜空气。
我坐在笼子里唱歌给**他**听，
是**他**把我关在那里。
我是一个很好满足的囚犯，
我的主啊，因为这令**你**满意！

"我可做的没有其他事情，
只是整日歌唱不止。

而**他**，我最渴望满足的人，
确实在听我唱的歌曲。
是**他**捉住我，将我挥动自如的翅膀束缚，
可**他**仍躬身听我歌唱不止。”

072 Edgar Albert Guest
埃德加·艾伯特·格斯特

◆ *The Poet's Profile* （诗人小档案）

埃德加·艾伯特·格斯特（1881—1959）：生于英国的美国多产诗人。格斯特在20世纪前半叶很受欢迎，以“人民的诗人”而为人所知。1891年，格斯特随家人从英格兰搬到了美国。1902年，他加入美国国籍。格斯特的诗在北美被广泛阅读，他的诗富有情感、乐观向上，跟尼克·肯尼的轻松诗一脉相承。肯尼是格斯特同时代的报业辛迪加的专栏作家。

◆ *Love*

Truth went forth on a search one day
For the source of love that he might say
He had found its depth and its breadth for aye.

He met a miser, bent and old,
And his mission to him he promptly told;
"Love," said the miser, "is yellow gold."

He sought a maiden, young and fair,
With orange blossoms in her hair,
Who whispered, "My love is waiting there."

To a struggling youth at last Truth came,
As he toiled and studied and spoke his name;

"Love," said the youth, "is a thing called fame."

"Love!" mocked a man with features sour,
Before whom others were made to cower,
"Love! yes, love is worldly power."

A pale, weak woman Truth chanced to see,
Rocking a baby on her knee;
"Only a mother knows love," said she.

◆ *Annotations* （原诗注释）

1. for aye: forever 永远

2. miser: *n.* a person who hoards wealth and spends as little money as possible 守财奴；财迷；吝啬鬼

3. promptly: *adv.* with little or no delay 立即地；迅速地

4. maiden: *n.* （archaic or poetic/literary） a girl or young woman, especially an unmarried one （古旧用法或诗/文用法）少女；（尤指未婚的）年轻妇女

5. fair: *adj.* （archaic） beautiful; attractive （古旧用法）美丽的；动人的；有魅力的 （e.g. the fairest of her daughters 她女儿中最漂亮的一位）

6. toil: *v.* work extremely hard or incessantly 苦干；辛勤劳动 （e.g. We toiled away. 我们劳碌不停。）

7. feature: *n.* （usu. features） a part of the face, such as the mouth or eyes, making a significant contribution to its overall appearance 五官；容貌；长相

8. mock: *v.* tease or laugh at in a scornful or contemptuous manner 嘲笑；讥笑；嘲弄

9. sour: *adj.* bad-tempered and morose 坏脾气的；别扭的

10. cower: *v.* crouch down in fear 畏缩；退缩 （e.g. Children cowered in terror as the shoot-out erupted. 枪战爆发时，孩子们害怕得缩成一团。）

11. worldly: *adj.* （worldlier, worldliest） of or concerned with material values or ordinary life rather than a spiritual existence 世俗头脑的；追名逐利的

12. chance: *v.* do something by accident or without design 偶然；碰巧（e.g. He was very effusive if they chanced to meet. 他们若是巧遇，他总会表现得热情过头。）

13. rock: *v.* cause （someone or something） to move gently to and fro or from side to side 轻轻摇动；使轻轻摆动；使轻轻晃动 （e.g. She rocked the baby in her arms. 她轻摇怀中的婴儿。）

◆ *A Lead-in Note* （简明导读）

诗人将“真知”赋予生命，令其去探寻爱的内涵。经过与财迷、少女、拼搏青年、寻常男子以及婴儿的母亲一番接触后，真知公开宣布：“爱的深度和广度，他永久寻到。”爱，无所不包，无所不在，又因人而异，千差万别。

◆ 爱

有一天，**真知**前去寻找
爱的源泉后，他或许明表：
爱的深度和广度，他永久寻到。

他遇到一个财迷，驼背又年迈，
向其说明来意后，财迷立刻表态：
“爱嘛，就是金子，黄黄的色彩。”

他寻到一位少女，年轻而娇美，
头发上插着一簇簇橘黄色的花蕊。
她低语：“我的爱在那儿等我相会。”

最后，**真知**来到一位拼搏青年身旁，青年道出自己的姓名，辛勤苦读寒窗。
青年说："爱，是一种东西，叫声望。"

"爱!"一名男子蔑视道，面露怒气。
在这名男子面前，其他人畏缩不敢语。
"爱！没错，爱就是世俗的权力。"

真知碰巧看见一位苍白、虚弱的女子，
这位女子轻轻摇着膝盖上的婴儿。
"只有做母亲的才了解爱。"她发出此语。

073 Henry Wadsworth Longfellow 亨利·沃兹沃斯·朗费罗

◆ *The Poet's Profile* （诗人小档案）

亨利·沃兹沃斯·朗费罗（1807—1882）：美国诗人和教育家。朗费罗写了很多具有音乐感的抒情诗篇，还写过神话和传奇故事。在他生活的那个时代，他是最受欢迎的美国诗人之一。朗费罗的代表作品有《海斯布罗斯残骸》《村中铁匠》和《海华沙之歌》等。

◆ *The Arrow and the Song*

I shot an arrow into the air,
It fell to earth, I knew not where;
For, so swiftly it flew, the sight
Could not follow it in its flight.

I breathed a song into the air,
It fell to earth, I knew not where;
For who has sight so keen and strong,
That it can follow the flight of song?

Long, long afterward, in an oak
I found the arrow, still unbroke;
And the song, from beginning to end,
I found again in the heart of a friend.

◆ *Annotations* （原诗注释）

1. breathe: *v.* say something with quiet intensity （低声细气地）说出；吐露

2. oak: *n.* （also as "oak tree"） a large tree which bears acorns and typically has lobed deciduous leaves. Oaks are dominant in many north temperate forests and are an important source of hard and durable timber used chiefly in building, furniture, and （formerly） ships. （亦作 "oak tree" ）栎；橡树

3. unbroke = unbroken

◆ *A Lead-in Note* （简明导读）

此诗的诗意取向，存在一定的争议。在此，不妨将其视作一首爱情诗。就这方面而言，一提到箭，人们自然想到爱神丘比特之箭。丘比特之箭射中谁，谁就会坠入爱河，当然有时也会身受其伤。年轻的时候，不知爱为何物，胡乱射出一支箭，随口哼出一首歌。很久很久后的某一天，发现那支箭完好无损，那首歌完整依然。有人会把那支箭保存完好，有人会把那首歌珍藏心中，曲调依然。

◆ 箭与歌

我向空中射出一支箭，
箭下落，不知落在哪个地段。
因为飞得太快，眼睛
无法跟上其飞行路线。

我向空中哼出一首歌，
歌飘落，不知落在什么处所。
谁的视力会如此敏锐与犀利，
跟得上疾驰如飞的歌？

很久很久后，在一棵橡树的枝叶间，
我找到了那支箭，完整依然。
而那首歌，从开头到结尾，
我又在一个朋友的心中发现。

074 Charles Hanson Towne
查尔斯·汉森·汤

◆ *The Poet's Profile* （诗人小档案）

查尔斯·汉森·汤（1877—1949）：美国作家、诗人和编辑。除了承担一些杂志的编辑职责外，汤还是一位多产的作家，写了诸多诗集、小说、戏剧、旅行杂记，还写了多部歌曲套曲、音乐剧唱词、轻歌剧及回忆录等。他的作品大多歌颂纽约市，最著名的当属《曼哈顿：一首诗》及一些对往事追忆的书。

◆ *Love and Time*

I said, "Love laughs at Time," before I knew
The perfect joy of wholly loving you;
So swift the days went hurrying to that Day
When we were one—Love swept us on the way.

But now—Time laughs at Love; for swifter yet
Speed years that seem as hours! The sun will set,
The final curtain fall, our lives be done;
We will have lived—long years that seemed as one!

◆ *Annotations* （原诗注释）

1. swift: *adv.* （poetic/literary except in combination） swiftly （除了组合用法外为诗/文用法）迅速

2. sweep: *v*. to win overwhelmingly in 获全胜

◆ *A Lead-in Note* （简明导读）

当初，爱情嘲笑时间，爱情战胜一切。转眼间，时间嘲笑爱情，“我们的人生会终结，但我们将永驻——千年万年似一年之少”。我们的爱情永恒，漫漫岁月似乎是短暂的一瞬。

◆ 爱情与时间

说出“爱情嘲笑时间”之时，我不知道
全身心爱你时绝佳的喜悦与美妙。
匆匆的岁月疾驰而过，转眼之间
到了你我融为一体的那天——途中，爱情将我们横扫。

可现在，时间嘲笑爱情，因那些年
似几小时飞过！太阳会落下而不再闪耀，
帷幕最后会落下，我们的人生会告终，
但我们将永驻——千年万年似一年之少。

075 Sara Teasdale 萨拉·蒂斯代尔

◆ *The Poet's Profile* （诗人小档案）

萨拉·蒂斯代尔（1884—1933）：美国诗人，出生时的名字为萨拉·特雷弗。她的诗收录于《〈特洛伊的海伦〉及其他诗歌集》《百川入海》《爱歌》《火焰与影子》和《奇异的胜利》等诗集中。蒂斯代尔以抒情诗篇赢得了大众的钦佩，她的诗主要围绕女子对美、对爱情以及死亡的感受而展开。蒂斯代尔的诗就是她自己人生发展的曲线图——诗中有她年轻时在圣路易斯家中生活的经历，有她在纽约市成为一位知名作家却越来越感到忧虑不安的体会，也有她忧郁之中理想幻灭以至于想自杀的人生体验。最终在1933年，她服下了过量的安眠药，了此一生。尽管后来的许多批评家并不认同蒂斯代尔是一位举足轻重的诗人，但在她生活的那个时代，她却很受大众和批评家的青睐。1918年，蒂斯代尔是获得“哥伦比亚诗歌奖”的第一人，这个奖项就是后来的“普利策诗歌奖”。

◆ *After Love*

There is no magic any more,
We meet as other people do,
You work no miracle for me
Nor I for you.

You were the wind and I the sea—
There is no splendor any more,

I have grown listless as the pool
Beside the shore.

But tho' the pool is safe from storm
And from the tide has found surcease,
It grows more bitter than the sea,
For all its peace.

◆ *Annotations* （原诗注释）

1. magic: *n.* the power of apparently influencing the course of events by using mysterious or supernatural forces 魔法；法术；巫术；魔力（e.g. Suddenly, as if by magic, the doors start to open. 突然，像是谁施了魔法，门开启了。）

2. miracle: *n.* a highly improbable or extraordinary event, development, or accomplishment that brings very welcome consequences 奇迹；人间奇迹（e.g. It was a miracle that more people hadn't been killed or injured. 更多的人未遇难或受伤，这是一个奇迹。）

3. splendor: *n.* great light or luster; brilliance 光辉；光彩

4. listless: *adj.* （of a person or their manner） lacking energy or enthusiasm （人或行为方式）无力的；无精打采的（e.g. bouts of listless depression 一阵阵无精打采的抑郁情绪）

5. tho' = though

6. surcease: *n.* （archaic or US） cessation （古旧用法或美国用法）停止（e.g. He teased us without surcease. 他没完没了地嘲笑我们。）

◆ *A Lead-in Note* （简明导读）

诗人用形象化的语言和意象写出了爱恋过后的一种状态。相遇的激烈之火燃烧过后，一切趋于平静："为我，你没有奇迹可创造，为你，我也创造不出奇迹。"当初的爱恋已不见踪影，"我已变成岸边一个水洼，无力而倦怠。"这片水洼因为没有了往日的暴风骤雨般爱情的洗礼，盐分大为增加，

“却比海水更为苦涩，只因池中一片静谧”。当初爱情的甜蜜，如今变得苦涩无比，这就是爱恋过后的状态。

◆ 爱恋过后

你我相遇，其他人亦如此，
不再产生什么魔力。
为我，你没有奇迹可创造，
为你，我也创造不出奇迹。

你是那时风，我是那时海，
再也放不出什么光彩。
我已变成岸边
一个水洼，无力而倦怠。

可是，尽管水洼离开暴风骤雨，
离开海潮，成了安全的静水一池，
却比海水更为苦涩，
只因池中一片静谧。

076 Emily Elizabeth Dickinson
埃米莉·伊丽莎白·狄更生

◆ *The Poet's Profile* （诗人小档案）

埃米莉·伊丽莎白·狄更生（1830—1886）：美国女诗人。狄更生的诗采用的是省略的语言形式，注重谐音和头韵，而非尾韵，这反映了她在隐居生活中奋力拼搏的心情。在她写作的那个时代，她的诗独具一格：诗行短小，一般没有标题，经常使用近似押韵的方式和一些非常规的大写及标点。狄更生很多诗的主题是死亡和永生，这两大主题在她写给朋友的信中也反复出现过。

◆ *If You Were Coming in the Fall*

If you were coming in the Fall,
I'd brush the Summer by
With half a smile, and half a spurn,
As Housewives do, a Fly.

If I could see you in a year,
I'd wind the months in balls—
And put them each in separate Drawers,
For fear the numbers fuse—

If only Centuries, delayed,
I'd count them on my Hand,
Subtracting, till my fingers dropped

Into Van Dieman's Land,

If certain, when this life was out—
That yours and mine, should be
I'd toss it yonder, like a Rind,
And take Eternity—

But now, all ignorant of the length
Of time's uncertain wing,
It goads me, like the Goblin Bee—
That will not state—its sting.

◆ *Annotations* （原诗注释）

1. spurn: *n*. an act of rejecting with disdain or contempt 轻蔑地拒绝；蔑视

2. wind: *v*. repeatedly twist or coil （a length of something） around itself or a core 卷；卷绕 （e.g. Anne wound the wool into a ball. 安妮把毛线绕成一个球。）

3. fuse: *v*. join or blend to form a single entity 合并；使融为一体 （e.g. Intermarriage had fused the families into a large unit. 联姻把几个家庭合并为一个大家庭。）

4. Van Diemen's Land: 凡戴曼流放地

Van Diemen's Land was the original name used by most Europeans for the island of Tasmania, now part of Australia. In 1803, the island was colonised by the British as a penal colony with the name Van Diemen's Land, and became part of the British colony of New South Wales.

凡戴曼流放地是多数欧洲人对塔斯马尼亚岛的称呼，这个岛现为澳大利亚的一部分。1803年，这个岛成为英国的殖民地，作为惩罚囚犯的关押地，取名“凡戴曼流放地”，并成为英国殖民地中新南威尔士的一部分。

5. yonder: *adv*. （archaic or dialect） at some distance in the direction indicated; over there （古旧用法或方言用法）在那边（指一定距离以外）（e.g. There's a ford

south of here, about nine miles yonder. 从这里往南大约15千米远的地方有一个浅滩。)

6. rind: *n.* the tough outer skin of certain fruit, especially citrus fruit （尤指柑橘属果实的）果皮

7. eternity: *n.* a state to which time has no application; timelessness 永恒

8. goad: *v.* provoke or annoy （someone） so as to stimulate some action or reaction 刺激；激怒；惹恼；驱使 （e.g. He goaded her on to more daring revelations. 他鼓动她更大胆地进行揭露。)

9. goblin: *n.* a mischievous, ugly, dwarf-like creature of folklore 小精灵（民间传说中淘气、丑陋、矮小的动物）

◆ *A Lead-in Note* （简明导读）

此诗的主题是等待以及等待所带来的极度痛苦。“假若”一词的不断重复，加深了这种等待的不确定性。即使此生等不到你，诗人说“我会像抛果皮一样将此生抛远，选择来生等你”。多么痴情的女子！从此诗的最后一节可以推测，诗人的这场等待似乎无望，因而更受折磨：“这折磨着我，如居心叵测的蜂——硬是不告诉你，如何叮咬。”多么生动形象的刻画！

另外，此诗作者“Dickinson”在《世界人名翻译大辞典》中的翻译是“迪金森”，但该词条下做了特殊说明，即Dickinson指这位诗人时译作“狄更生”，此应为规范性的译法。

◆ 假若秋天你归来

假若秋天你归来，
我会微笑着，面带蔑视之情，
将夏日拂开，
如主妇对待一只苍蝇。

假若时隔一年才见到你，
我会把岁月缠成一团又一团，

再分别放进不同的抽屉，
唯恐将一个个数字弄乱。

假若见你只是推延了几百年，
我就用手一天一天数日子，
一天一天数，直到把手指数断，
落入凡戴曼流放地。

假若此生肯定无缘再见，
因你我终有一死，
我会像抛果皮一样将此生抛远，
选择来生等你。

但时至今日，时隔多久完全不明，
何时归来无以推敲。
这折磨着我，如居心叵测的蜂——
硬是不告诉你，如何叮咬。

077 Ella Wheeler Wilcox 埃拉·惠勒·威尔科克斯

◆ *The Poet's Profile* （诗人小档案）

埃拉·惠勒·威尔科克斯（1850—1919）：美国女诗人和小说家。威尔科克斯写了多部浪漫体诗集，其中《激情诗集》最为成功。最经久不衰的一首诗是《孤独》，其中有这样的诗行："你笑，全世界都跟着你笑；你哭，就你一人独自在哭。"1918年，也就是她去世前一年，她的自传《我与这个世界》出版。

◆ *Time and Love*

Time flies. The swift hours hurry by
And speed us on to untried ways;
New seasons ripen, perish, die,
And yet love stays.
The old, old love—like sweet at first,
At last like bitter wine—
I know not if it blest or curst,
Thy life and mine.

Time flies. In vain our prayers, our tears,
We cannot tempt him to delays;
Down to the past he bears the years,
And yet love stays.
Through changing task and varying dream

We hear the same refrain,
As one can hear a plaintive theme
Run through each strain.

Time flies. He steals out pulsing youth,
He robs us of our care-free days,
He takes away our trust and truth,
And yet love stays.
O Time! Take love! When love is vain,
When all its best joys die—
When only its regrets remain—
Let love, too, fly.

◆ *Annotations* （原诗注释）

1. ripen: *v.* become or make ripe 成熟；催熟 （e.g. Honeydew melons ripen slowly. 甜瓜缓慢地成熟了。）

2. perish: *v.* （of rubber, a foodstuff, or other organic substance） lose its normal qualities; rot or decay （橡胶、食品或其他有机物质）老化；腐烂；腐朽 （e.g. Most domestic building was in wood and has perished. 大部分的住宅是木质结构而且已经腐朽了。）

3. blest = blessed

4. curst = cursed

5. thine: *pron.* （form of "thy" used before a vowel） archaic form of yours; the thing or things belonging to or associated with thee （元音之前同 "thy" ）（古旧用法）你的（同 "yours" ）;（ "thou" 的物主代词）你（您）的东西

6. refrain: *n.* a repeated line or number of lines in a poem or song, typically at the end of each verse （诗歌中，尤指在节末）叠句;（歌曲中重复演唱，尤指在末尾）叠歌；副歌

7. plaintive: *adj.* sounding sad and mournful 伤心的；哀伤的 （e. g. a plaintive cry 悲号）

8. stain: *n.* （usu. strains） the sound of piece of music as it is played or performed 旋律；曲调 （e.g. From within the flat could be heard the strains of country and western music. 可以听到从公寓里面传来的乡村音乐和西部音乐的旋律。）

◆ *A Lead-in Note* （简明导读）

此诗每一节都以“时间飞逝”开始，再写与时间飞逝有关的一些情形，以与久长的爱情形成对比。时间飞逝，但诗人的爱情久长，不受影响。时间飞逝，夺走了许多人生的美好，但爱情伟大，可战胜一切。然而，并非所有爱情都是如此。徒劳无果的爱情，剩下的只有遗憾，那就让时间把这种爱情带走吧。

◆ 时间与爱情

时间飞逝。时间总是匆匆而去，
催促着我们踏上未知之旅。
季节到来、成熟、腐烂、消亡，
但爱情久长。
愈来愈老的爱——始于甘露，
终似酒苦。
你的生活，还有我的生活，
得到保佑或受到诅咒？我很迷惑。

时间飞逝。对时间祈祷或哭泣皆徒劳，
无法诱使其延迟分秒。
埋入过去的是一年又一年的时光，
但爱情久长。
不断换工作再改梦想，如此生活

如听同一段副歌。
可以听出其中感伤的主题
贯穿每一首曲子。

时间飞逝。时间偷走我们脉动的青春，
夺去我们无忧日子里的纯真。
还带走了我们的真理和信仰，
但爱情久长。
啊，时间，带走爱情吧！当爱情无果，
当爱情所有的美妙消亡，
当爱情只剩下遗憾，
那也让爱情飞翔。

078 Ellis Parker Butler 埃利斯·帕克·巴特勒

◆ *The Poet's Profile* （诗人小档案）

埃利斯·帕克·巴特勒（1869—1937）：美国作家。巴特勒写了2000多篇小说和散文及其他体裁的书30多本。其中最著名的是短篇小说《猪就是猪》。巴特勒的职业生涯横跨40多年，其小说、诗歌及其他文章在200多家杂志上发表过。尽管巴特勒的著作数量巨大，可充其一生不过是一名业余作家而已。他的专职工作是银行家。在当地社区，他是一位活跃人物。

◆ *Golden Silence*

I told her I loved her and begged but a word,
One dear little word, that would be
For me by all odds the most sweet ever heard,
But never a word said she!

I raged at her then, and I said she was cold;
I swore she was nothing to me;
I prayed her the cause of her silence unfold,
But never a word said she!

I covered with kisses her delicate hand,
But she only glanced down where the sea
Low murmured in ripples of love on the sand,
And never a word said she!

I cast her hand from me with rage unsuppressed,
And she turned her blue eyes up to me
And smiled as she laid her fair head on my breast;
"What need of a word?" asked she.

◆ *Annotations* （原诗注释）

1. by all odds: （N. Amer.） certainly （北美用法）肯定地；无疑地

2. rage: *v.* feel or express violent uncontrollable anger 发怒；发火；怒斥（e.g. He raged at the futility of it all. 他为一事无成而狂怒。）

3. pray: *v.* （archaic） to ask （someone） imploringly for something; beseech （古旧用法）请求；恳求

4. unfold: *v.* reveal or disclose （thoughts or information） 透露；展现（思想或信息）（e.g. Miss Eva unfolded her secret exploits to Mattie. 埃娃小姐把自己的秘密透露给玛蒂。）

◆ *A Lead-in Note* （简明导读）

此诗是对"沉默是金"的诠释。情侣之间脉脉含情，沉默不语，一切尽在不言中，这是一种爱的境界。此诗中，诗人爱恋的这位女孩，达到了这种境界。诗人多次让她开口说话，哪怕只说一个字也行，"但她一直闭口不语"。诗的最后，她以问代答，道出了这种爱的境界："有何必要说一个字？"

◆ 似金的沉默

我告诉她我爱她还请求她只说一个字，
一个亲切可爱的字，对我那无疑是
最为甜蜜的字眼儿——我从未听闻，
但她一直闭口不语！

我就对她发了怒，说她冷漠无情，
我发誓说她没有什么了不起。
我恳请她透露沉默的缘由，
但她一直闭口不语！

我一次次吻她那纤柔的手，
可她只是低头向着大海看去。
大海低语，爱的波浪轻拂沙滩，
但她一直闭口不语！

我怒气无可忍，把她的手甩开，
可她抬头看着我，蓝眼神采奕奕。
她微笑着将娇美的头靠在我的胸膛，
问："有何必要说一个字？"

079 Sylvia Plath 西尔维亚·普拉思

◆ *The Poet's Profile* （诗人小档案）

西尔维亚·普拉思（1932—1963）：美国女诗人和小说家。1956年，她嫁给了同时代诗人特德·休斯。夫妇俩住在美国，后又搬到英格兰居住。他们生有两个孩子：弗里达和尼古拉斯。普拉思成年后生活大部分时间里患有抑郁症，并于1963年自杀身亡。在她死后的1982年，她因《普拉思诗选》获得普利策诗歌奖。普拉思的作品之所以著名，缘于其对极端心态和痛苦心理的描述。她的代表作品有诗集《精灵》和小说《钟形罐子》。

◆ *Mad Girl's Love Song*

"I shut my eyes and all the world drops dead;
I lift my lids and all is born again.
(I think I made you up inside my head.)

The stars go waltzing out in blue and red,
And arbitrary blackness gallops in:
I shut my eyes and all the world drops dead.

I dreamed that you bewitched me into bed
And sung me moon-struck, kissed me quite insane.
(I think I made you up inside my head.)

God topples from the sky, hell's fires fade:

Exit seraphim and Satan's men:
I shut my eyes and all the world drops dead.

I fancied you'd return the way you said,
But I grow old and I forget your name.
（I think I made you up inside my head.）

I should have loved a thunderbird instead;
At least when spring comes they roar back again.
I shut my eyes and all the world drops dead.
（I think I made you up inside my head.）"

◆ *Annotations*（原诗注释）

1. drop dead: die suddenly and unexpectedly 突然倒毙；猝死（e.g. She had seen her father drop dead of a heart attack. 她曾看见她父亲因心脏病发作而猝死。）

2. lid: *n.*（often lids） an eyelid 眼皮（e. g. Eyes now hooded beneath heavy lids. 此刻被沉沉下垂的眼皮遮住了双眼。）

3. waltz: *v.* move or act lightly, casually, or inconsiderately 轻快地走动；无拘束地行动

4. arbitrary: *adj.* based on random choice or personal whim, rather than any reason or system 随机选择的；随心所欲的；无理由的；无系统的（e.g. His mealtimes were entirely arbitrary. 他吃饭完全不定时。）

5. gallop: *v.*（galloped, galloping）（of a horse） go at the pace of a gallop（马）飞跑；疾驰

6. bewitch: *v.*（often be bewitched） gain control over （someone） by casting a spell on them 施魔力于（某人）；蛊惑；使鬼迷心窍（e. g. His relatives were convinced that he was bewitched. 他的亲属确信他是着了魔。）

7. moonstruck or moon-struck: *adj.* unable to think or act normally, especially because of being in love （尤指因恋爱）迷乱的；茫然的，发呆的

8. insane: *adj.* in a state of mind which prevents normal perception, behaviour, or social interaction; seriously mentally ill 精神错乱的；有严重精神病的；发疯的

9. topple: *v.* overbalance or become unsteady and fall slowly 失去平衡；不稳而缓慢倒下（e.g. She toppled over when I touched her. 当我碰她时，她就倒了下来。）

10. seraph: *n.*（pl. seraphim or seraphs） an angelic being, regarded in traditional Christian angelology as belonging to the highest order of the ninefold celestial hierarchy, associated with light, ardour, and purity（基督教的）六翼天使

11. Satan: *n.* the Devil; Lucifer 魔鬼；撒旦

12. fancy: *v.* imagine; think 设想；想象；认为（e.g. He fancied he could smell the perfume of roses. 他想象着自己闻到了玫瑰花香。）

13. thunderbird: *n.* a mythical bird thought by some North American Indians to bring thunder（神话中引起雷雨的）雷鸟；巨鸟

◆ *A Lead-in Note*（简明导读）

此诗是普拉思在史密斯学院上大学期间写的。此诗是一首半退让、半心碎性质的诗，严格按照"维拉内拉诗体"（16世纪法国的一种十九行诗体，为田园抒情诗，特点是二韵加叠句）形式写成，诗体包含很多生动形象的拟人修辞手法。此诗首次刊登于1953年8月的《小姐》（*Mademoiselle*）杂志上，当年六月，普拉思在纽约市任此杂志客座编辑。这件事在普拉思的小说《钟形罐子》中有描述。具体而言，此诗写于诗人普拉思第一次企图自杀前，即1953年8月24日前。

◆ 疯癫女孩的情歌

"我双眼一合，全世界瞬间倒毙；
双眼一睁，一切皆重生。
(我想，你为我大脑所虚拟!)

蓝星星，红星星，纷纷轻舞散去，
无形无际的黑暗如马狂奔而来：
我双眼一合，全世界瞬间倒毙。

梦中的我上了床，因你施展魔力；
还给我唱情迷之歌，吻我之举太失常。
(我想，你为我头脑所虚拟!)

上帝慢慢倒下，地狱之火渐渐退去；
六翼天使和魔鬼撒旦的侍从纷纷离开。
我双眼一合，全世界瞬间倒毙。

在我想象之中你该归来，如你所许，
但我已老，记不起你的名。
(我想，你为我头脑所虚拟!)

我本应爱上传说中的雷鸟，取而代你，
因至少在春回之际，雷鸟会呼啸着归来。
我双眼一合，全世界瞬间倒毙。
(我想，你为我头脑所虚拟!)"

080 Langston Hughes
兰斯顿·休斯

◆ *The Poet's Profile* （诗人小档案）

兰斯顿·休斯（1902—1967）：美国诗人、小说家、剧作家和专栏作家。休斯多产的文学生涯就是从《萎靡的布鲁斯》开始的。这本书由一系列以黑人为主题的诗歌组成，是休斯运用布鲁斯和爵士乐韵律完成的。他的诗集有《黑人母亲》等。

◆ *Quiet Girl*

I would liken you
To a night without stars
Were it not for your eyes.

I would liken you
To a sleep without dreams
Were it not for your songs.

◆ *Annotations* （原诗注释）

1. liken: *v.* （liken someone/thing to） point out the resemblance of someone or something to 把……比作 （e.g. Racism is likened to a contagious disease. 种族主义被比作传染病。）

2. Were it not for your eyes = If it were not for your eyes

3. Were it not for your songs = If it were not for your songs

◆ *A Lead-in Note* （简明导读）

休斯所写以黑人为主题的诗歌，多用布鲁斯和爵士乐韵律完成。此诗具有这样的韵律，如歌谣般简洁、明快，朗朗上口。如果排除黑人解放运动方面的政治性解读，此诗其实是诗人对自己喜欢的一位恬静的黑人女孩的真实描写。没有星星的夜晚，漆黑一片，恬静的黑人女孩不声不响。她的存在，那双一闪一闪的迷人双眼能证明。黑夜里，女孩沉睡，做着神秘的梦。何以见得？因为睡梦中，她露出洁白的牙齿，唱着动人的歌。

◆ 恬静的女孩

我未将你
比作没有星星的夜晚，
多亏了你的双眼。

我未将你
比作没有梦境的沉睡，
多亏了你的歌相随。

081 Claude McKay
克劳德·麦凯

◆ *The Poet's Profile* （诗人小档案）

克劳德·麦凯（1889—1948）：牙买加裔美国作家和诗人。麦凯是美国黑人“哈莱姆文艺复兴运动”中一位有巨大影响力的人物。1921年，麦凯赴美国游学，就读于塔斯基吉学院，但只学了几个月就离开了，去了堪萨斯州立大学学农科。在20世纪20年代，麦凯前往俄罗斯和法国游历。在法国，他见到了埃德娜·圣文森特·米莱及辛克莱·刘易斯。1934年，他返回美国，居住在纽约市哈莱姆区。后来，麦凯关注哈莱姆区各式精神和政治领袖的学说，最终皈依天主教。除了一些长篇小说作品，麦凯还创作了一些诗集、一部短篇小说集、两部自传（《漫长离家路》和《牙买加我绿色的山丘》）以及一部非虚构的社会历史学著作《哈莱姆：黑人的大都市》。麦凯于1922年出版的诗集《哈莱姆阴影》是美国黑人“哈莱姆文艺复兴运动”时期首批出版的图书。在他去世后的1953年，《麦凯诗选》得以出版。

◆ *Romance*

To clasp you now and feel your head close-pressed,
Scented and warm against my beating breast;

To whisper soft and quivering your name,
And drink the passion burning in your frame;

To lie at full length, taut, with cheek to cheek,

And tease your mouth with kisses till you speak

Love words, mad words, dream words, sweet senseless words,
Melodious like notes of mating birds;

To hear you ask if I shall love always,
And myself answer: Till the end of days;

To feel your easeful sigh of happiness
When on your trembling lips I murmur: Yes;

It is so sweet. We know it is not true.
What matters it? The night must shed her dew.

We know it is not true, but it is sweet—
The poem with this music is complete.

◆ *Annotations*（原诗注释）

1. romance: *n.* a feeling of excitement and mystery associated with love （与爱情相联系的）动人心魄的离奇、神秘感受；浪漫气氛；传奇气氛 （e.g. I had a thirst for romance. 我渴望感受浪漫的气氛。）

2. clasp: *v.* hold （someone） tightly 紧握；紧抱 （e.g. He clasped Joanne in his arms. 他双臂紧抱乔安妮。）

3. scented: *adj.* filled or impregnated with perfume 香味的；洒了香水的

4. frame: *n.* a person's body with reference to its size or build （人的）身躯；体格 （e.g. A shiver shook her slim frame. 她打了个哆嗦，纤细的身躯颤抖了一阵。）

5. taut: *adj.* stretched or pulled tight; not slack 拉紧的 （e.g. The fabric stays taut without adhesive. 不用黏合剂，布料也能保持紧绷。）

6. tease: *v.* tempt （someone） sexually with no intention of satisfying the desire aroused 挑逗；撩拨

7. melodious: *adj.* of, producing, or having a pleasant tune; tuneful 产生优美旋律的；悦耳的 （e.g. the melodious chant of the monks 僧侣们优美的吟诵）

8. note: *n.* a bird's song or call, or a single tone in this （鸟的）鸣声 （e.g. The tawny owl has a harsh flight note. 灰林鸮飞行时会发出刺耳的鸣声。）

9. easeful: *adj.* （poetic / literary） providing or offering comfort or peace （诗/文用法）舒适的；安闲的 （e.g. Life was easeful at that time. 那时生活安逸。）

10. dew: *n.* tiny drops of water that form on cool surfaces at night, when atmospheric vapour condenses 露；露滴；露水 （e.g. The grass was wet with dew. 草地被露水打湿了。）

◆ *A Lead-in Note* （简明导读）

此诗正如诗题所示，描写的是爱情中的鱼水之欢，是一首地地道道的浪漫激情之歌。柏拉图式的爱情应该不是完整的爱情，完整的爱情既有精神方面也有物质方面，是精神和物质的完美结合，也是爱情的完美体现。

◆ 浪漫激情

现在抱紧你，感受到你的头紧靠在我胸膛；
你的头芳香、温暖，紧靠我跳动的心房。

轻声低语中，颤抖地道出你的名，
陶醉于你胴体中燃烧的激情。

伸直身体彼此紧贴躺着，面颊贴着面颊，
一个又一个吻撩拨你的嘴，引你发话——

情话，疯话，梦话，还有甜蜜却无意义的话语，
如求偶之中鸟儿的鸣叫声，自成旋律。

听见你问我，是否爱你到永远，
听见我自己回答：直至海枯石烂。

感受到你的幸福和舒服的喘息，
就在我于你发抖的舌尖轻语“是的”之时。

这感觉如此甜蜜，但你我知道这是虚幻。
这又有什么关系？露水的生成就在夜晚。

你我知道这是虚幻，可这感觉甜蜜——
本诗以及与之相配的音乐完毕。

082 Philip Henry Savage
菲利普·亨利·萨维奇

◆ *The Poet's Profile* （诗人小档案）

菲利普·亨利·萨维奇（1868—1899）：美国诗人。萨维奇在哈佛大学英语系当过英语讲师，从而有能力于1895年出版第一部诗集《第一批诗歌及未完成诗歌集》。萨维奇拒绝了到麻省理工学院当英语讲师这一职位后，开始在波士顿公共图书馆工作。先是当馆长的秘书，后于1899年成为该馆的档案管理员。

◆ *Love Is a Life You Cannot Trace*

Love is a life you cannot trace
Nor find by gazing in the face.
You cannot sum it, pence by pence,
Nor find it in its elements.

◆ *Annotations* （原诗注释）

1. trace: *v.* find or describe the origin or development of 追溯；追究；查考（e.g. Bob's book traces his flying career with the RAF. 鲍勃的书追溯了他在英国皇家空军的飞行生涯。）

2. pence: *n.* plural form of penny "penny"的复数

penny: *n.* （pl. for separate coins pennies, for a sum of money pence /pens/） a British bronze coin and monetary unit equal to one hundredth of a pound 便士

（英国铜硬币和货币单位，100便士等于1英镑）

3. element: *n.* a part or aspect of something abstract, especially one that is essential or characteristic （抽象事物的）基本组成部分；要素 （e.g. The death had all the elements of a great tabloid story. 这一死亡事件具备小报新闻需要的一切要素。）

◆ *A Lead-in Note* （简明导读）

爱情是微妙的，说不清道不明之物。即便你说得头头是道，也只是说出其某一方面，犹如盲人摸象，很不全面。爱情更不可能具体到几个便士就可以数清楚的程度。更有甚者，"在其成分中也无法查出线索"。

◆ 爱情是一种你无法明察的生活

爱情是一种你无法明察的生活，
凝视其面孔也无法查出结果。
你无法几个便士、几个便士将其累加，
在其成分中也无法查出线索。

Chapter 03

Short Love Verse by Poets from the Other English-speaking Countries

第三章

其他英语国家诗人的韵体爱情短诗

083 Robert William Service 罗伯特·威廉·瑟维斯

◆ *The Poet's Profile* （诗人小档案）

罗伯特·威廉·瑟维斯（1874—1958）：英裔加拿大诗人和作家。瑟维斯经常被人称为“育空河吟游诗人”（育空河源于加拿大西北部育空地区）。他对育空河及其流域人们形象化的描述，让人似乎感觉他就是克朗代克河（加拿大西北部育空地区育空河的支流）淘金热中的一位淘金老手，而瑟维斯实际上是那里的一位银行职员。

◆ *Old Sweethearts*

Oh Maggie, do you mind the day
We went to school together,
And as we stoppit by the way
I rolled you in the heather?
My! but you were the bonny lass
And we were awfu' late for class.

Your locks are now as white as snow,
And you are ripe and wrinkled,
A grandmother ten times or so,
Yet how your blue eyes twinkled
At me above your spectacles,
Recalling naughty neck-tickles!

It must be fifty years today
I left you for the Yukon;
You haven't changed—your just as gay
And just as sweet to look on.
But can you see in this old fool
The lad who made you late for school?

Oh Maggie, ask me in to tea
And we can talk things over,
And contemplate the nuptial state,
For I am still your lover:
And though the bell be slow to chime
We'll no be grudgin' o' the time.

◆ *Annotations*（原诗注释）

1. sweetheart: *n.* a person that one is in love with 恋人；情人（e.g. The pair were childhood sweethearts. 这一对是青梅竹马的恋人。）

2. oh: *interj.* used to express a range of emotions including surprise, anger, disappointment, or joy, or when reacting to something that has just been said（表示惊讶、愤怒、失望、高兴等感情）噢；啊；哦；唉；哎呀

3. stoppit: 疑似“stopped”之误，也许是诗人有意为之，别有用心吧。另外，文中还有几处类似用法，估计是仿苏格兰英语的用法。

4. heather: *n.* a purple-flowered Eurasian heath that grows abundantly on moorland and heathland. Many ornamental varieties have been developed 石南

5. bonny: *adj.*（also bonnie）（bonnier, bonniest） attractive or beautiful 吸引人的；漂亮的（e.g. a bonny lass 一位漂亮的少女）

6. lass: *n.*（chiefly Scottish & N. English） a girl or young woman（主要为苏格兰或北英格兰用法）女孩；少女（e.g. He married a lass from Yorkshire. 他娶了一个约克夏女孩。）

7. awfu' = awful

awful: *adv.* （informal, chiefly N. Amer.） awfully; very （非正式用法或主要为北美用法）很；非常 （e.g. We're an awful long way from the motorway. 我们离高速公路还远着呢。）

8. lock: *n.* （chiefly poetic/literary） （locks） a person's hair （主要为诗/文用法）头发 （e.g. flowing locks and a long white beard 发随风舞，白髯垂胸）

9. twinkle: *v.* （of a star or light, or a shiny object） shine with a gleam that changes constantly from bright to faint （星星、光或发光物）闪烁；闪耀 （e.g. The lights twinkled in the distance. 远处有灯光闪烁。）

10. tickle: *n.* a sensation like that of being lightly touched or prodded 痒（感）（e.g. I had a tickle between my shoulder blades. 我感觉肩胛骨间有点痒。）

11. Yukon: *n.* a river of NW North America, which rises in Yukon Territory, NW Canada, and flows 3, 020 km （about 1, 870 miles） westwards through central Alaska to the Bering Sea 育空河（位于北美西北部的河流，源于加拿大西北部育空地区，全长3020千米，约1870英里，向西流经阿拉斯加中部，汇入白令海。）

12. lad: *n.* （informal） a boy or young man （often as a form of address）（非正式用法）少年；男青年

13. contemplate: *v.* have in view as a probable though not certain intention 预期；打算 （e.g. He was contemplating action for damages. 他正打算采取破坏行动。）

14. nuptial: *adj.* of or relating to marriage or weddings 婚姻的；婚礼的 （e.g. moments of nuptial bliss 幸福婚姻的美妙时刻）

15. chime: *v.* （of a bell or clock） make melodious ringing sounds, typically to indicate the time （钟、铃、时钟）发出和谐响声（尤指报时）

16. no: *adv.* （Scottish） not （苏格兰用法）不 （e.g. I'll no be a minute. 我要不了一分钟就好。）

17. grudgin' = grudging

grudge: *v.* to feel envy towards or for; bear a grudge; harbor ill feelings 嫉妒；怨恨；怀恨

18. o' = of

◆ *A Lead-in Note* （简明导读）

遥想当初，你我两小无猜、天真无邪：“石南丛中，我将你翻来滚去。”但是，我们终究没能走到一起，“想必那是五十年前的今天，我离开你，去育空闯荡一番”。如今，你我已老，“可你蓝色的双眼闪着光芒”。你我已是老情人，“尽管想起一些事有点儿迟缓，可我们并不抱怨年华”。

◆ 老情人

哎呀，玛吉，那天你是否在意？
当时我们上学，走在一起。
路上我们停了下来，
石南丛中，我将你翻来滚去。
天呐，可你是多么漂亮的女孩！
那天我们进入课堂，迟到无疑。

如今，你发白如雪霜，
变得成熟，皱纹布脸庞，
多次当上祖母，约有十次，
可你蓝色的双眼闪着光芒！
那双眼，从眼镜上方看着我，
想起在脖子上挠痒痒的顽皮时光。

想必那是五十年前的今天，
我离开你，去育空闯荡一番。
但你没变——还是那样欢快；
无论怎么看，你都甜蜜依然。
可是，在我这个老笨蛋身上，
你能否辨出曾让你上课迟到的少年？

哎呀，玛吉，请我进屋喝茶，
我们可细谈一些事，在你家；
再审视一下婚姻的状况，
因我仍是你的情人啊——
尽管想起一些事有点儿迟缓，
可我们并不抱怨年华。

084 George William Russell
乔治·威廉·拉塞尔

◆ *The Poet's Profile* （诗人小档案）

乔治·威廉·拉塞尔（1867—1935）：爱尔兰作家、编辑、画家和爱尔兰民族主义人士。拉塞尔是爱尔兰文学复兴的代表人物。他的第一部诗集《归乡：途中诗歌集》奠定了他在“爱尔兰文学复兴”中的地位。他的诗歌和戏剧之所以有名，是因为神秘的笔调、优美的旋律以及对人类精神本质的看法。

◆ *Freedom*

I will not follow you, my bird,
I will not follow you.
I would not breathe a word, my bird,
To bring thee here anew.

I love the free in thee, my bird,
The lure of freedom drew;
The light you fly toward, my bird,
I fly with thee unto.

And there we yet will meet, my bird,
Though far I go from you
Where in the light outpoured, my bird,
Are love and freedom too.

◆ *Annotations* （原诗注释）

1. breathe: *v.* to utter, especially quietly （悄悄）说出

2. word: *n.* （a word） even the smallest amount of something spoken or written 一个字（所说或所写的最小量）(e.g. Don't believe a word of it. 一个字也别信。)

3. thee: *pron.* [second person singular] archaic or dialect form of you, as the singular object of a verb or preposition （古英语"thou"的宾格，同"you"）你；汝

4. anew: *adv.* （chiefly poetic literary） in a new or different and typically more positive way （主要为诗/文用法）重新；再次（多含积极意义）

5. lure: *n.* the strongly attractive quality of a person or thing 诱惑力；吸引力；魅力 （e.g. the lure of the exotic East 异域东方的诱惑力）

6. unto = to

7. outpour: *v.* to flow out rapidly; pour out 倾泻；泻出

◆ *A Lead-in Note* （简明导读）

此诗中，"我的鸟儿"指代已经不在人世的一个女子，也是诗人拉塞尔深爱的一个女子。人世间的负累太多，自由不易，而来世应该是一个自由自在的世界。"我的鸟儿，我不会跟随你，我不会跟随你"，因为诗人还活着，但也许精神和灵魂已经随她而去了。"我的鸟儿，我不愿说出一个字要你重新到这里"，因为这里不如你那里，可以呼吸到更多自由的空气。但是，"自由的诱惑逼近，已成定局"，人必有一死，诗人也不例外。到那时，"我的鸟儿，在那里我们终会相见"，一同呼吸自由的空气。

◆ 自　由

我的鸟儿，我不会跟随你，
我不会跟随你。

我的鸟儿，我不愿说出一个字
要你重新到这里。

我的鸟儿，我爱你的自由自在，
自由的诱惑逼近，已成定局。
我的鸟儿，我随你一同
飞到你向往的光明之地。

我的鸟儿，在那里我们终会相见，
尽管离你很远，我也去。
我的鸟儿，那儿的光明里面
有爱，也有自由倾泻如雨。

085 Lucy Maud Montgomery 露西·莫德·蒙哥马利

◆ *The Poet's Profile* （诗人小档案）

露西·莫德·蒙哥马利（1874—1942）：加拿大女作家。蒙哥马利最为知名的作品是她于1908年开始发表的系列小说《绿山墙的安妮》（也有其他版本的译文，如《秀气佳人》《清秀佳人》《红发安妮》《绿屋的安妮》等）。此系列小说，一经出版即获成功。这一系列作品中的中心人物是孤女安妮·舍利。舍利让小说的作者蒙哥马利名气大振、蜚声海外。蒙哥马利的文学作品、日记和书信被全世界的学者和读者阅读并研究。

◆ *Love's Prayer*

Beloved, this the heart I offer thee
Is purified from old idolatry,
From outworn hopes, and from the lingering stain
Of passion's dregs, by penitential pain.

Take thou it, then, and fill it up for me
With thine unstinted love, and it shall be
An earthy chalice that is made divine
By its red draught of sacramental wine.

◆ *Annotations* （原诗注释）

1. prayer: *n.* a solemn request for help or expression of thanks addressed to

God or an object of worship 祷告；祈祷；祷文；祷辞

2. beloved: *n.* a much loved person 钟爱的人：心爱的人 （e.g. He watched his beloved. 他注视着自己的心上人。）

3. thee: *pron.* [second person singular] archaic or dialect form of you, as the singular object of a verb or preposition （古英语“thou”的宾格，同“you”）你；汝

4. purify: *v.* remove contaminants from 使纯净；净化

5. idolatry: *n.* extreme admiration, love, or reverence for something or someone 崇拜 （e.g. We must not allow our idolatry of art to obscure issues of political significance. 我们不能听任对艺术的盲目崇拜遮掩了政治意义上的问题。）

6. outworn: *adj.* no longer usable or serviceable 不能再用的 （e.g. outworn lead flashings 破烂不堪的铅制防雨板）

7. lingering: *adj.* lasting for a long time or slow to end 犹存的；苟延残喘的

8. dregs: *n.* the remnants of a liquid left in a container, together with any sediment or grounds 残渣；残滓

9. penitential: *adj.* relating to or expressing penitence or penance 悔罪的；悔过的；忏悔的；苦修的；补赎的 （e.g. penitential tears 悔罪的眼泪）

10. thou: *pron.* [second person singular] archaic or dialect form of you, as the singular subject of a verb （古旧用法或方言用法）（作动词的单数主语）你（同“you”）

11. thine: *pron.* （form of “thy” used before a vowel） archaic form of yours; the thing or things belonging to or associated with thee （元音之前同“thy”）（古旧用法）你的（同“yours”）；（“thou”的物主代词）你（您）的东西

12. unstinted: *adj.* given without restraint; liberal 不吝啬的；慷慨的；无限制的 （e.g. They received unstinted praise. 他们获得了慷慨的赞扬。）

13. earthy: *adj.* terrestrial; not heavenly or divine 人间的；尘世的

14. chalice: *n.* （historical） a large cup or goblet, typically used for drinking wine （历史上的用法）大酒杯；高脚杯

15. divine: *adj.* devoted to God; sacred 敬神的；神圣的 （e.g. divine liturgy 圣餐仪式）

16. draught: *n.* （poetic / literary or archaic） a quantity of a liquid with

medicinal properties （诗/文用法或古旧用法）饮剂；（药水）剂量

17. sacramental: *adj.* relating to or constituting a sacrament or the sacraments 圣事的；圣礼的；圣餐的；圣餐用的

◆ *A Lead-in Note* （简明导读）

我这颗心历经风吹雨打，也饱经风霜。如今，我这颗心得以净化，“净化自古老的崇拜仪式”——这颗心以前有很多人崇拜过、爱过。现在，这颗心已经回归，已经“改邪归正”。只有你慷慨的爱才能将它填满，让它发生改变而“成为一只凡间的高脚杯，却因装入圣餐用的红酒而神圣非凡”。此时，爱的祈祷灵验了。

◆ 爱的祈祷

钟爱的人，我把这颗心给你——
它得以净化，净化自古老的崇拜仪式，
净化自破灭的希望，净化自激情残渣中
残存的污斑，经历了忏悔的苦痛洗礼。

那么你收下它吧，为我将它填满
你慷慨的爱，它将改变，
成为一只凡间的高脚杯，
却装入圣餐用的红酒而神圣非凡。

086 Duncan Campbell Scott
邓肯·坎贝尔·斯科特

◆ *The Poet's Profile* （诗人小档案）

邓肯·坎贝尔·斯科特（1862—1947）：加拿大诗人、散文家和短篇小说家。斯科特是19世纪末20世纪初加拿大文学领域的一位重要人物。他曾是“联盟诗人”团体的成员。这个团体的成员还包括查尔斯·乔治·道格拉斯·罗伯茨、布利斯·卡曼、阿奇博尔德·兰普曼等人。

◆ *A Love Song*

I gave her a rose in early June,
Fed with the sun and the dew,
Each petal I said is a note in the tune,
The rose is the whole tune through and through,
The tune is the whole red-hearted rose,
Flush and form, honey and hue,
Lull with the cadence and throb to the close,
I love you, I love you, I love you.

She gave me a rose in early June,
Fed with the sun and the dew,
Each petal she said is a mount in the moon,
The rose is the whole moon through and through,
The moon is the whole pale-hearted rose,
Round and radiance, burnish and blue,

Break in the flood-tide that murmurs and flows,
I love you, I love you, I love you.

This is our love in early June,
Fed with the sun and the dew,
Moonlight and roses hid in a tune,
The roses are music through and through,
The moonlight falls in the breath of the rose,
Light and cadence, honey and hue,
Mingle, and murmur, and flow to the close,
I love you, I love you, I love you.

◆ *Annotations* （原诗注释）

1. feed: *v.* provide an adequate supply of food for 为……提供充足的食物；养活 （e.g. The island's simple agriculture could hardly feed its inhabitants. 这座岛农业单一，无法养活岛上的居民。）

2. dew: *n.* tiny drops of water that form on cool surfaces at night, when atmospheric vapour condenses 露；露滴；露水 （e.g. The grass was wet with dew. 草地被露水打湿了。）

3. petal: *n.* each of the segments of the corolla of a flower, which are modified leaves and are typically coloured 花瓣

4. through and through: in every aspect; thoroughly or completely 完全；彻底 （e.g. Harriet was a political animal through and through. 哈丽雅特是个彻头彻尾的政治动物。）

5. flush: *n.* a fresh growth of leaves, flowers, or fruit （叶、花或果）茂盛生长

6. form: *n.* the body or shape of a person or thing （人或物）形体；体型；身材 （e.g. His eyes scanned her slender form. 他双眼扫了一下她苗条的身材。）

7. lull: *n.* a temporary interval of quiet or lack of activity 暂时平息；暂时平静；暂停

8. cadence: *n.* （Music） a sequence of notes or chords comprising the close of a musical phrase （音乐用语）终止式；终止 （e.g. the final cadences of the Prelude 前奏曲的最后终止式）

9. throb: *n.* a strong, regular beat or sound; a steady pulsation 跳动；搏动；有节奏的震动（或颤动）

10. mount: *n.* a mountain or hill （archaic except in place names） （除用于地名外均为古义）山；丘

11. radiance: *n.* light or heat as emitted or reflected by something 发光；明亮；热射 （e.g. The radiance of the sunset dwindled and died. 落日余晖渐渐减弱直至消失。）

12. burnish: *n.* the shine on a highly polished surface 光泽；光亮

13. flood tide or flood-tide: an incoming tide 涨潮；升潮

14. murmur: *v.* make a low continuous sound 持续发出轻声（e.g. The wind was murmuring through the trees. 风吹过树木发出沙沙响声。）

15. breath: *n.* the air taken into or expelled from the lungs 气息；呼出（或吸入的）空气 （e.g. I was gasping for breath. 我大口喘气。）

◆ *A Lead-in Note* （简明导读）

这是一首宛转、悠扬的爱之歌，副歌部分“我爱你，我爱你，我爱你如初”，进一步升华了主题。玫瑰在西方象征着爱情，所以诗人将玫瑰这一意象融进了整首歌中。这朵玫瑰是曲调，花瓣是音符。诗人又进一步将一朵朵花瓣想象成一座座小山，连在一起构成了月亮。这样，整朵玫瑰便成了月亮：“圆润而光亮，泛光且发蓝。”最后，诗人将爱、玫瑰和月亮融合到一起：“月光落进玫瑰的气息里——照亮至曲终，似蜜且色殊。相混融，语轻轻，流动至结尾：我爱你，我爱你，我爱你如初。”

◆ 爱之歌

我送给她一朵玫瑰，那是六月之初；
玫瑰沐浴过阳光，滋润过露珠。
我说，每一枚花瓣都是音符，合成曲调；
玫瑰是曲调，包含一个个花瓣音符。
曲调是整朵玫瑰，花蕊红润——
鲜嫩而形美，似蜜且色殊。
曲暂歇欲终止，跳跃至结尾：
我爱你，我爱你，我爱你如初。

她送给我一朵玫瑰，那是六月之初；
玫瑰沐浴过阳光，滋润过露珠。
她说，每一枚花瓣都是一座小山，围成月亮；
玫瑰是月亮，包含一座座花瓣小山。
月亮是整朵玫瑰，花蕊浅白——
圆润而光亮，泛光且发蓝。
曲调断于潮起，潮水流动、轻语：
我爱你，我爱你，我爱你如初。

这就是我们的爱之歌，那是六月之初；
我们的爱沐浴过阳光，滋润过露珠。
月光和朵朵玫瑰藏在曲调里，
朵朵玫瑰是音乐，包含一个个玫瑰音符。
月光落进玫瑰的气息里——
照亮至曲终，似蜜且色殊。
相混融，语轻轻，流动至结尾：
我爱你，我爱你，我爱你如初。

087 James Joyce 詹姆斯·乔伊斯

◆ *The Poet's Profile* （诗人小档案）

詹姆斯·乔伊斯（1882—1941）：爱尔兰作家。乔伊斯是现代主义运动中最重要的一位作家，1914年完成的短篇小说集《都柏林人》令他一举成名。小说《尤利西斯》使现代小说结构产生了巨大的变革并发展了意识流创作技巧。乔伊斯的代表作品有《青年艺术家肖像》和《芬尼根的苏醒》等。

◆ *Alone*

The noon's greygolden meshes make
All night a veil,
The shorelamps in the sleeping lake
Laburnum tendrils trail.

The sly reeds whisper to the night
A name—her name—
And all my soul is a delight,
A swoon of shame.

◆ *Annotations* （原诗注释）

1. greygolden = grey golden
2. mesh: *n.* material made of a network of wire or thread 网；网状物
3. veil: *n.* a piece of fine material worn by women to protect or conceal the

face 面纱；面罩（e.g. a white bridal veil 新娘的白色面纱）

4. shorelamps = shore lamps

5. laburnum: *n.* a small European tree which has hanging clusters of yellow flowers followed by slender pods containing poisonous seeds. The hard timber is sometimes used as an ebony substitute. 毒豆；金链花

6. tendril: *n.* a slender thread-like appendage of a climbing plant, often growing in a spiral form, which stretches out and twines round any suitable support （植物的）卷须蔓

7. trail: *v.* （typically of a plant） grow or hang over the edge of something or along the ground （尤指植物）蔓生；蔓延 （e.g. The roses grew wild, their stems trailing over the banks. 玫瑰一阵疯长，茎蔓延到了堤上。）

8. sly: *adj.* （of a remark, glance, or facial expression） showing in an insinuating way that one has some secret knowledge that may be harmful or embarrassing （言语、眼光或面部表情）诡异的；狡黠的 （e.g. He gave a sly grin. 他狡黠地咧嘴一笑。）

9. swoon: *n.* an occurrence of fainting 昏厥 （e.g. Her strength ebbed away and she fell into a swoon. 她的力气越来越小，然后就昏倒了。）

◆ *A Lead-in Note* （简明导读）

独自一人时，人的思绪奇特，行为也奇特。恋爱中的人独自一人时，更是会具有奇特的遐思和冥想。诗人乔伊斯正是如此。诗人独自一人时，想象力无比丰富，思维颇为奇特：灰黄的网、夜晚的面纱、湖岸的灯、毒豆花的须藤。就连芦苇也变成了一个神秘的耳语者，对戴着面纱的夜晚的耳朵提及她的芳名，爱和羞愧一下子涌上诗人的心头："于是，我整个人开始欢喜，昏迷般的羞怯感升腾。"

◆ 独自一人时

正午灰黄的网，
织成整个夜晚的面纱。
湖岸的灯照在沉睡湖面上，
宛若毒豆花的须藤蔓爬。

诡秘的芦苇对夜晚耳语，
提及一个名字——她的芳名。
于是，我整个人开始欢喜，
昏迷般的羞怯感升腾。

088 William Butler Yeats 威廉·巴特勒·叶芝

◆ *The Poet's Profile* （诗人小档案）

威廉·巴特勒·叶芝，亦作W.B.叶芝（1865—1939）：爱尔兰诗人和剧作家。叶芝的剧作《凯瑟琳伯爵夫人》和短篇故事集《凯尔特的黄昏》推动了爱尔兰的戏剧和文学的复兴。他著名的诗歌集有《钟楼》（收录了《拜占庭之航》《勒达与天鹅》等诗篇）和《盘旋的楼梯》。1923年，叶芝获诺贝尔文学奖。

◆ *When You Are Old*

When you are old and grey and full of sleep,
And nodding by the fire, take down this book,
And slowly read, and dream of the soft look
Your eyes had once, and of their shadows deep;

How many loved your moments of glad grace,
And loved your beauty with love false or true,
But one man loved the pilgrim soul in you,
And loved the sorrows of your changing face;

And bending down beside the glowing bars,
Murmur, a little sadly, how Love fled
And paced upon the mountains overhead
And hid his face amid a crowd of stars.

◆ *Annotations* （原诗注释）

1. nod: *v.* let one's head fall forward when drowsy or asleep （瞌睡时）垂着头（e.g. Anna nodded over her book. 安娜对着书本垂头打瞌睡。）

2. shadow =eyeshadow

eyeshadow: *n.* a coloured cosmetic, typically in powder form, applied to the eyelids or to the skin around the eyes to accentuate them 眼影

3. pilgrim: *n.* a person who journeys to a sacred place for religious reasons 朝圣者

4. bar: *n.* a long rod or rigid piece of wood, metal, or similar material, typically used as an obstruction, fastening, or weapon（木或金属等）长杆；棒（尤指用作障碍、系结物或武器）

◆ *A Lead-in Note* （简明导读）

此诗是诗人写给自己爱过的一位女子的，所以以第二人称“你”直呼对方。此诗写的是诗人与这位女子曾经拥有的爱。据推测，这位女子是爱尔兰有名的革命家和爱国人士莫德·冈妮。不幸的是，冈妮最终另嫁他人。通读全诗可以看出，此诗旨在告诉自己所爱之人：我们之间的爱没有长久下去，曾经的爱已经可望而不可即了，你应该感到遗憾。结尾两行说爱神（大概指诗人自己）“转眼就踱步于高耸的山间，将头埋到一群星星里边”。

◆ 当你春华不再

当你春华不再，发白又易困，
取此诗集读于壁炉前，头时起时垂。
你仍缓缓读着，梦里看到你
年轻时双眸的柔情和眼影的深邃。

不知多少人爱过你悦雅的春华，

还爱过你的美，假意或真心难辨。
只有一个人虔诚爱过你至心灵，
爱过你凄楚中饱经风霜的脸。

你躬身闪烁的炉火旁，低语轻哼，
有点儿伤感，感爱神逃离如风。
转眼就踱步于高耸的山间，
将头埋到一群星星里边。

089 Emily Pauline Johnson
埃米莉·保利娜·约翰逊

◆ *The Poet's Profile* （诗人小档案）

埃米莉·保利娜·约翰逊（1861—1913）：加拿大女诗人、女作家和表演艺术家。约翰逊在19世纪后期负有盛名，很受欢迎，一般以E.保利娜·约翰逊这个名字为人所知，或者被称为保利娜·约翰逊。约翰逊以其诗歌和表演而著称，颂扬的是她所属土著部落的传统。约翰逊是拥有广泛读者的一代作家中的一员，这一代作家对加拿大文学的发展起了重要的推动作用。尽管约翰逊的文学名望在她死后开始下降，但自20世纪后期起，她的生平和作品重新燃起了世人的兴趣。2002年，约翰逊的诗歌全集出版，其中收录了她所创作的知名诗篇。

◆ *The Lost Lagoon*

It is dusk on the Lost Lagoon,
And we two dreaming the dusk away,
Beneath the drift of a twilight grey,
Beneath the drowse of an ending day,
And the curve of a golden moon.

It is dark in the Lost Lagoon,
And gone are the depths of haunting blue,
The grouping gulls, and the old canoe,
The singing firs, and the dusk and—you,
And gone is the golden moon.

O! lure of the Lost Lagoon, —
I dream to-night that my paddle blurs
The purple shade where the seaweed stirs,
I hear the call of the singing firs
In the hush of the golden moon.

◆ *Annotations* （原诗注释）

1. lagoon: *n.* a stretch of salt water separated from the sea by a low sandbank or coral reef （由沙丘或珊瑚礁与海隔开的）咸水湖；潟湖

2. dream: *v.* （dream time away） waste one's time in a lazy, unproductive way 虚度

3. drift: *n.* a continuous slow movement from one place to another （缓慢的）流动 （e.g. There was a drift to the towns. 曾有一股人流涌向城镇。）

4. twilight: *n.* the soft glowing light from the sky when the sun is below the horizon, caused by the reflection of the sun's rays from the atmosphere 暮光；曙光

5. drowse: *n.* a light sleep; a condition of being half asleep 假寐；瞌睡；打盹

6. curve: *n.* a line or outline which gradually deviates from being straight for some or all of its length 曲线；曲形轮廓

7. depth: *n.* （the depths） a point far below the surface 深处

8. haunting: *adj.* poignant; evocative 产生强烈印象的；唤起美好回忆的 （e.g. the sweet haunting sound of pan pipes 美妙难忘的排箫声）

9. blue: *n.* （the blue） （poetic/literary） the sky or sea, or the unknown （诗/文用法）天空；大海；未知世界 （e.g. Far out upon the blue were many sails. 大海远处有许多帆船。）

10. gull: *n.* a long-winged web-footed seabird with a raucous call, typically having white plumage with a grey or black mantle 鸥

11. canoe: *n.* a narrow keelless boat with pointed ends, propelled by using a paddle or paddles 小划子；独木舟

12. fir: *n.* （also as "fir tree"） an evergreen coniferous tree with upright cones and flat needle-shaped leaves, typically arranged in two rows. Firs are an important source of timber and resins. 冷杉；枞树

13. o: *interj.* used to express surprise or strong emotion 哦；哟；啊；唉；哎呀（表示惊讶或强烈的情感）

14. lure: *n.* the strongly attractive quality of a person or thing 诱惑力；吸引力；魅力

15. paddle: *n.* an act of using a paddle in a boat 划桨 （e.g. a gentle paddle on sluggish water 在缓缓的流水中轻轻地划桨）

16. shade: *n.* a colour, especially with regard to how light or dark it is or as distinguished from one nearly like it （色彩的）深浅浓淡 （e.g. various shades of blue深浅不同的蓝色）

17. seaweed: *n.* large algae growing in the sea or on rocks below the high-water mark 海藻；海草

18. stir: *v.* move or begin to move slightly 移动；微动 （e.g. Nothing stirred except the wind. 除了风以外，一切都静止不动。）

19. hush: *n.* a silence 寂静；安静 （e.g. A hush descended over the crowd. 人群顿时一片寂静。）

◆ *A Lead-in Note* （简明导读）

失落的潟湖代表着失落的爱情。黄昏启幕，预示着爱情的落幕。失落的潟湖里，一切都失去了踪迹，更是找寻不见你的影子，甚至"金色的月，亦不见停留"。爱就这样结束，爱就这样落幕，但"失落的潟湖魅力永固"。在今夜的梦中，诗人在失落的潟湖里划桨行船，"我听见召唤，发自欢唱的冷杉树，而金色的月则静悄悄"。

◆ 失落的潟湖

失落的潟湖之上，黄昏启幕，
我们俩却将黄昏虚度——
灰色微光缓缓流淌，
昏沉的一天行将结束，
金色的月露出弯曲的模样。

失落的潟湖里，黑暗模糊：
不见常驻的蓝天深深映入，
不见成群的鸥鸟和老独木舟，
不见欢唱的冷杉和黄昏，以及——你，
金色的月，亦不见停留。

啊！失落的潟湖魅力永固——
今夜我欲入梦：紫色的阴暗处
海藻微动，我划桨模糊了那色调。
我听见召唤，发自欢唱的冷杉树，
而金色的月则静悄悄。

090 Thomas Moore
托马斯·穆尔

◆ *The Poet's Profile* （诗人小档案）

托马斯·穆尔（1779—1852）：爱尔兰诗人和音乐家。时至今日，穆尔最为知名的当属抒情诗歌《吟游少年》和《夏日里的最后一朵玫瑰》。穆尔写过一些爱国歌曲和怀旧歌曲，其中著名的有《竖琴曾穿越塔拉宫厅堂》和《吟游少年》，他也因其所著的东方浪漫诗《拉拉·鲁克》而著名。穆尔常被称作“阿那克里翁·穆尔”。阿那克里翁是古希腊抒情诗人，以歌颂爱情和美酒而闻名。

◆ *Thee, Thee, Only Thee*

The dawning of morn, the daylight's sinking,
The night's long hours still find me thinking
Of thee, thee, only thee.
When friends are met, and goblets crown'd,
And smiles are near, that once enchanted,
Unreach'd by all that sunshine round,
My soul, like some dark spot, is haunted
By thee, thee, only thee.

Whatever in fame's high path could waken
My spirit once, is now forsaken
For thee, thee, only thee.
Like shores, by which some headlong bark

To the ocean hurries, resting never,
Life's scenes go by me, bright or dark,
I know not, heed not, hastening ever
To thee, thee, only thee.

I have not a joy but of thy bringing,
And pain itself seems sweet when springing
From thee, thee, only thee.
Like spells, that nought on earth can break,
Till lips, that know the charm, have spoken,
This heart, howe'er the world may wake
Its grief, its scorn, can but be broken
By thee, thee, only thee.

◆ *Annotations* （原诗注释）

1. thee: *pron.* [second person singular] archaic or dialect form of you, as the singular object of a verb or preposition （古英语"thou"的宾格，同"you"）你；汝

2. dawning: *n.* the beginning or first appearance of something 黎明；开端；曙光 （e.g. the dawnings of civilization 文明的开端）

3. morn = morning

4. goblet: *n.* （archaic） a metal or glass bowl-shaped drinking cup, sometimes with a foot and a cover （古旧用法）（金属或玻璃的）碗状酒杯

5. crown'd = crowned

crown: *v.* rest on or form the top of 给……加顶；占据（覆盖）……的顶端 （e.g. The distant knoll was crowned with trees. 远处的圆丘顶部被树木覆盖。）

6. enchant: *v.* （often as "be enchanted"） fill （someone） with great delight; charm 使陶醉；使入迷（e.g. Isabel was enchanted with the idea. 伊莎贝尔对那个想法着了迷。）

7. Unreach'd = Unreached

8. haunt: *v.* (of a person) frequent (a place)(人)常去(某地)(e.g. He haunts street markets. 他经常去街市转悠。)

9. waken: *v.* to rouse from sleep; awake 唤醒；弄醒

10. forsake: *v.* (past forsook; past participle forsaken) (chiefly poetic / literary) abandon (someone or something) (主要为诗/文用法)抛弃；遗弃(人或物)(e.g. He would never forsake Tara. 他永远不会抛弃塔拉。)

11. headlong: *adj.* in a rush; with reckless haste 匆忙地(的)；草率地(的)(e.g. a headlong dash through the house 匆忙冲着穿过房子)

12. bark: *n.* (archaic or poetic/literary) a ship or boat (古旧用法或诗/文用法)船；小舟

13. heed: *v.* pay attention to; take notice of 注意；留心；关注；理会 (e.g. He should have heeded the warnings. 他本应听从警告才是。)

14. thy: *adj.* (also "thine" before a vowel) archaic or dialect form of your (元音前亦作"thine")(古旧用法或方言用法)你(您)的(同"your")

15. hasten: *v.* move or travel hurriedly 匆忙赶去 (e.g. We hastened back to Paris. 我们急忙赶回巴黎。)

16. spell: *n.* a form of words used as a magical charm or incantation 符咒；咒语

17. nought = naught

naught: *pron.* (archaic) nothing (古旧用法)无；没有什么 (e.g. He's naught but a worthless fool. 他是一个不中用的笨蛋。)

18. charm: *n.* an object, act, or saying believed to have magic power 魔物；魔法；魔咒

19. howe'er = however

20. wake: *v.* (figurative) cause (something) to stir or come to life (比喻用法)引起；激起；唤起 (e.g. It wakes desire in others. 这引起了他人的欲望。)

◆ *A Lead-in Note* （简明导读）

“你，你，唯有你”，并无其他，“你”就是焦点所在。没有你，我与朋友聚不会开心；没有你，一切都可以错过而奔向你。有了你，“痛苦本身变得甜蜜，若痛苦从你，你，唯有你那里涌出”。我的心只会因你而破碎不堪。

◆ 你，你，唯有你

天放亮，日西倾，
还有漫长的夜晚，我始终
想着你，你，唯有你。
朋友相遇，酒杯满盈，
张张笑脸现眼前，曾令人着迷，
而我的灵魂，远不及周围灿烂的笑容，
像某个暗黑的所在——
你，你，唯有你，光顾其中。

在名望这条高高的通衢之上，
一度唤醒我心智的所有，已经
为了你，你，唯有你而被抛弃。
某只小船途经一个个海岸，匆匆
驶向海洋，永不停歇。
如同海岸，人生或明或暗的场景
与我擦肩，我不知不顾，踏上了奔向
你，你，唯有你的旅程。

除了你带来的快乐，我无快乐而言，
痛苦本身变得甜蜜，若痛苦从
你，你，唯有你那里涌出。

知悉咒语的唇若不启封，
这样的魔法，地球上无一能破解。
如同魔法，我这颗心，无论世人如何唤醒，
其悲伤及所受的蔑视，只会
因你，你，唯有你而破碎成空。

091 Oscar Wilde
奥斯卡·王尔德

◆ *The Poet's Profile* （诗人小档案）

奥斯卡·王尔德（1854—1900）：爱尔兰剧作家、小说家、诗人和哲人。他倡导“为艺术而艺术”的主张，在其唯一的一部长篇小说《道林·格雷的肖像》中得以彰显。作为剧作家，他以两部喜剧：《少奶奶的扇子》和《认真的重要性》取得了巨大成功。1895—1897年，王尔德因同性恋受指控而入狱，最后死于流放中。

◆ *Her Voice*

The wild bee reels from bough to bough
With his furry coat and his gauzy wing.
Now in a lily-cup, and now
Setting a jacinth bell a-swing,
In his wandering;
Sit closer love: it was here I trow
I made that vow,

Swore that two lives should be like one
As long as the sea-gull loved the sea,
As long as the sunflower sought the sun, —
It shall be, I said, for eternity
'Twixt you and me!
Dear friend, those times are over and done,
Love's web is spun.

Look upward where the poplar trees
Sway and sway in the summer air,
Here in the valley never a breeze
Scatters the thistledown, but there
Great winds blow fair
From the mighty murmuring mystical seas,
And the wave-lashed leas.

Look upward where the white gull screams,
What does it see that we do not see?
Is that a star? or the lamp that gleams
On some outward voyaging argosy, —
Ah! can it be
We have lived our lives in a land of dreams!
How sad it seems.

Sweet, there is nothing left to say
But this, that love is never lost,
Keen winter stabs the breasts of May
Whose crimson roses burst his frost,
Ships tempest-tossed
Will find a harbour in some bay,
And so we may.

And there is nothing left to do
But to kiss once again, and part,
Nay, there is nothing we should rue,
I have my beauty, —you your Art,
Nay, do not start,
One world was not enough for two
Like me and you.

◆ *Annotations* （原诗注释）

1. reel: *v.* to go round and round in a whirling motion 旋转着移动；绕圈移动

2. bough: *n.* a main branch of a tree 树枝；大树枝 （e.g. apple boughs laden with blossom 开满了花的苹果树枝）

3. furry: *adj.* （furrier, furriest） covered with fur 被毛皮覆盖的

4. gauzy: *adj.* （gauzier, gauziest） resembling gauze; thin and translucent 薄纱似的；薄而透明的 （e.g. a gauzy dress 一件薄纱衣服）

5. jacinth = hyacinth

hyacinth: *n.* a bulbous plant of the lily family, with strap-like leaves and a compact spike of bell-shaped fragrant flowers. Native to western Asia, hyacinths are cultivated outdoors and as house plants 风信子属植物；风信子

6. bell: *n.* the corolla of a bell-shaped flower 钟状花冠

7. trow: *v.* （archaic） think or believe （古旧用法）想；相信 （Why, this is strange, I trow! 咦，我想这太奇怪了！）

8. eternity: *n.* a state to which time has no application; timelessness 永恒

9. 'twixt = betwixt

betwixt: *prep.* archaic term for between （古旧用法）同"between"

10. poplar: *n.* a tall, fast-growing tree of north temperate regions, widely grown in shelter belts and for timber and pulp 白杨；杨树

11. thistledown: *n.* light fluffy down which is attached to thistle seeds, enabling them to be blown about in the wind 蓟种子冠毛；蓟花的冠毛

12. fair: *adj.* （of the wind） favourable （风向）顺的 （e.g. They set sail with a fair wind. 他们顺风起航。）

13. lea: *n.* （poetic/literary） an open area of grassy or arable land （诗/文用法）草地；耕地 （e.g. The lowing herd winds slowly o'er the lea. 发出低沉叫声的牛群在草地上蜿蜒慢行。）

14. gleam: *v.* shine brightly, especially with reflected light （尤指反光的）发光；闪烁（e.g. Her eyes gleamed with satisfaction. 她的眼里流露出满意的神情。）

15. voyage: *v.* （archaic） sail over or along （a sea or river） （古旧用法）

在海或河上航行，沿海或河船行

16. argosy: *n.* （poetic/literary） a large merchant ship, originally one from Ragusa （now Dubrovnik） or Venice （诗/文用法）（原指从拉古萨——今杜勃罗文克或威尼斯起航的）大商船

17. ah: *interj.* used to express a range of emotions including surprise, pleasure, sympathy, and realization 啊；呀（用于表示惊讶、喜悦、同情和意识到等一系列情绪）

18. keen: *adj.* （of the air or wind） extremely cold; biting （空气或风）严寒的；刺骨的

19. burst: *v.* cause a break, especially by puncturing 戳破 （e.g. He burst the balloon in my face. 他当着我的面把气球戳破了。）

20. crimson: *n.* of a rich deep red colour inclining to purple 深红色的；绯红色的 （e.g. She blushed crimson with embarrassment. 她窘得满脸通红。）

21. tempest: *n.* a violent windy storm 大风暴；暴风雨；暴风雪

22. nay: *adv.* （archaic or dialect） no （古旧用法或方言用法）不 （e.g. Nay, I must not think thus. 不，我可不能那样想。）

23. rue: *v.* bitterly regret （something one has done or allowed to happen） and wish it undone 对……感到懊悔；对……感到后悔；对……感到悔恨（e.g. She might live to rue this impetuous decision. 她可能会对一时冲动做出的这个决定后悔一辈子。）

24. start: *v.* give a small jump or make a sudden jerking movement from surprise or alarm 惊起；惊跳 （e.g. "Oh my!" she said, starting. 她吃惊地说："哦，我的天！"）

◆ *A Lead-in Note* （简明导读）

这首《她之语》可与王尔德的姊妹篇《我之语》（*My Voice*）参看，因为此诗的"她"就是《我之语》中的"你"。此诗中，诗人"我"站在"她"的角度，揭示了"她"对他们之间这段恋情的看法。曾经，"她"跟"我"许过诺言，认为我们的爱永恒不变。许诺的地方（也许是座花园），有一只野蜂"始终不停地飞去飞来"采蜜。如今，"爱之网编织完毕"，一切都已结

束。“我”没有显得多么不安，反倒认为爱只不过是幻梦一场，并且带有伤感之意。同时，“我”认为“我”也是这么想的。分手之际，“我”寻求到安慰：“不，我们没什么可怨恨，我有我的美丽，而你有你的才艺。”“我”最后给出了分手的理由：“世界只一个，不足以容下两个物体，比如我和你。”

◆ 她之语

野蜂绕飞于大枝杈间，
外衣毛茸茸，扑打着薄纱般的翅膀。
他时而钻入百合杯形花里，时而将
风信子的钟形花朵摇晃，
始终不停地飞去飞来。
爱人，再坐近些：就在此处，我想
我许过那个誓言，

坚定地认为两个生命应合为一体，
只要海鸥爱大海，
只要葵花向日。
当时我说爱永恒，你我应该
相爱到底！
亲爱的朋友，那些时光已过且不再来，
爱之网编织完毕。

看上方，那里的白杨
在夏日天空中摇来摇去。
这里的山谷中无一丝微风
吹起蓟花的冠毛，但那里
有强劲的顺风
从浩瀚的大海吹来——大海低沉神秘，

从被海浪冲击的岸边草地吹来。

看上方，那里有白鸥唱鸣，
白鸥看到的，我们没看到，那是何物？
是星星吗？或者是闪烁的灯
挂在某艘出海航行的大商船上。
啊！有可能
我们生活的地方是梦中的一块陆地！
那看起来多么伤情。

亲爱的，再无什么可说，
只剩这些：爱还是那样；
严冬刺中了五月的心胸；
五月的深红玫瑰刺穿寒霜；
大船被暴风雨肆虐后，
将在某个海湾找个避风港。
我们也会如此。

再无什么可做，
只是再吻一次，然后离去。
不，我们没什么可怨恨，
我有我的美丽，而你有你的才艺。
不，莫吃惊，
世界只一个，不足以容下两个物体，
比如我和你。

092 Oliver Goldsmith
奥利弗·哥尔德斯密斯

◆ *The Poet's Profile* （诗人小档案）

奥利弗·哥尔德斯密斯（1728—1774）：爱尔兰小说家、诗人、散文家和剧作家。哥尔德斯密斯的代表作品有长篇小说《威克菲尔德的牧师》、田园诗《荒村》以及两部戏剧：《善性之人》和《她屈身求爱》。

◆ *When Lovely Woman Stoops to Folly*

When lovely woman stoops to folly,
And finds too late that men betray,
What charm can soothe her melancholy,
What art can wash her guilt away?

The only art her guilt to cover,
To hide her shame from every eye,
To give repentance to her lover,
And wring his bosom—is to die.

◆ *Annotations* （原诗注释）

1. stoop to something or stoop to doing something: to do something bad or unpleasant in order to gain an advantage for yourself （为私利）不择手段；卑鄙（或堕落）到做某事 （e.g. He's the kind of person who would stoop to making personal attacks on a rival. 他是那种能卑鄙到对竞争对手进行人身攻击的人。）

2. folly: *n.* a foolish act, idea, or practice 蠢行；傻念头；蠢事（e.g. the follies of youth 青年人的傻事）

3. betray: *v.* be disloyal to 对……不忠；辜负（e.g. the men who have betrayed British people's trust 这些辜负了英国人民信任的人）

4. charm: *n.* an object, act, or saying believed to have magic power 魔物；魔法；魔咒

5. soothe: *v.* relieve or ease （pain） 减轻（疼痛）(e.g. It contains a mild anaesthetic to soothe the pain. 它含有温和的麻醉剂，能够减轻疼痛。)

6. melancholy: *n.* a deep, pensive, and long-lasting sadness 忧思；愁思

7. art: *n.* a skill at doing a specified thing, typically one acquired through practice （多指通过训练而得的）技术；技艺；技巧（e.g. the art of conversation 交谈的技巧）

8. guilt: *n.* a feeling of having committed wrong or failed in an obligation 内疚；不安（e.g. He remembered with sudden guilt the letter from his mother that he had not yet read. 他记起母亲的信还未读，心中突然感到内疚。）

9. repentance: *n.* remorse or contrition for past conduct or sin 悔悟；悔改；后悔；忏悔

10. wring: *v.* squeeze and twist （something） to force liquid from it 绞；拧

11. bosom: *n.* the chest of a human 胸；胸部

◆ *A Lead-in Note* （简明导读）

女子委身于男子，到了犯傻的地步，却痛苦地发现对方背叛了自己。于是，她哀伤，她为自己堕落性的委身感到愧疚，但为时已晚。怎么办？答案就在最后一节，颇具戏谑口吻，同时又残忍得令人心痛，却很难想象到——“就是：她自己去死”。

◆ 美丽女子堕落到犯傻时

美丽女子堕落到犯傻时，
发现男子都会变心，却为时晚矣。
什么魔力能抑制她的哀伤？
什么办法可将她的愧疚洗去？

把她的愧疚和耻辱藏起，
把忏悔推给她的爱侣，
再扭绞他的心——唯一的办法
就是：她自己去死。

Chapter 04

Free Verse of Love by Poets from English-speaking Countries

第四章

英语国家诗人的自由体爱情短诗

093 Samuel Taylor Coleridge 塞缪尔·泰勒·柯尔律治

◆ *The Poet's Profile* （诗人小档案）

塞缪尔·泰勒·柯尔律治（1772—1834）：英国诗人、评论家和哲学家。柯尔律治和威廉·华兹华斯合著的《抒情歌谣集》是英国浪漫主义诗歌的里程碑，其中包括诗歌《古舟子咏》。柯尔律治的代表作品有《克丽斯特贝尔》和《忽必烈汗》等。

◆ *The Exchange*

We pledged our hearts, my love and I,
I in my arms the maiden clasping;
I could not tell the reason why,
But, O, I trembled like an aspen!

Her father's love she bade me gain;
I went, and shook like any reed!
I strove to act the man—in vain!
We had exchanged our hearts indeed.

◆ *Annotations* （原诗注释）

1. pledge: *v.* （Law） give as security on a loan （法律用语）用……作抵押（e.g. the creditor to whom the land is pledged 本土地的抵押债权人）

2. maiden: *adj.* being or involving the first attempt or act of its kind 首次的；

处女的（e.g. the Titanic's maiden voyage 泰坦尼克号的处女航）

3. clasp: *v.* hold（someone）tightly 紧握；紧抱（e.g. He clasped Joanne in his arms. 他双臂紧抱乔安妮。）

4. o: *interj.* used to express surprise or strong emotion 哦；哟；啊；唉；哎呀（表示惊讶或强烈的情感）

5. aspen: *n.* a poplar tree with small rounded long-stalked leaves that tremble in the breeze 颤杨；山杨

6. bid: *v.*（bidding; past bid or bade; past participle bid）（archaic or poetic/literary）command or order（someone）to do something（古旧用法或诗/文用法）命令；吩咐（e.g. I did as he bade me. 我按他的吩咐行事。）

7. reed: *n.* a tall, slender-leaved plant of the grass family, which grows in water or on marshy ground 芦苇

8. in vain: without success or a result 徒劳地（e.g. They waited in vain for a response. 他们白等回音。）

◆ *A Lead-in Note*（简明导读）

陷入爱河之中的少男少女，双方都要面临一个问题：拜见未来的岳父岳母或公公婆婆。这尤其是小伙子最紧张的时刻。此诗寓含的正是这样一个人生中的爱情哲理。诗人以贴近实际生活的比喻揭示了这样的哲理，同时揭示了真爱需要真心对待。

◆ 互　换

我和我的爱人以真心相许，
我的臂弯紧拥着这位少女。
可是，无法说出什么理由，
哎呀，我如颤杨般抖动不已！

我照吩咐要讨未来岳父欢心；

我前去，抖得跟芦苇无差异！
任我怎么尽显男子气概，皆徒劳！
我们的真心真的互换给了彼此。

094 Edward Estlin Cummings
爱德华·埃斯特林·卡明斯

◆ *The Poet's Profile* （诗人小档案）

爱德华·埃斯特林·卡明斯（1894—1962）：美国诗人和小说家。卡明斯毕业于哈佛大学，获得文科硕士学位。第一次世界大战期间，他被派往欧洲，却因军事原因被拘押很长时间。战争结束后，他没有回国，而是到欧洲很多地方去旅行，并开始接触欧洲现代主义艺术。卡明斯从画家巴勃罗·毕加索的作品以及其他现代主义者那里获得了灵感，开始在自己的诗作中对形式、标点甚至是新句法（结构及语言规则）进行创新试验——有时是荒诞性的试验。卡明斯的诗歌幽默、文雅，歌颂爱情和性爱，富有创意和吸引力。他的诗采用极不寻常的间距和缩格，并完全不用大写字母。卡明斯用词不复杂，对象的选择也无隐晦之意。卡明斯的诗读起来都有闻所未闻的感觉，感觉像诗人自己在发明语言。卡明斯至今仍然是一位受人欢迎的美国诗人。

◆ *i carry your heart with me*

i carry your heart with me(i carry it in
my heart)i am never without it(anywhere
i go you go,my dear;and whatever is done
by only me is your doing,my darling)
                                                    i fear
no fate(for you are my fate,my sweet)i want
no world(for beautiful you are my world,my true)
and it's you are whatever a moon has always meant

and whatever a sun will always sing is you

here is the deepest secret nobody knows
(here is the root of the root and the bud of the bud
and the sky of the sky of a tree called life;which grows
higher than soul can hope or mind can hide)
and this is the wonder that's keeping the stars apart

i carry your heart(i carry it in my heart)

◆ *Annotations* （原诗注释）

1. First of all, the commas and brackets "（）" without spaces in this poem are not a mistake. That is how Cummings liked it. （Normally, you need a space after a punctuation mark.）要做出解释的是，这首诗中的逗号和括号使用中应该空格的地方没有空格，不是打字和排版错误，卡明斯喜欢这样做，有意而为之（通常标点符号后面要有一个空格）。

2. sweet: *n.* used as an affectionate form of address to a person one is very fond of 宝贝；亲爱的（用作爱称）(e.g. Hello, my sweet. 你好，我的宝贝儿。)

3. bud: *n.* a compact knob-like growth on a plant which develops into a leaf, flower, or shoot 芽；蓓蕾

◆ *A Lead-in Note* （简明导读）

此诗是情诗中的典范，表达的是诗人对心爱之人炽热的爱。"你"就是爱的全部，"我随身带着你的心"，而且"一刻不能没有它"。有了"你"，"我"可以舍弃一切，"而且这就是奇迹就是让众星分立而不碰撞的奇迹"。

◆ 我随身带着你的心

我随身带着你的心（随我内心带着
你的心）一刻不能没有它（我走到哪里
你就走到哪里，我亲爱的；只要我做什么
你就做什么，我的亲爱之人）
　　　　　　　　　　我不怕
什么命运（因你是我的命运，我的宝贝）我不要
什么世界（因漂亮的你是我的世界，我的真爱）
而且无论月亮意味着什么总是取决于你意味着什么
而且无论太阳歌唱的是什么总是为你而唱

这儿有最深藏的秘密没有谁会知道
(这儿有根部中之根部也有蓓蕾中之蓓蕾
而且有棵叫作生命之树的上空中之上空；这棵树长得
高过灵魂所能期许的或者心灵所能掩藏的高度)
而且这就是奇迹就是让众星分立而不碰撞的奇迹

我带着你的心（随我内心带着你的心）

095 Walt Whitman
沃尔特·惠特曼

◆ *The Poet's Profile* （诗人小档案）

沃尔特·惠特曼（1819—1892）：美国诗人、散文家和新闻记者。作为一名人文主义者，惠特曼参与到超验主义和现实主义过渡时期的活动中，将这两种主义者的观点融入自己的作品之中。惠特曼是一位极具影响力的诗人，常被称作“自由体诗之父”。1855年，惠特曼自费出版了自由体诗集《草叶集》，集内收有《我对令人兴奋的躯体歌唱》和《自我之歌》这两首诗。在他有生之年，该诗集又出了八个增订本。

◆ *Sometimes with One I Love*

Sometimes with one I love I fill myself with rage for fear I effuse unreturn'd love,

But now I think there is no unreturn'd love, the pay is certain one way or another

(I loved a certain person ardently and my love was not return'd,

Yet out of that I have written these songs).

◆ *Annotations* （原诗注释）

1. rage: *n.* (poetic/literary) intense feeling, especially prophetic, poetic, or martial enthusiasm or ardour （诗/文用法）（尤指预示的、诗意的或武力的）激情；狂热

2. effuse: *v.* give off (a liquid, light, smell, or quality) 倾出；溢出；出

（液体、光或气味）；显出（某特征）

3. unreturn'd = unreturned

4. ardently: *adv.* in an ardent manner 热心地；热烈地；热情地

5. return'd = returned

◆ *A Lead-in Note* （简明导读）

恋爱之人都有这样的顾虑：自己爱恋对方，怕对方没有回应而没有结果。诗人也有这样的担心，但同时也找到了平衡点："但现在我认为根本不存在无果的爱恋"。诗人认为，爱恋总会有结果的。即使没有爱的结果，也会有其他方面的结果。例如，诗人从无果的爱恋中写出了很多诗歌，包括这首《有时候跟我爱的人在一起》。也就是说，无果的爱恋给诗人的创作带来了素材和灵感，算是对诗人无果之爱所给予的补偿。另外，惠特曼所写的相当一部分爱情诗，其主题都是爱恋无果，得不到对方的回应。

◆ 有时候跟我爱的人在一起

有时候跟我爱的人在一起，我满心狂热却又担心爱恋最终无果，

但现在我认为根本不存在无果的爱恋，肯定会从一方面或另一方面得到结果

（我热情似火地爱上某个人，我的爱恋没有结果，

然而从那过程中我写出这么多诗歌）。

096 William Carlos Williams 威廉·卡洛斯·威廉斯

◆ *The Poet's Profile* （诗人小档案）

威廉·卡洛斯·威廉斯（1883—1963）：美国诗人。威廉斯与现代主义和意象派有着紧密的联系。他视自己的诗歌作品为具有独特美国特征的作品。他的诗作之中，被收入诗集最多的一首是《红色手推车》，它是体现意象主义运动风格和原则的诗歌典范（亦见《那就是说》）。但是，这首诗于1923年作为诗集《春天及一切》的一部分发表时，威廉斯早就摈弃了意象主义运动的风格。威廉斯的主要诗集有《春天及一切》《〈沙漠音乐〉及其他诗集》等。

◆ *Marriage*

So different, this man
And this woman:
A stream flowing
In a field.

◆ *Annotations* （原诗注释）

1. marriage: *n.* the formal union of a man and a woman, typically recognized by law, by which they become husband and wife 结婚 （e.g. The news of their marriage was not made public until three months later. 他们结婚的消息三个月后才公开。）

2. stream: *n.* a small, narrow river 小河；小溪 （e.g. We picnicked beside a bubbling stream. 我们在流水潺潺的小溪旁野餐。）

◆ *A Lead-in Note* （简明导读）

在短短的四行自由体诗中，诗人对婚姻做出了自己独特的诠释。在诗人看来，婚姻就是男女结合成为一体，然后两个人就密不可分了。而且，诗人以形象化的意象来诠释这种婚姻关系。此诗中，诗人以小溪和田野这两个意象来喻指男女。男女的婚姻就是“一条小溪流淌在田野之中”：小溪和田野彼此紧密联系在一起，不可分割，这就是婚姻。

◆ 婚　姻

如此不同寻常，此男
与此女：
一条小溪流淌在
田野之中。

097 Amy Lowell
埃米·洛厄尔

◆ *The Poet's Profile* （诗人小档案）

埃米·洛厄尔（1874—1925）：美国女诗人。洛厄尔是美国马萨诸塞州布鲁克赖恩的印象派诗人，在她死后的第一年，即1926年，获得普利策诗歌奖。洛厄尔从未上过大学，因为她的家人认为女子上学有失体统。因此，她如饥似渴地阅读加以弥补，而且不断收集图书，几乎到了入魔的程度。作为印象派中的一位领军人物，洛厄尔以散文诗和令人愉悦的意象而闻名。

◆ *The Bungler*

You glow in my heart
Like the flames of uncontrolled candles.
But when I go to warm my hands,
My clumsiness overturns the light,
And then I stumble
Against the tables and chairs.

◆ *Annotations* （原诗注释）

1. bungler: *n.* a clumsy person 笨拙者；经验不够的人

2. glow: *v.* give out steady light without flame （没有火焰地）发光 （e.g. The tips of their cigarettes glowed in the dark. 他们的烟头在黑暗中闪光。）

3. stumble: *v.* trip or momentarily lose one's balance; almost fall 绊脚；绊跌；绊倒（e.g. Her foot caught a shoe and she stumbled. 她的脚碰到一只鞋，绊了一跤。）

◆ *A Lead-in Note* （简明导读）

此诗具有意象派的典型特征。此诗中，蜡烛是典型的意象，象征着爱情。一个笨拙的行为可能会使烛光——爱之光变得可望而不可即。本来“我走过去，要温暖一下双手”，想得到爱的温暖，“可却笨手笨脚令蜡烛翻仰：跌翻了椅子，撞到了桌子”，一发而不可收，局面失控，爱情消失。

◆ 笨拙之人

你在我的心中闪亮，
就像无拘无束燃烧的烛光。
我走过去，要温暖一下双手，
可却笨手笨脚令蜡烛翻仰：
跌翻了椅子，撞到了桌子。
我一路跌跌撞撞。

098 Stephen Crane
斯蒂芬·克莱恩

◆ *The Poet's Profile* （诗人小档案）

斯蒂芬·克莱恩（1871—1900）：美国作家。克莱恩一生短暂，但作品颇丰。他的著名作品具有现实主义风格，是美国自然主义和印象派的早期典范。现代批评家认为，克莱恩是他那个时代最具创新力的作家之一。他以长篇小说《红色英勇勋章》而著名。这篇小说讲述了美国南北战争时期一个新兵的故事，被誉为心理现实主义的杰作——虽然克莱恩本人并无战争经历。

◆ *Love Walked Alone*

Love walked alone.
The rocks cut her tender feet,
And the brambles tore her fair limbs.
There came a companion to her,
But, alas, he was no help,
For his name was heart's pain.

◆ *Annotations* （原诗注释）

1. tender: *adj.* （of a part of the body） sensitive to pain （身体部位）易痛的；一触即痛的

2. bramble: *n.* a prickly scrambling shrub of the rose family, especially a blackberry 悬钩子属有刺灌木（尤指黑莓）；荆棘

3. fair: *adj.* （archaic） beautiful; attractive （古旧用法）美丽的；动人的；

有魅力的（e.g. the fairest of her daughters 她女儿中最漂亮的一位）

4. alas: *interj.*（chiefly poetic/literary or humorous） an expression of grief, pity, or concern（主要为诗/文用法或幽默用法）哎呀；唉（表示悲痛、遗憾或关心）(e.g. Alas, my funds have some limitations. 唉，我资金有限。)

◆ *A Lead-in Note*（简明导读）

她的名字叫“爱”。她在独自行走，走得异常艰难：“石头划破她那一触即痛的双脚，荆棘刺破她那娇美的肢体。”她需要有人陪伴，走过人生的旅程。这时，他走了过来，她满心欢喜。可是，他最终带给她的是爱的伤痛，“因他的名字就叫心痛”。爱，还得独自行走下去。

◆ 爱，独自行走

爱，独自行走。
石头划破她那一触即痛的双脚，
荆棘刺破她那娇美的肢体。
一个伙伴向她走来，
唉，可他根本不起什么作用，
因他的名字就叫心痛。

099 Carl Sandburg
卡尔·桑德堡

◆ *The Poet's Profile* （诗人小档案）

卡尔·桑德堡（1878—1967）：美国诗人和传记作家。桑德堡的诗收录在《芝加哥诗集》《烟与钢》《桑德堡诗歌全集》和《蜜与盐》等四部诗集中。桑德堡也以1926—1939年完成的亚伯拉罕·林肯的传记而闻名。此传记共分为六卷，其中包括《亚伯拉罕·林肯：北美大草原岁月》（共两卷）以及《亚伯拉罕·林肯：战争岁月》（共四卷）。

◆ *Dream Girl*

You will come one day in a waver of love,
Tender as dew, impetuous as rain,
The tan of the sun will be on your skin,
The purr of the breeze in your murmuring speech,
You will pose with a hill-flower grace.

You will come, with your slim, expressive arms,
A poise of the head no sculptor has caught
And nuances spoken with shoulder and neck,
Your face in a pass-and-repass of moods
As many as skies in delicate change
Of cloud and blue and flimmering sun.

Yet,
You may not come, O girl of a dream,
We may but pass as the world goes by
And take from a look of eyes into eyes,
A film of hope and a memoried day.

◆ *Annotations* （原诗注释）

1. waver: *n.* the action of wavering 飘动；闪动

2. dew: *n.* tiny drops of water that form on cool surfaces at night, when atmospheric vapour condenses 露；露滴；露水 （e.g. A cold, heavy dew dripped from the leaves. 一滴滴冰冷、沉重的露珠从树叶上滚落。）

3. impetuous: *adj.* moving forcefully or rapidly 激烈的；猛烈的；迅疾的（e.g. an impetuous but controlled flow of water 迅疾但受控制的水流）

4. tan: *n.* a golden-brown shade of skin developed by pale-skinned people after exposure to the sun （日晒后变成的）棕褐色皮肤

5. purr: *n.* a low continuous vibratory sound, typically that made by a cat or vehicle（猫发出的）呼噜声；（车辆发出的）咕隆声；咕噜声

6. pose: *v.* assume a particular attitude or position in order to be photographed, painted, or drawn 摆出姿态（或姿势）（e.g. The prime minister posed for photographers. 那位首相摆好了姿势让摄像师拍照。）

7. poise: *n.* graceful and elegant bearing in a person 优雅的姿势

8. sculptor: *n.* an artist who makes sculptures 雕刻家；雕塑家

9. nuance: *n.* a subtle difference in or shade of meaning, expression, or sound（意义、表情或声音的）细微差别；微妙的变化 （e.g. the nuances of facial expression and body language 面部表情和肢体语言的细微差别）

10. flimmering: 此词疑为"glimmering"之误，故按照"glimmering"之意译出。

11. film: *n.* （archaic） a fine thread or filament （古旧用法）细纹；细丝（e.g. films of silk 细丝线）

12. memoried: *adj.* filled with memories 充满回忆的

◆ *A Lead-in Note* （简明导读）

在诗人的意念中，心仪的女孩会飘然而至：“你会到来，纤细的手臂富有情感；一颦一笑，连雕刻家都难以捕捉。”多么优雅美丽的女孩。也许，这个女孩只能停留在诗人的梦中，不会到来。也许，即使相遇，也是擦肩而过，但“目光交融之时，我看到一线希望，留下了充满回忆的一天”。这样，也很美好。

◆ 梦中的女孩儿

会有那么一天，你带着爱飘然而至，
柔如露水，疾如雨滴。
太阳会晒黑你的皮肤，
你的喃喃细语如微风徐徐，
你的姿态似山坡上的花儿优雅。

你会到来，纤细的手臂富有情感；
一颦一笑，连雕刻家都难以捕捉。
香肩玉颈微妙，胜似言语万千。
你的面庞情绪多样，瞬息即变，
堪比天空复杂多变的气象：
忽而多云，忽而碧蓝，忽而阳光闪耀。

然而，
你或许不会到来。啊，梦中的女孩儿！
或许跟世人一样，我们只是擦肩而过。
目光交融之时，我看到一线希望，
留下了充满回忆的一天。

100 Hilda Doolittle
伊尔达·杜利特尔

◆ *The Poet's Profile* （诗人小档案）

伊尔达·杜利特尔（1886—1961）：美国女诗人和小说家。杜利特尔与20世纪早期先锋意象派诗人有交往。这些意象派诗人包括埃兹拉·庞德、理查德·奥尔丁顿等。杜利特尔以笔名“H. D.”发表作品。第二次世界大战期间，她兄弟去世，她与诗人理查德·奥尔丁顿的婚姻破裂，这两件事令她陷入痛苦之中，对她后来的诗作也产生了重要影响。意象派权威人士格伦·休斯曾这样写道：“她的孤独从其诗中叫喊而出。”杜利特尔对古希腊文学深感兴趣，她经常从希腊神话和古典诗人那里获取诗歌素材。杜利特尔的作品中，她经常借助自然景色和物象来表达特定的情感或心绪。

◆ *Never More Will the Wind*

Never more will the wind
cherish you again,
never more will the rain.

Never more
shall we find you bright
in the snow and wind.

The snow is melted,
the snow is gone,
and you are flown:

Like a bird out of our hand,
like a light out of our heart,
you are gone.

◆ *Annotations* （原诗注释）

1. nevermore or never more: never again 决不再
2. cherish: *v.* hold （something） dear 珍爱；珍视
3. melt: *v.* become liquefied by heat 融化；熔化

◆ *A Lead-in Note* （简明导读）

简短的诗行，简洁的语言，道出的是爱的失意。风和雨都不再珍惜你的时候，“你永远不会闪亮在雪中和风中”。这样，随着雪的消融，你也将消融不见，无迹可寻。“如同鸟儿从手里飞走，如同光线从心中消失”，一切似乎都不曾发生过。

◆ 风永远不会

风永远不会
再珍惜你，
雨也永远不会。

我们将发现
你永远不会闪亮在
雪中和风中。

雪融化，

雪消失，
你消融不见：

如同鸟儿从手里飞走，
如同光线从心中消失，
你消失不见。

101 Maxwell Bodenheim
马克斯韦尔·博登海姆

◆ *The Poet's Profile* （诗人小档案）

马克斯韦尔·博登海姆（1892—1954）：美国诗人和小说家。博登海姆的父亲所罗门·博登海姆生于德国，母亲卡丽生于法国的阿尔萨斯-洛林地区。卡丽于1881年移民到美国，所罗门直到1888年才移民到美国。1900年，博登海姆跟家人一起从密西西比州搬到了芝加哥市。在芝加哥，博登海姆遇到了美国作家本·赫克特，并与他成为朋友。他们共同创办了《芝加哥文学时报》，其撰稿人包括卡尔·桑德堡、威特·宾纳、韦切尔·林赛等知名人物。博登海姆后来去了纽约。在纽约，他以"格林威治村波西米亚之王"而著称。在20世纪20年代的"爵士乐时代"，博登海姆的作品为他赢得了国际声誉。但是，继20世纪20年代和30年代的成功之后，博登海姆的情况开始急转直下了。

◆ *Love*

You seemed a caryatid melting
Into the wind-blown, dark blue temple of the sky.
But you bent down as I came closer, breaking the image.
When I passed, you raised your head
And blew the little feather of a smile upon me.
I caught it on open lips and blew it back.
And in that moment we loved,
Although you stood still waiting for your lover,
And I walked on to my love.

◆ *Annotations* （原诗注释）

1. caryatid: *n.* （pl. caryatides or caryatids） （Architecture） a stone carving of a draped female figure, used as pillar to support the entablature of a Greek or Greek-style building （建筑学）女像柱（用作支撑希腊或希腊风格建筑的柱上楣构）

2. temple: *n.* a building devoted to the worship, or regarded as the dwelling place, of a god or gods or other objects of religious reverence 庙宇；寺院；圣堂；神殿

◆ *A Lead-in Note* （简明导读）

失之交臂的爱，是短暂相恋之后的分道扬镳。你姿态优美而神秘，"我靠近之时，你却弯下腰，打破了原有的形象"。于是，我们相恋、相爱。然后，你恢复原有的形象，继续等待你爱的人，"而我继续向前，走向我的爱"。这就是爱所经历的过程。

◆ 爱

你看似一尊女子像柱，融进
被风吹拂的、深蓝色的空中神殿。
我靠近之时，你却弯下腰，打破了原有的形象。
我路过时，你抬起头，
将一枚微笑的羽毛吹向我。
我张开双唇将之接住，吹了回去。
就在那一刻，我们相爱了——
尽管你静静站立等待你爱的人，
而我继续向前，走向我的爱。

Main Bibliography
主要参考文献

[1] LARKIN P. Collected poems [M]. New York, NY: Farrar, Straus & Giroux Inc, 2004.

[2] LONGFELLOW W. et al. 300 Classic poems [M]. Tianjin, China: Tianjin Renmin Press, 2014.

[3] NEGRI P. Great short poems [M]. Mineola, NY: Dover Publications, 2012.

[4] SMITH P. 100 Best-loved poems [M]. Mineola, NY: Dover Publications, 1995.

[5] 哈代.哈代诗选：英汉对照[M].飞白，译.北京：外语教学与研究出版社，2014.

[6] 黄杲炘.英诗汉译学[M].上海：上海外语教育出版社，2007.

[7] 柯尔律治.柯尔律治诗选：英汉对照[M].杨德豫，译.北京：外语教学与研究出版社，2013.

[8]《新牛津英汉双解大词典》编译出版委员会.新牛津英汉双解大词典[M].上海：上海外语教育出版社，2007.

[9] 新华通讯社译名室.世界人名翻译大辞典[M].修订版.北京：中国对外翻译出版公司，2007.

[10] 周定国.世界地名翻译大辞典[M].北京：中国对外翻译出版公司，2008.

Epilogue
后　记

译事之难，难于上青天。这样说，一点都不为过。

译诗之难，乃难中之难，更是难于上青天了。译诗是文学翻译领域的难点，可谓难上加难。

我们从浩如烟海的英语国家众多诗人中筛选出101位，再从每位诗人的作品中筛选出一首爱情短诗。这101位诗人不一定都十分出众，也不一定都名垂诗史，但是他们的诗都短小精悍，都寓含一定的爱情哲理，让人读后有所思考。对这些诗的汉译探索，即译诗，我们首先力求在意义和意象方面的贴切，再考虑形式因素，特别是押韵方面。

在筛选、研究和翻译英语国家这101位诗人所作的101首爱情短诗过程中，我们下了不少工夫，特别是在翻译过程中，不时会遇到这样或那样的“坎坷”。诗人在创作过程中，为了格律的需要，避开了一些常用词，转而采用生僻的诗歌专用词，这就逼着译著者去琢磨这样的词。另外，在译诗过程中，还要观照原诗的形式，特别是韵律方面，同时还要兼顾译语（即汉语）诗歌的形式，特别是汉语读者的诗歌审美习惯。对于这样的“坎坷”，译著者下笔前会来回踱步、反复思量、仔细斟酌。正如鲁迅先生在译完《死魂灵》谈到翻译时所言：“我向来总以为翻译比创作容易，因为至少是无须构想。但到真的一译，就会遇着难关，譬如一个名词或动词，写不出，创作时候可以回避，翻译上却不成，也还得想，一直弄到头昏眼花，好像在脑子里面摸一个急于要开箱子的钥匙，却没有。”（鲁迅《杂文集·且介亭杂文二

集·“题未定”草》）

此外，还会遇到语言及文化差异方面的“绊脚石”，处理起来颇费脑筋。正如严复在谈《天演论》翻译的《译例言》中所言：“新理踵出，名目纷繁，索之中文，渺不可得，即有牵合，终嫌参差，译者遇此，独有自具衡量，即义定名。”在翻译中须认真加以思考，甚至经过了很长时间才“创造性”地下笔定论，可谓“一名之立，旬月踟蹰。我罪我知，是存明哲”（严复《译例言》）。由此可见，译事之难也好，或译诗之难也罢，不亚于李白笔下的“蜀道之难，难于上青天”了！

幸运的是，在对这101位诗人所作的101首爱情短诗进行筛选、研究和翻译过程中，我们得到了许多朋友和同事热情的帮助和有力的支持，感激之情无以言表。特别感谢远在大洋彼岸、旅居美国的师姐钟亚梅女士，大学恩师路南女士以及同窗兄弟Peter You，感谢大连职业技术学院公共外语教学部及渤海大学外国语学院的领导和同事，感谢安徽师范大学出版社汪碧颖编辑在出版方面所做的工作。

当然，由于时间和能力所限，错误在所难免，还望读者赐教、斧正，并多提宝贵意见。

记得《礼记·中庸》里有言：“君子之道，譬如行远必自迩，譬如登高必自卑。”我们努力践行之。

解　红　王永胜

2020年4月